MR FINCHLEY DISCOVERS
HIS ENGLAND

Victor Canning's first novel, *Mr Finchley Discovers His England*, was published in 1934, since which time he has been a full-time author. He now has over thirty novels to his credit, of which *The Great Affair* is the latest. He is also the author of many short stories and serials which have been published in the principal newspapers and magazines of England and America.

Born in Plymouth in 1911, Victor Canning was a features writer for the *Daily Mail* before the Second World War, during which he was commissioned in the Royal Artillery. He has worked as a scriptwriter in Hollywood and now lives in Kent.

His recent novels include *Doubled in Diamonds*, *The Python Project*, *The Melting Man* and *Queen's Pawn*.

D0870664

MR FINCHLEY DISCOVERS HIS ENGLAND

VICTOR CANNING

UNABRIDGED

PAN BOOKS LTD : LONDON

First published 1934 by Hodder and Stoughton Ltd.
Republished 1970 by William Heinemann Ltd.
This edition published 1972 by Pan Books Ltd,
33 Tothill Street, London, SW1.

ISBN 0 330 23396 3

Printed in Great Britain by
Cox & Wyman Ltd, London, Reading and Fakenham

CONTENTS

Of the Beginning of the Discovery, and of the Triumph of Habit over Circumstance

EDGAR FINCHLEY was forty-five, short, with a comfortable face such as you might see on the fringe of any crowd, and a tonsure that surprised you when he raised his hat. He was panting slightly as he came to the top of the hill. He had lived in London all his life and, since Mr Bardwell had made him chief clerk ten years ago, he had never had a week's holiday. Mr Bardwell himself never took a holiday and he fostered the practice among his clerks. Mr Finchley had succumbed meekly to the conviction that he was indispensable to the office, a conviction which Mr Bardwell had encouraged. When Mr Bardwell had died it was generally anticipated that Mr Sprake would continue the tradition. But Sprake (he was only referred to as Mr Sprake in the presence of clients) had developed surprising attributes. Mr Finchley took out his yellow silk handkerchief and wiped his forehead as he mused over the astonishing change which had come over Sprake. He came to the office in tweeds. He smoked all day, scattered his ash in deed boxes, and looked more like a bookmaker than a lawyer. Mr Finchley had witnessed in silence the desecration and waited anxiously for the practice to decline. The practice did not decline. Business increased. Sprake grew jollier and the checks on his golfing suits larger. And then – it was hot even in the shade now and Mr Finchley decided to rest on the seat at the end of the avenue – there came the day when Sprake had called him into his room.

'Ah, Finchley, I wanted to have a chat with you,' he said. 'Of course, you know that things have changed a bit since poor Bardwell packed up . . . good man, Bardwell, but he was inclined to regard things from the solicitor's point of view too much instead of looking at 'em from the point of view of a man, eh? Still, we all have our little ways. Have a cigarette? Yes, things have changed a little since Bardwell went.'

'Yes sir,' Mr Finchley answered quietly; 'things have changed a little—'

'And for the best, eh, Finchley, eh?' For the moment Mr Finchley thought that Sprake was going to dig him in the stomach in the familiar manner which is commonly construed as friendly.

'Yes, sir, decidedly for the better.'

'Nobody's grumbling about that, I hope, eh, Finchley, eh?' Sprake roared comfortingly.

'Not that I know of, sir.'

'And a good thing, too! Now here's what I wanted to speak to you about. While Bardwell was alive he ran this office on his lines and no one said anything – he was head man! But now I'm running this office, and it's going to be run on my lines, eh, Finchley, eh?'

Mr Finchley nodded, not thinking it necessary to reply. The ghost of Bardwell himself could not have stopped Sprake from doing as he willed now.

'Well, what do you think I'm going to do, Finchley? What do you think I want to speak to you about?'

'I really couldn't say, sir,' Mr Finchley muttered.

'Holidays, Finchley . . . holidays!' Sprake put his head on one side in an absurd manner and cooed at Mr Finchley.

'Holidays, sir?'

'Yes, holidays, Finchley. Holidays! A proper system of holidays! Can't expect my staff to do their jobs if they ain't fit! Must have holidays . . . eh?'

Holidays. The whole idea, even now, seemed a little strange to Mr Finchley. For the first time he was going to have a holiday. For three weeks – it was now Saturday, the twenty-ninth of July – he was to forget the office, forget deeds and bills of cost; forget everything but the sunshine and that he had money in his pocket to spend any way he liked.

He sat down on a green-painted bench between two elms to rest himself. The climb up the long hill and the heat of the noon had made him tired. Yes, Sprake was a good

8

fellow. His clerks meant something to him. It was astonishing how different the atmosphere of the office had become in the last few months. The thought of holidays had filled everyone with a new spirit. That very morning Sprake had called him in and asked where he was going. Even the office-boy had said to him as he left:

''Ave a good holiday, Mr Finchley – and don't do anything I wouldn't do!'

Mr Finchley had smiled. A man about to start his holidays can forgive much.

It was pleasant on the bench and the cool shade of the trees made him reluctant to hurry away. He glanced at his watch. His train did not go until late in the afternoon and there was no Mrs Patten waiting to scold him if he were late for lunch. Mrs Patten was his housekeeper. Not for anything would Mr Finchley have admitted that she bullied him. But she did, of course. Though entirely for his own good. But now he was on holiday. On the opposite pavement a dog lay stretched against the warm flagstones. From an open window came the sound of a woman singing, and there was a deep quality in her voice which seemed to drug the street in a quiet peace. Mr Finchley puffed at his pipe and the smoke lost itself against the still elm leaves. An errand-boy pedalled down the street raising little whorls of dust behind him, the sleeping dog stirred and suddenly the singing woman ceased her song to shout something to someone within the house. A hand shook the shoulder of sleeping peace and the street leaped to life. A furniture lorry rumbled like a tumbril down the street and stopped fifty yards from Mr Finchley's seat, while a little girl in blue crawlers wriggled up area steps to tease the dog, and the sun evading the trees began to slant its rays across Mr Finchley. He moved along the bench to avoid the heat and idly watched the small girl. The furniture men dropped the tail-board of their van and the noise echoed along the street like badly wrought thunder. As the sound died its place was taken by a high roar from the direction of the main thoroughfare two hundred yards away. The roar rose to a majestic fury, dropped to nothing and then

9

was taken up in a lower key. Mr Finchley sat up. He knew what the sound was, and in his heart was a feeling of envy for the man who controlled the pulsing machine which produced it. The noise rose in a regular crescendo and then stopped. With a high-pitched protest of tyres against the road surface, a low green six-litre Bentley drew up at the kerb alongside Mr Finchley's bench.

He watched the driver ease himself out of the seat and throw his coat and gloves into the back of the car. Slamming the door, the man turned away and, as he did so, he saw Mr Finchley. Mr Finchley saw him hesitate for a second as though a thought had suddenly occurred to him. He looked at Mr Finchley: perhaps he saw a neatly clad, harmless-looking little man sunning himself on a bench, perhaps he saw the admiration in Mr Finchley's eyes as he took in the rakish lines of the car, but whatever he saw it conquered his hesitation. He stepped up to Mr Finchley and addressed him.

'Awful cheek on my part, but I've got to transact some business down the road for half an hour and if you're going to be here for a while would you mind keeping an eye on her?' He nodded lovingly towards the car. 'You see,' he explained, 'I've only just had her and one hears so many stories of car thefts these days.'

Mr Finchley's heart warmed to the stranger. He was a modest man, and any display of confidence in him by others inevitably filled him with a secret pride which made him anxious to justify the confidence.

'That's all right,' he replied. 'I'm just getting a little sun before lunch, but I'll keep an eye on her so long as I'm here ... no, no bother, I assure you!'

'Thanks! Have a cigarette? No, of course, you're smoking a pipe ... awfully good of you to—' The man's words trailed away into the distance as he started down the street.

The street relapsed into peace again. Away on his right London muttered to itself as the morning slid into the afternoon. In the elm above Mr Finchley the shadows moved and played, courting the blazing sun as it swung over the houses. Mr Finchley finished his pipe, polished the bowl with his handkerchief and put the pipe in his pocket. The shadows of the houses cut odd geometrical designs on the asphalt. The sleeping dog roused itself and walked stiffly across the roadway. It stood before Mr Finchley who made friendly passes at the animal and was rewarded with an insolent yawn. The dog pricked up its ears and trotted away. By now the whole length of the bench was bathed in sunshine and the woodwork was hot under Mr Finchley's hand. He looked at his watch. Time was passing, and he had to have his lunch and catch a train. The stranger had been gone twenty minutes. Mr Finchley rose and dusted his trousers. He walked round the car slowly, inspecting it. The paintwork of the body was new and glossy and the brightly polished headlamps and fittings bravely defied the sun with their dazzle. He leaned over the driving seat. The speedometer showed a total mileage of seven hundred and fifty-four miles. It was a car such as Mr Finchley often dreamed that he might one day have. He noticed that the back seat of the car was still in the shade. At any other time Mr Finchley would have thought twice about such an action, but now something inspired him with a somnolent disregard for the conventions with which his life was so much wrapped about. He opened the low door, stepped into the car and stretched himself comfortably along the back seat.

Ten minutes passed, but the stranger did not return. The dog wandered back to the elms and settled down under the bench and from the area of the house opposite the clatter of dishes was mixed with the petulant crying of a child. Mr Finchley did not see the dog return. He did not hear the dishes or the child. He was sleeping. His left trouser-leg was wrinkled up his calf, showing his suspender, his hands were crossed upon his waistcoat and his felt hat had slipped forward thirty degrees. Mr Finchley slept and the dog scratched its flank lazily in the shade of the bench.

TWO

The Justification of a Life of Crime, and the Revolt of Circumstances against Habit

Mr Finchley had a dream. He was in an aeroplane, beneath him lay water.

Something was happening. The plane dipped at an acute angle towards the sea which rose at him like a vicious blue hand. He shut his eyes and waited for the impact. *Bump!* He was struck in the back by some hard object.

He opened his eyes, and realized that he was no longer dreaming. He was lying on the floor in the back of the Bentley. A persistent droning filled his ears, and without warning he was suddenly thrown violently against the low seat. The car was moving.

Startled, he raised himself on to the back seat. The car was rushing at a terrific speed along a wide road bordered by neat, regular grass patches and sentinelled by young trees. It swerved unexpectedly around another car and Mr Finchley was again flung violently to one side. As he fell he hurt his hand.

The pain annoyed him and he flushed with a sudden anger. What did the fellow mean?

'Hey!' He started forward and shook the driver by the shoulder. His action nearly wrecked the car. The driver jumped nervously and turned. Seeing Mr Finchley standing over him he stared as though he were confronting his own ghost. His hands dropped from the wheel and the car snaked madly across the width of the tarmac.

'Look out! Look out! You'll kill us!' cried Mr Finchley frantically. As he spoke the man recovered himself and grabbed the wheel. The car came back on her course. Mr Finchley breathed again.

'What—' he shouted through the wind, 'what's the idea? What do you mean by driving off with me?'

This time the driver leaned back cautiously:

'If I were you I'd sit down and keep my mouth shut for a while,' he shouted.

Mr Finchley lost his temper. He remembered his lunch and also that he had a train to catch.

'Here, do you hear me? Stop this car at once! You can't do this! I'll have the police after you! Stop the car, do you hear!'

The man did not reply. They were approaching a cross-road. Mr Finchley had a glimpse of automatic signals . . . a red light shone out. From the other road a lorry nosed its way round the corner. The driver, ignoring the warning light, accelerated. The engine screamed and they whirled around the back of the lorry with the back wheels drawing screams from the smooth surface of the road . . . Mr Finchley's heart jumped twice quickly and his hands grasped the back of the front seat to save himself from being flung out.

They were clear of the crossroads. The car, travelling faster than Mr Finchley had ever gone in his life, tore up the road, threading a mad passage through the other traffic. The driver took absolutely no notice of anything else on the road. His face running with perspiration, Mr Finchley beat a tattoo upon the other's shoulder:

'Are you mad? Stop the car at once before you smash into something! What' – his anger emboldened him – 'the dickens is the idea?'

The driver turned. For the first time Mr Finchley saw that it was not the same man who had asked him to look after the car. The other had been wearing a cap. The present driver wore a long, smartly cut black coat and a black felt hat was pulled well down over his eyes. At his throat a white-spotted silk muffler bellied as the wind cut across the low wind-screen.

'You'd better sit down and keep quiet,' he said. 'I'll explain later—'

'I'll do nothing of the sort!' broke in Mr Finchley angrily. 'Stop this car at once!'

For reply the other started to laugh. And the car continued its mad way along the road, swerving, screaming, turning and roaring. The more the man laughed the angrier became Mr Finchley. He stamped his feet on the floor and beat the back of the seat with his fist.

'I'll have the police on you for this . . . do you hear me? The police! THE POLICE! I won't stand such foolery!' he shouted.

'You're too late!' the reply came, high above the roar of the car.

'What do you mean? I believe you must be mad.'

The car made a leap between two long-distance coaches before the other answered. He was no longer laughing.

'I mean you're too late to set the police on me. They are already. Look—' He took one hand off the wheel and pointed backwards.

Mr Finchley thought he was joking. But he looked back. Behind them the road was almost free of traffic. It was a long straight by-pass road. There were only two cars; one was the motor-coach they had passed, and just in front of it was another car. Mr Finchley watched it. The car was travelling at a high speed and as he looked he thought he saw the glint of buttons in the sun.

'I shouldn't advise you to stand up—' The driver was shouting at him again. 'If they get close enough they might take a pot shot at us. But I shouldn't worry about that. I picked a good car. This bus'll touch a hundred! Better sit tight for a while.'

It took Mr Finchley some little time to convince himself that the other was neither joking nor mad; and even when he did he found it difficult to reconcile his present position with his sense of dignity. It was inconceivable that he, Mr Finchley, should be chased by the police. He had gone peacefully to sleep in the back of the car and now he was awakened to find himself heading up the Watford by-pass road at a speed well over eighty miles an hour.

He sat back in his seat, wiped his face carefully and pressed his hat tighter upon his head. This was very disturbing. This was a fine start to his first holiday. Somebody was going to suffer for this. Carrying him off in a car! The idea! He, he . . . He thumped the upholstery in his rage. What would Sprake say? – and Mrs Patten?

The driver turned round and smiled at him. He had a thin face and deep crow's feet gave him a puckish expression. His eyes sparkled as he nodded affably. It was evident that he bore Mr Finchley no ill-will. The smile disarmed him, and his answering glare wavered. The driver lifted his eyebrows and turned to his wheel. Mr Finchley gripped the cushions and tried to still his churning thoughts. After all, he had done no wrong and the police, even if they caught him, could not blame him. Still ... it was not so much what the police might do as what people might say. People like Sprake – no, Sprake would understand. But there were others. Mrs Patten now, she would not understand ... Why did this have to happen to him?

They were tearing down a steady incline. At the bottom the road forked. In the fork was a petrol-station; a low pleasant bungalow with yellow stucco walls and trim box hedges. Along the ridge of the roof ran a line of wooden foxhounds. The petrol pumps saluted them like red and green giants as they flashed by. The road curved quickly to a hump-backed bridge. Mr Finchley had a vision of water, quiet cool shadows, a canal barge and a man easing at a lock gate to let the barge through.

Despite his natural indignation, he could not entirely suppress a growing appreciation of the other's skill in handling the car. Gradually his anger began to leave him. He was not the type of man to be angry for long. The motion of the car, now that he had time to settle down, was a joy to him. He knew from the way in which the other handled the car that he was in safe hands. The driver was taking risks, but he was not taking them rashly. The man turned and looked back along the road. The police car was not yet in sight. A bend of the road hid them from the incline. Mr Finchley heard the engine note rise and the car hurtled forward like a green rocket; faster, faster ... the hedges danced by, the trees swept down to them and laughed, the sky tilted to one side and laughed with the trees and everything was blurred to a pleasant polychrome of speed. An AA sign started up from the road like an unexpected sun, and Mr Finchley read – King's Langley. The next moment they had entered a long straggling street lined on either side by untidy houses, shops with ragged boards flanking the windows and a few weary trees. Their speed dropped quickly. The other raced down through his gears with a sureness of touch that Mr Finchley knew came only from experience and a love of engines. A hand was flung out, brakes sung, and they had swung off the main road and were climbing a steep hill. Halfway up the hill the man turned round in his seat:

'That'll probably do 'em. But I can't afford to take any chances. I'm afraid I must ask you to be patient a little longer.'

He did not wait for Mr Finchley's reply. Perhaps it was as well that he did not, for Mr Finchley himself was not at all sure what he might have said. One half of him was annoyed at the prospect of missing his train, while the other half was beginning to revel in the pleasure of the ride and the exhilaration of breaking the law, of flouting convention at another's risk. Mr Finchley grunted and settled back in the car. Whether he agreed or not, it would obviously make very little difference to the young man.

The car raced up the hill, swung round a narrow corner and soon they were whipping through a maze of narrow lanes with high dust-covered hedges and frightening corners that hid farm carts and wavering cyclists; but the driver avoided all with a mad dexterity. For nearly half an hour by Mr Finchley's wristwatch they seemed to pursue an endless course through the tangle. They flashed by dark copses and over little white bridges where streams broke into cool lashers, by the side of a long park rich with huge oaks and browsing deer which stared at the sound of the engine and tossed their heads, and over village commons, to scatter the ducks as they waddled from their pools. Mr Finchley was convinced that they had passed the same public-house four times, but each time the sign over the low doorway held a different legend to disprove him. Then, without warning, the car bumped off the road as they were crossing a small heath, dipped down a slope, the mudguards slashing a trail of gold from the gorse bushes, and came to a stop well out of sight under a clump of tall trees.

The driver jumped from his seat and came round to Mr Finchley.

'And now—' began Mr Finchley, but the other cut him short.

'Just give me a few more minutes. If they're still on my trail we shall hear them go by in a short while. There's a main road just beyond here and they'll think I'm making for that. I'll explain everything to you later.'

He slipped away from the car, and as he went Mr Finchley saw that one hand was thrust deeply into his right coat pocket, as though he were holding something . . . as though, Mr Finchley told himself with a cold thrill, he might be holding a revolver. With an odd feeling in his throat Mr Finchley suddenly was aware of the potential danger of his position. Fear crept in where before had been anger. He watched the man make his way up the bank and then lie down in the cover of a gorse bush from where he could observe the roadway without being seen.

Mr Finchley waited anxiously. He did not know what to do. Suppose the police were not taken in? Suppose they saw the marks where the car had left the road? They could not very well blame him for what had happened, but it might be difficult to explain things satisfactorily to them. And if the police did not discover them – what then?

The driver was still lying motionless, almost indistinguishable against the black twisted limbs of the bushes. A twig fell from a tree and hit Mr Finchley sharply on the head. He put his hat on with a stealthy movement and looked up. He expected – now that the engine had stopped and a curious silence was all around him his nerves were acting strangely – to see a policeman stretched along the boughs. A small green chestnut-case dropped on to his hand and he saw a browny-grey shape flirt between two branches, like a duster jerked quickly out of a backroom window and withdrawn. From deeper within the wood which fringed the heath a jay suddenly made the silence rock with noise and Mr Finchley start violently. How much longer had he to wait before this farce was finished? A grasshopper sang *never, never, never, never,* mockingly, and from a blackthorn a chaffinch confided lazily to him that it had only just begun.

At last, when he had decided that they must have shaken off the police car, there came a high whine from the far side of the heath and he heard a car race quickly along the road. He saw his companion stiffen and, as the noise died away, roll over on to his back and give a loud whoop of joy.

He came slowly back to the car and leaning over the side smiled at Mr Finchley.

'And that's that. They won't come back. And now I must apologize for the rude way in which I have treated you, though I think you will agree that in the circumstances I had little option to do otherwise. When a man's hunted he hasn't time or inclination to think of others. That's one of the few things which annoy me in my profession. I so seldom get an opportunity to observe the courtesies and politenesses which make life easy for civilized beings . . .'

'That may be so, young man,' said Mr Finchley. 'I'm afraid I don't know what your profession is, but I can guess. I only know that you have considerably upset my arrangements . . . considerably upset them and I am going to report the whole matter to the police and have you taken in charge.' As he spoke Mr Finchley gradually recaptured some of his former annoyance and anger and forgot his fear. 'You nearly killed me, you nearly wrecked a new car which does not belong to you and you are undoubtedly avoiding the police. And apart from all this, you have made me miss my lunch, and a train I was to have caught this afternoon to Margate.'

'What,' said the other, 'do you expect me to do? I had to take the car – I didn't know you were in it!'

'I don't want any excuses,' snorted Mr Finchley, relieved at the contrite tone. 'I want to get back to London as soon as possible and I also want to see you in the hands of the police. You're a public menace!'

'Oh, sir!' There was a sly gleam in the other's eyes. 'You wouldn't give me up to the police, just because I was unfortunate enough to make you miss a train—'

'—and my lunch!' put in Mr Finchley hastily.

'And your lunch. You'd willingly see me in prison for doing that?'

'Well, perhaps—' In the face of the other's calmness Mr Finchley began to lose his choler.

'I knew you wouldn't. You're not that sort—'

'I'm a private citizen, and I expect to be treated as such. I suppose as you're ... a ... a ... crook, you wouldn't understand what I mean.' Mr Finchley felt a curious sadness suddenly envelop him as he faced the tall, pleasant-faced young man.

'You know,' he said in a different voice, 'you're very young to be leading this kind of life. Very young. Can't you do anything else? Can't you see you're on the wrong path . . .' Mr Finchley was working into a loquacious admonition when he was interrupted by a banana, which the other produced from his pocket.

'Don't do it, sir!' the other said, offering him the banana.

'Don't do what?' asked Mr Finchley, looking hard at the fruit.

'Don't start all that "Have you been saved?" "What of your soul, young man," business. It's been done before without success. A man makes his own life and once he's started he sticks to it. I'm awfully sorry about your lunch. I've missed mine, too. Won't you share my banana?'

He did not wait for Mr Finchley to refuse, but peeled the fruit quickly, broke it, and handed him a half. Mr Finchley took it mechanically.

'Aren't you going to eat it?' asked the other, as Mr Finchley held the banana awkwardly as though it were a baby's dummy, sticky and redolent.

'Why – why – I . . .'

'Oh! It's quite a good one – and I paid for it!' He laughed as Mr Finchley grew red with unnecessary embarrassment.

'I suppose I shall,' Mr Finchley muttered, and took a bite of the banana.

'I'm sorry about all this,' the other said between mouthfuls; 'but what was I to do? Surely you appreciate that, Mr—?'

'Mr Finchley's my name,' he replied, and held the remainder of his banana in his mouth as he fumbled from force of habit for a card.

'Don't bother,' the other laughed 'Mine's Beck. Wally Beck. Or, at least, that's one of 'em. It's the one my friends know me by. The police have lots of 'em. I've been Count Giovanni Stroom. Vivian P. Lesterdahl, Lucien Titley, and once I was just a number, but not for long. You've been a friend – so I give you the right name.'

'I've been a friend?' said Mr Finchley in amazement.

'Why, of course,' came the reply. 'There are few people would have viewed this incident, had they been in your place, with the same calm and understanding as you have ... very few, indeed. Men are like that, you know. They've lost all feeling for the adventurous and all love of danger – they're just clods. Then there are others. They may appear to be conservative, quiet and peace-loving – they are, but at the same time they have a longing for adventure. And when it comes to them they don't shout and call for the police. No, sir! They are men, even though they live the life of clerks, and when life offers 'em excitement they take it with both hands and ask for more. Don't you think so?'

Mr Finchley finished his banana before he replied. He was not such a fool as not to see that Wally was flattering him. He was not annoyed now. In fact, he was a little amused. It might be flattery he told himself, but it held a grain of reason and was true enough in theory. No; it was true! Few men could meet the unexpected with equanimity. It took a man of understanding, a man in whom there rested courage to see the other side of life.

'Yes, what you say may be very true,' he admitted, 'but it doesn't altogether solve my difficulties, does it? You've to admit that it doesn't. This is the first day of my holidays and I can afford to forgive a lot. I shall say nothing to the police, and I expect I can catch a later train. But one last word to you, young man, before I leave you and find the nearest bus station – you're leading a wicked, not a dangerous, life. You are breaking the law. Surely you could find your danger and adventure inside the law?'

Actually Mr Finchley was enjoying the experience of lecturing a law-breaker. Being a bachelor, he had been denied the self-imposed task of fathers to correct their own children; but as a law-abiding citizen and an upholder of the law, he discovered an overwhelming satisfaction in safely upbraiding (the gun in Wally's pocket had proven to be the banana) his companion. At first he had been angered and then a little afraid for himself in the presence of a self-confessed criminal. Wally's pleasant manner, and the puckish expression playing like cat's paws round his eyes had, however, proved to Mr Finchley that Wally was a human being in spite of his anti-social profession.

'You'll regret it,' he said; 'and then, perhaps, it'll be too late to alter things. Think it over. I say this, not because you have caused me any inconvenience, but for your own sake. Goodbye!'

Mr Finchley stepped from the car and held out his hand. Smiling curiously, Wally shook it. Mr Finchley waggled his head seriously and walked away. He felt that he had definitely scored. He had encountered a motor-bandit and emerged from the affair without any loss of dignity. As he walked away the smell of the gorse bushes washed over him pleasantly and from the wood at his back the jay began to laugh loudly and indecently.

THREE

How Mr Finchley Becomes a Felon and Sleeps in a Strange Bed

As he reached the foot of the rise, Wally's voice rang out: 'Stop!'

Mr Finchley turned and the world spun slightly under his feet. Wally was standing, tall and insolent, his legs apart, his black-coated figure picked out against the bright green of the car and in his left hand he held a small automatic.

'It won't do, Mr Finchley,' he said. 'You'd better come

back.' The tone of Wally's voice, coupled with the lift of his automatic, made it clear that he was not joking. Mr Finchley walked back again.

'It won't do, at all,' repeated Wally.

'Now look here—' began Mr Finchley. He was interrupted by a gesture of Wally's weapon.

'Don't argue for the minute. I'm thinking.'

He crinkled his eyebrows, tilted his slouch hat backward and scratched his head with the automatic. It was some time before the puzzled look passed from his face. Then he addressed Mr Finchley.

'You're a sportsman, aren't you?'

'Don't you think I've acted like one so far?' Mr Finchley asked sharply.

'Sure, I do! That's what makes it difficult. You've been a sport and I'm grateful to you.'

'Then I don't see what you're puzzled about. What's the meaning of the gun and calling me back? I thought this foolery was over!'

Wally looked at the gun as though he had forgotten that it was ever in his hand. He laughed quickly and put it into his pocket.

'Force of habit,' he explained. 'When I say "stop", I usually have to pull it out. Look here, we've got to get this thing straight!' He put one arm affectionately round Mr Finchley and guided him into the front seat of the car.

'Have a cigarette?' he asked, when they were both seated, and thrust one upon the unwilling Mr Finchley.

'Now what's the matter? I'm anxious to get away!' Mr Finchley waved his unlighted cigarette.

'I know,' said Wally. 'That's the trouble. Now let's talk this matter out comfortably and sanely. This is the position as I see it. You've missed a train—'

'And my lunch,' insisted Mr Finchley.

'And your lunch,' agreed Wally gloomily. 'You're going off to Margate to start your holidays. Not married? No. Luggage gone in advance? Yes. Good! House all locked up and nothing to worry about there? Well – that makes things better. You go from here and catch a Green Line bus from the main road up there—' He jerked a thumb over his shoulder. 'By the way, how did you come to be in the car if it isn't yours?'

Mr Finchley told him.

'Um! Then probably before you get home the police will have identified you, and, although you have done no wrong, you'll have to answer questions. That means that within four hours the police will be here looking for me—'

'What of it? You won't be here!'

'That's just it!' Wally drew at his cigarette. 'I shall be here. If I stir before it's dark they'll nab me. If I wait until dark I can get clear in the car easily.'

'But what about me?' asked Mr Finchley, growing anxious again. 'I can't stop here until nightfall. It'll be too late to get a train to Margate. I know there's no food in the house and my housekeeper has gone.'

'Yes, that's difficult. But I've got an idea!' replied Wally. 'That's why I asked you if you were a sport. You must stay here with me and then come back to our place for the night – we're quite civilized – and I'll send a wire to your hotel at Margate to say that you are coming tomorrow. Tomorrow afternoon I'll take you there in a different car . . .'

'No!' Mr Finchley replied firmly. 'I can't do it. I won't do it! It's preposterous! If you imagine you can keep me here . . . !'

'Why not?' broke in Wally. 'It solves all the difficulties.'

'Does it! Even if I agreed, as soon as I got to Margate the police would be after me. It won't take them long to discover from the owner of the car's description who I am. How am I to explain things? I shall have to tell the truth then! Besides, what about the car? Are you actually going to steal it?'

Wally started incredulously for a moment and burst into laughter.

'What a game! What a day!' he cried. 'Don't you see – you don't have to explain anything! This is what happened and you could do nothing to prevent it. You went to sleep in a car, quite innocently, and woke up to find yourself being driven off by an armed desperado – it's always an armed desperado – who took you to a lonely common, where he lay hidden all day and forced you to remain at the point of an automatic!' Wally jabbed him playfully in the side with the gun and grinned. 'At night he blindfolded you and drove off to a house in the country – you don't know where it is. You don't care; all you are worrying about is your holiday at Margate. You had supper. It was drugged – anyone who reads thrillers will confirm that. You slept, and when Sunday came you recovered to find yourself being driven into Margate in a strange car.'

'Easy! And the rest?'

'You are left at your hotel and immediately inform the police. You become, if you wish, the day's news. And here's a tip. If you get right on the phone to a daily paper that story ought to net you enough to pay for your holiday. Why, you're in clover. Gosh!' Wally was becoming enthusiastic. 'I almost wish I were you. What a glorious start to a holiday! As for this car ... she's a beauty, ain't she?' He rubbed the wheel slowly. 'She'll be found – since you insist and it's one way of repaying you – by the roadside in good condition. How's that?'

'It sounds all right, but—' Mr Finchley began doubtfully.

'And it is all right. You can't tell the police where you stopped the night, because you don't know. What do you say? The only other alternative is to go now, and that means I'm in for a long stretch, and your holiday may be crippled? You wouldn't do the dirty on me – would you?'

Mr Finchley was silent. It sounded all right, only ... There was something wrong. Was there? Or was it because it was all so strange? Was it ... was it because he was afraid? Afraid! He sneered at the thought. All his life he had lived in a narrow circle, looking to other men to provide the excitement and thrills in his life, sharing his experiences at second-hand with a thousand others. All his life he had secretly longed for something to happen to him that would mark him as a man apart from the rest of his fellows, a man upon whom life had thrust the honour of the unexpected and found him ready.

The sun splashed the boles of the chestnuts with fire. Across the golden air came the slow rumble of a train, and far in the woods two jays cursed one another heartily. Silence for the jays was a thing to be embroidered by noise, and life, Mr Finchley discovered, was nothing if it did not hold adventure and romance.

He turned to Wally. 'Since you put it that way, I see no other way out,' he replied hesitantly.

Wally swung round, and Mr Finchley saw that he was surprised.

'You'll do it?'

Mr Finchley nodded: 'I suppose so – but I still don't like the idea.'

'Shake!' cried Wally. 'You've got guts! You're a man I could love! You're a man after my own heart!' He pumped Mr Finchley's hand eagerly. He started to laugh. He laughed quietly; he chuckled; he laughed loudly so that the wrinkles sparked over his face. He laughed until his hat fell off and Mr Finchley smiled indulgently. Wally rocked and Mr Finchley grinned. Wally wiped his eyes and laughed louder than ever and Mr Finchley suddenly found himself laughing with him. Then they both roared with an excess of feeling that relieved the grotesqueness of the situation and broke down the last barrier between them.

The rest of the afternoon passed quickly. They talked, and found that their views on league football were the same. Mr Finchley confided to Wally about Mrs Patten and her tyrannies, though he could not accept the other's suggestion that he should poison her.

No one came to disturb them. They smoked and forgot their hunger while Wally told Mr Finchley some of his history. The darkness came, draping the trees in mystery, silencing the jays and chaffinch, until the grasshoppers alone sawed indefatigably at the moon, tilted like a blown feather against the night. A june-bug banged stupidly into the windshield of the car. Wally said it was time to go.

'Better bandage yourself,' he said, tossing a handkerchief to Mr Finchley, 'so that you won't have to tell any lies.'

Mr Finchley chuckled and tied the handkerchief about his eyes. He made himself comfortable on the back seat.

Wally stepped on the accelerator, moved the gear lever, and the car jolted backwards across the turf to the road. The engine raced and they were off. To Mr Finchley, lying in the car, the exhilaration of that moment was a thing of mystery. It seemed that there had never been any Sprake or Margate; nothing but a wearisome greyness in which he had moved dream-fashion. Now he was alive.

For two hours he lay in the back of the car, with a rug over him to protect him from the cold. Once the car stopped while Wally bought petrol and oil. Mr Finchley had not the slightest idea of the direction in which they were driving and, for the sake of his own conscience when the police should come to question him, he did not attempt to trace the car's progress. He was aware that they must have travelled nearly a hundred miles, and was wondering how soon the journey would be over, when he heard the note of the wheels change as they churned across soft gravel.

'All right! You can take the curtains off!'

Mr Finchley removed the handkerchief, to find that the car was in a garage, a small fibre-walled, lath-lined hut. He wriggled stiffly from the car.

'This way!'

Wally took his arm and led him from the garage. They were at the top end of a drive which led to a large house.

'There's no one here but the maid,' he explained, as he fitted a key into the door. 'The others were in London with me. They will probably arrive in the morning.'

'You keep a maid?'

'Why not?' asked Wally. 'To the world we are just three independent gentlemen. She thinks I'm a stockbroker. Even if I told her that I was a crook, she wouldn't believe me. I'm too respectable. You might remember that.'

They passed through the hall to the back of the house. Wally led the way to the kitchen.

'Can't wake the girl now. We'll just forage for ourselves. I'm hungry!'

'I'm hungry, too. It's a long time since I ate anything.'

'We'll soon cure that—' Wally opened a cupboard door. 'Here, take this!'

Mr Finchley found himself burdened with a large plate holding a piece of cold beef. He deposited it on the table. A loaf of bread followed. Butter, lettuce, onions, a jar of mixed pickles, cheese; and then Wally stepped back.

'You'll find plates and stuff over there.' He pointed to another cupboard and, leaving Mr Finchley to discover them, he scuttled from the kitchen.

Mr Finchley was surprised to find himself setting the table as though it were his normal manner to eat with a thief every evening. He even found time between the cupboard and the table to feel a little proud of his adventure.

Wally returned, nursing three bottles.

'India pale ale!' he remarked laconically, and fetched a couple of glasses. They sat down to eat. There was that silence between them that grows around men who eat because they are hungry; men eating from need and not from habit. The beef was tough, but neither noticed it. The lettuce and onions were gone, and the cheese crippled before Wally leaned back, shook his head approvingly and reached for a bottle.

'The pleasures of the other senses are nothing compared with a good appetite. Ten minutes ago I would have swopped a Corot for a cold chicken.'

'Yes.' Mr Finchley was expansive with food. 'Hunger is the best sauce. When you always have regular meals, you lose your appreciation for food. Too much of a good thing spoils it.'

'Like keeping a harem, eh?' Wally laughed.

'I don't know about that.' Mr Finchley fought shy of such a topic.

'Well, I can't say that I do either,' laughed Wally. 'Here pass your glass and we'll drink.'

Mr Finchley entered into his companion's mood. He was beginning to enjoy himself a little. He raised his glass:

'Here's to the first day of my holiday,' he said boldly, 'and to the first crook of my life: they're both turning out different from what I expected.'

They drank.

'And here,' said Wally, rising, 'is to a man who lives as he wills and yet keeps the laws!'

They drank again and finished the bottles.

'Now it's time you were drugged and flung into the dungeon. I'll show you where you sleep.'

Mr Finchley was shown his bed in a small, blue-papered room. He sat down on the edge of the bed, the sight of which reminded him that he was tired.

'Here, catch!' Wally popped his head round the door and threw Mr Finchley a pair of pyjamas, green with black silk facings, lordly things which were cold to the touch. 'Good-night, sleep well!'

'Goodnight!'

Mr Finchley was suddenly anxious for bed. The door closed behind Wally, and that impulsive young man departed from Mr Finchley's life.

FOUR

Of Roses and Honesty

THE sound of water escaping from a broken gutter awakened Mr Finchley. He turned over, still half asleep, and saw through the window that it was raining hard. A grey sky was pressing down over a tall poplar that tossed like a horse's tail in the wind. The drone of the rain on the window and the subtle orchestration of the escaping water came pleasantly to him. He reflected that it was very comforting to lie in bed on a wet Sunday morning.

Somewhere within the house a clock struck ten. Mr Finchley sat up in bed and yawned. He must get up. In a few hours Wally would be taking him to Margate. There was a new cake of soap, a new toothbrush and towels on the wash-stand. They had not been there when he had gone to bed.

'Must have come in while I was asleep,' he murmured.

He started to wash, and, as he did so, he hummed to himself. The cold water fired his skin and the soap worked into his eyes.

'Bother the soap!'

He grabbed a towel blindly and wiped his eyes. There was a laugh behind him. Mr Finchley's head broke through the folds of the towel like a seal breaking water.

'Eh?'

'Go on with your washin'! I didn't say anything.'

A short man, wearing brown plus-fours and an open-necked shirt, was sitting sideways on the bed watching Mr Finchley. This must be one of the others Wally had spoken about. Mr Finchley went on with his dressing. The man took a bite from an apple he was eating and waved his hand.

'Go on, don't mind me! I'm used to it.'

Mr Finchley saw that the left side of his face was covered completely by a hideous scarlet naevus.

'I suppose,' said Mr Finchley, trying to hide his confusion, 'Wally told you about me?'

'He did!' The tone was rather surprising.

Mr Finchley began to be uneasy.

The other rose and threw his core into the empty grate.

'Yes, Wally told me. A pity. In fact the whole affair's a pity. I wanted to kill you and clear the mess up, but Wally said that wouldn't be playing the game, so we let it go ...' His words merged into a murmur as he leaned on the window-ledge and looked out into the garden. The whole delivery of the remark had been so matter of fact that Mr Finchley decided he must be joking.

'That was very good of Wally to put it like that.'

The man turned from the window, and his lips twisted as he spoke. 'Wally's a fool, and most fools talk about playing the game. Killing you would have been much easier, don't you think so?'

Mr Finchley was alarmed at the man's attitude. He talked of killing Mr Finchley in the same detached manner in which one might talk of drowning kittens.

'I suppose you're going to adopt Wally's suggestion about Margate. It appeared to be the only sensible thing to do ...'

'I don't know ... killing would have been easier. Funny

how misfortune never comes alone. Ever noticed it?'

'Well ... well ... I don't ...'

'Oh, it does very often! For example: we come home and find you here, and on top of that the wind and the rain in the night – you slept through it, I expect – battered down three of my General McArthurs. Spoilt every bloom!'

He sat down on the bed and lit a cigarette without offering one to Mr Finchley.

'Well, I'd like to know what you are going to do!' Mr Finchley was amazed to find himself asking the question almost truculently. He had had enough fooling for one morning. 'I want to go to Margate!'

'I'm not stopping you,' the other said. 'That's where you all ought to go. It's only when you start to crowd in at the other places that I get annoyed.'

'I'm glad of that,' replied Mr Finchley.

'Of what?'

'That I can go to Margate. I should have been there yesterday. What do you say, Mr ...?'

'Thornton.'

'Mr Thornton ... to my having some breakfast now. Wally said he would drive me to Margate today.'

'Breakfast ... yes, I'll send it up to you. I'm afraid, though – Mr Finchley, isn't it? – you can't go to Margate today.'

Mr Finchley started forward. 'Look here—' He broke off, suspicion crowding into his mind: 'I see, I suppose you think that as soon as I get to Margate, I shall tell the truth to the police and then they'll get you? Does Wally think that way, too?'

'My dear Mr Finchley, you misjudge us,' Mr Thornton said sadly. 'We know quite well that you'll play your part all right; but it won't work!'

'And why not?'

'You couldn't do it. It would be quite impossible for you to make the police believe your story. I'm afraid you'd make a poor liar. Wally should have thought of that. He's a fool. The police would see through your story at once. Killing would have been so simple ...'

Mr Finchley was angry. His face went red, and his podgy hands trembled at his coat lapels.

'You think I can't do it, do you?' he shouted. 'And I suppose you think I started on this fool's game because I had to? You think I agreed to Wally's suggestion because I had to and not because I wanted to help him? And you think that when a man's done everything he can to help you out of a scrape, when he's run practically against the law, for no other reason on earth except that he happens to be a little soft-hearted, that you can sit down and insult him freely! By thunder, sir! I ... I feel ... I feel like punching you on the nose!' It was the most warlike expression Mr Finchley could command. He waved his fist under Mr Thornton's nose. 'In fact' – he stamped angrily – 'unless you apologize to me – I WILL!'

Mr Thornton confronted him, his face immobile.

'Don't punch me on the nose!' he said gravely. 'It would be unpleasant. Besides, you couldn't do it while I have this ...' He spun an automatic round his index finger airily and then replaced it in his pocket. 'I apologize, if I *have* insulted you.'

'Uh! I'm glad you've had the decency to apologize!' snorted Mr Finchley, calming down considerably.

'Perhaps we'd better let this subject rest for a while,' continued Mr Thornton. 'I'll see about your breakfast and shaving arrangements.'

The door shut behind him. Mr Finchley heard a faint click and, trying the handle, he found, as he had expected, that the door was locked.

He sat down on the bed and kicked petulantly at the mat. He had still not recovered himself. It was a good thing for the fellow that he had gone when he did! A bad liar ... He took out his pipe and began to fill it. If he saw Wally again it would be to say something nasty to him. There was a limit beyond which no man would willingly go ...

The tobacco and the silence of his room gradually restored Mr Finchley. It was not his nature to be angry for long, and by the time the room was grey with smoke he had recovered some of his former calm. But he was still far from happy. It had been promised that he should be taken to Margate. He had carried out his part of the bargain, and he was determined that not Wally, nor Mr Thornton, nor anyone should prevent him from reaching Margate.

The door opened suddenly and a short man came into the room carrying a tray. He had a crop of curly red hair, a freckled face, a battered nose and the large, misshapen ears of a pugilist. He winked at Mr Finchley and placed the tray on a small table which stood by the window.

'That'll be the water for yer shavin' and yer breakfast. And if it's a wise boy you are, you'll be shavin' first. The water'll be cold enough to christen Lucifer if you wait till ye've eaten the sausages . . .'

'But—'

'Jackson's the name, if you'll be after thankin' me,' the man interrupted him. 'There's a nice taste of home-made marmalade for you, too. I didn't exactly make it, but I showed the girl.'

Mr Finchley stood open-mouthed. Jackson was gone and the door locked before he could make any move, but there was a jug of coffee, sausages under a cover, toast, butter and marmalade on the tray and shaving water and razor.

'Better shave first, I suppose,' grunted Mr Finchley.

He shaved carefully. The water was not very hot, and a safety razor came strangely to his hand. Then he ate his breakfast. He had hardly finished before Mr Thornton opened the door and entered the room.

'Feel better now?' he inquired.

'I'm all right. I'm only anxious to know how long it's going to be before we start,' replied Mr Finchley.

Mr Thornton shook his head:

'There's no starting today, or tomorrow. You'll have to stop here a few days while we make arrangements to get away. In three days we shall be gone and then you can go to Margate or the police.'

'You mean I've got to stay here, in this room, for several days?' demanded Mr Finchley.

'That's what I've been trying to tell you.'

'I won't do it! This is ridiculous! An outrage! I'll have the law after you ... you!' Mr Finchley snapped his fingers in a futile attempt to command words biting enough to express his rage.

Mr Thornton cut in abruptly: 'I can't understand your objection. You'll be well fed and I've brought some books for you to read.' He tossed a couple of volumes on to the bed.

'Blast your books!' burst out Mr Finchley, his face purpling. 'I want to go to Margate!'

Indeed, so much did Mr Finchley want to go to Margate at that moment that he would have rushed at Mr Thornton in an attempt to make his way from the room by force. Mr Thornton was, however, dangling an automatic in one hand suggestively, as though he had half guessed Mr Finchley's intentions.

'So you can,' replied Mr Thornton, 'only I think you'd better read the books first!' And he left the room swiftly and locked the door.

Considering the affair as sanely as he could, Mr Finchley knew that even in the most favourable light it was preposterous. It was not right, it was neither decent nor civilized, that he, Mr Edgar Finchley, an Englishman, a taxpayer, a ratepayer and an honorary member of the Isthmians Cricket Club (one of the oldest and most dignified clubs in North London), should be associating with criminals. It did not now occur to him to be frightened. Mr Thornton had lightly suggested killing him. Mr Finchley had confidence in the British way of life which rightly regarded crimes, shooting and winning sweep-prizes as things that happen only on the pages of daily newspapers. Had Mr Thornton gone so far as to raise the automatic to shoot him, Mr Finchley knew that something would happen to save him. Things simply did not happen like that in England. Yes, the whole affair was preposterous; yet he was gratified to find that he was equal to such an occasion.

He reviewed the various schemes for escaping from the room and reaching Margate which came to his mind. He dismissed the idea of attacking Jackson when he came in again. Jackson, with his cauliflower ears, looked as though he would enjoy it. Even if he were to stun the man with a chair, he had to get clear of the house and Mr Thornton. The thought of Mr Thornton taking pot shots at him as he dodged down the drive was unnerving.

He discovered that the key was in the door, though on the outside, and – borrowing the method from the films – Mr Finchley decided to wait until nightfall. Then he would push a paper under the door directly beneath the keyhole and poke the key from its socket with his knife. The key would fall on the paper. He would draw it into the room and . . . Margate.

He walked about the room until he was tired. He smoked. He smoked so much that the room grew stuffy and he went to the window to let in fresh air. It was still raining. Below the level of the window ran a wooden balcony. Mr Finchley discovered that the window could be opened. Here he had been sitting scheming how to escape from the house for four hours, and all the time there had been a balcony for him to step on and a pillar down which he could slide to freedom!

'Fancy my not thinking of that,' he said, and darted away from the window quickly. Fortunately for him, his hat was in the room. He had no coat, but he did not mind getting wet if he could get away from the house.

He put on his hat and scrambled with difficulty to the sill. The balcony was four feet below him – not a long drop. But Mr Finchley, as he poised his hundred and fifty-five pounds on the sill, was unpleasantly aware of each of the forty-eight inches.

The sill was too narrow for him to turn and ease himself down. His heart beat lightly as he gradually let himself go. His grip on the wet ledge slipped and he fell with a dreadful thump which was amplified by the balcony-boards into running thunder.

He waited anxiously, but there came no sound. Five rainy minutes passed and he decided that he had not been heard.

Once on the balcony, the rain swept around him like a damp cloak, but he did not mind. He crept along the front of the house to the end of the balcony. Below was a lawn edged by damp laurel bushes and a few despondent lilac trees. He clambered awkwardly over the wooden rail and felt for the pillar. His feet found a grip around it. He looked round – the ground was a long way off. He eased himself downwards until his hands held the pillar and then proceeded to slide gravely and slowly to earth. As he neared the earth his spirits rose. If Mr Thornton thought he could cage him . . . ! He was not so weak and ineffectual as some people seemed to think!

Mr Finchley's feet touched the ground and, as they did so, a pair of strong arms caught him round the waist, pinioning his arms to his sides.

'Arrah! I was wondering if ye'd have the nerve for it!' A familiar voice boomed in his ear, and Mr Finchley twisting round, stared into the face of Jackson. His first shock over, he struggled and kicked to free himself, but Jackson held him as a mother holds a fractious child.

'Let go! Let go!' Mr Finchley kicked at the other's shins. Jackson only held the tighter. He laughed at Mr Finchley's efforts.

'Eh! A fine fighter, ain't ye now? But 'tis an awful row you make gettin' out of a windy! Come up, me beauty! Come up!'

With an easy movement he lifted Mr Finchley off his feet and carried him into the house and back to the old room. Mr Finchley recognized that he was beaten and watched Jackson close the window.

'I shouldn't be tryin' that again,' advised Jackson, and he left the room.

Later he brought Mr Finchley his tea. There was only the first scheme left now, and he waited for darkness.

He forced himself to read until his watch showed ten o'clock, then he undressed slowly and got into bed. He did not want to raise any suspicions and he was not sure whether Mr Thornton or Jackson would come into the room again before they retired. If everything went well, he was going to make his attempt at three o'clock, when the house would be asleep.

Mr Finchley lay musing in the darkness, until finally he dropped off to sleep. He was snoring when Mr Thornton passed his door at twelve and the sound made the man smile.

Mr Finchley woke at half past four and cursed himself for sleeping so long. Hurriedly he switched on the light and quietly commenced his operations. He had discovered an old newspaper under the mattress of the bed, and he pushed it silently under the door. He was surprised to find himself acting with a deft expertness. He almost wished that there was someone to see him and admire . . .

He opened his knife with steady fingers and inserted the thin blade into the keyhole. The blade met with no resistance. He turned it, puzzled. The draught from under the door cut across his bare ankles and made the newspaper belly like a sail. He pushed again, but no key fell on to the paper. A dark thought crept into his mind . . . Quickly he withdrew the knife and bending down looked through the keyhole. He could see nothing; all was dark, but through the hole whistled a draught strong and hearty like an express train roaring through a tunnel, and Mr Finchley knew that the key had been taken out . . . apparently Mr Thornton also visited the films.

This last check was more than Mr Finchley could stand at half past four in the morning. He swore, not caring who should hear him, kicked the door with his bare foot, switched off the light and got into bed again.

He was awakened at nine o'clock by the entry of Jackson with his breakfast and shaving water.

'Good mornin'!'

'Good morning,' replied Mr Finchley, sitting up in bed and rubbing the back of his head. 'How much longer am I to be kept in here?'

He was petulant at being awakened from a good sleep, and the sight of Jackson's merry, if uncouth, face irritated him.

'We can't bear to part with you,' grinned Jackson. He left the room laughing and Mr Finchley snorted.

For the rest of the day he was left alone. There was a

36

continual noise of hammering and scuffling in the house, and Mr Finchley guessed that the 'scoundrels' (by now he had no lack of forceful descriptions) were making their arrangements to leave the place.

He made no further efforts to escape; partly because he was not given an opportunity and partly because he had lapsed into an apathetic state of unconcern.

He picked up the books Thornton had flung him which had slipped on to the floor behind the bed, and examined them listlessly. They both dealt technically with the culture of roses. Mr Finchley opened one without enthusiasm. This was the third day of his holidays and he should be lazing in a deckchair on Margate front, with a Guards' band playing 'Humperdinck' agreeably in the distance, and pretty girls in scarlet costumes splashing about in the surf. He had no wish to learn about thrips. Mr Finchley sighed, and began to read.

Mr Thornton looked into the room at eleven and discovered Mr Finchley asleep, the light still burning.

He smiled. There was something in Mr Finchley that awakened a curious tenderness in him. Under different circumstances they might have spent a pleasant time talking of roses. A shadow slipped across his face ... this little man had, however, considerably upset his plans, hustled him indecently ... At the thought, his harshness swept back.

'It would have been easier to kill him ...' he muttered. The room was darkened and Mr Thornton locked the door silently. That was the last he saw of Mr Finchley.

FIVE

Of a Whistling Woman

MR FINCHLEY, waking, refused to believe his eyes. It certainly looked like a girl; medium height, black coat with a fur collar, a small black hat and a face which, had it not been troubled with a frown when he saw it, must ordinarily have been pleasant enough. Mr Finchley stared hard and sleepily at the phantom, shook his head reprovingly and rolled over on his side to sleep again. He would not read in bed again. Hardly had his head reached the pillow when the phantom gave evidence of its biological integrity.

'Hey! Rouse yourself – will you?'

Mr Finchley grunted. A savage gleam fired the girl's eye. She bent, lifted the bedclothes and plunged her hand swiftly into the bed.

'Aioooow! I—'

Mr Finchley jerked to life with a roar of anguish which was killed by the girl's placing her hand over his mouth.

'Sssssh! Be quiet. D'you want to wake the whole blessed house?'

She took her hand from his mouth. Mr Finchley rubbed his buttock without any doubt that he was awake and with less doubt about the girl – no ghost could pinch as she did.

'Can you drive a car?'

She asked the question while he was still troubling his mind with the metaphysics of the interruption.

'What are you doing in my room?' he asked. 'You can't come in here!'

'I don't care about can't. I'm here, and I didn't come for my own sake,' she replied.

'Then what did you come for? Did you come in that way?' He pointed to the window, now open.

'Yes. Yes. Oh! What a long time it takes you to think. Listen, can you drive a car?' Her feet moved impatiently.

'Yes, I expect so . . . at least . . . but what has that to do with it, whatever it is? Good gracious!' Mr Finchley was suddenly alarmed. 'You must get out of here, my girl. This is a dangerous house! If . . .'

'I know that, you mug! I've lived in this house for the last three years, but only since you came have I discovered just how dangerous it is . . .'

'You live here? Then what—'

'Oh! What a man! Listen, I'll explain. I'm the maid here. I knew they were keeping you here for something or the other, and all this packing made me suspicious. And then that

Jackson asked me yesterday to go to Paris. I told him that I'd give him an answer in the morning and decided to clear off tonight. Then I thought of you—'

'Very nice of you.'

'I'm like that,' she replied cheerfully. 'If you can drive a car it's easy – we'll pinch one of theirs. If not we walk.'

'I'll drive the car,' replied Mr Finchley, wondering if he could.

'That's that then—'

'But where am I to drive it?'

'Bristol first, to take me home; and then you can do what you like. I'm only interested in getting to Bristol. I shan't make a song to the police about them. They've treated me well up to now. But that Jackson mug, with his cauliflower ears, an' spittin' all over the place . . . ugh! Now get dressed quickly – and quietly. They're on the other side of the house, but we don't want to wake 'em!'

Once Mr Finchley thoroughly grasped the idea, it did not take him long to act, but it always took him some time to adjust himself. The girl leaned out of the window while he dressed. When he was ready she outlined her scheme to him.

'There's an Austin in the garage, we'll take that. I've seen that there's plenty of petrol and oil in her. You stop in the garage while I go down the drive and open the gate. When you hear me whistle you start her up and pick me up as you pass. Even if they hear us – which is likely enough – we shall be too far away for 'em to catch us. How's that?'

'Sounds all right to me,' admitted Mr Finchley. 'I'm as eager to get away as you, and, although I don't want to go to Bristol particularly, I'll do that for you. But I hope they don't hear us!'

'I thought you'd be game. Come on, then.' She swung herself agilely up over the window and dropped to the balcony. Mr Finchley followed, less agilely, and enlisted her help to reach the balcony. They crossed the balcony, with the moon throwing long shadows around them.

'You first,' whispered Mr Finchley, and he watched her mount the rail and slide down the pillar.

'All clear!' He heard her voice from below. He climbed on to the rail and his dark form merged with the pillar so that in the night it seemed to swell as though a snake were swallowing an egg. The egg moved uneasily down the snake's throat and Mr Finchley was standing by her side.

She moved away towards the garage with Mr Finchley following her.

'Here we are,' she said, 'I left the door open.'

Mr Finchley recognized the garage into which Wally had driven the Bentley.

'Sure you can manage the car?' she inquired.

'Yes,' Mr Finchley lied bravely. Theoretically his knowledge of car driving was complete. Actually, he knew as much about them as he did about women.

'Good. Now I'll slip down the drive and when you hear me whistle – step on it!'

'Leave it to me!'

The cool night air and the secret slipping away in the dark acted on his blood like wine. The girl disappeared into the darkness. He got into the car, and with the light from the dashboard he picked out the various controls and pedals.

A whistle vibrated across the night. He pressed the self-starter, and to his surprise the engine broke into song. Congratulating himself he engaged the gears. The resultant leap nearly marred the success of the night's exploit. The front wheels hit the grass bank on the other side of the drive and the nose of the car tilted upwards. He grabbed the wheel hard and slewed the car round. The car performed a series of short jerks along the sloping bankside, rolled playfully and decided to behave itself. He felt the wheels on firm gravel again and saw that half a laurel bush had been forced through the left side of the car into the empty seat at his side. Breathing heavily, he switched the headlights on. A black form darted out from the shadows of the trees by the drive gates.

'Good work!'

The man moved off and the girl sat down – on the laurel bush! 'What! What's all this?' She removed the debris from under her.

40

'Laurels,' said Mr Finchley, finding that the steering wheel demanded all his attention.

'Laurels!' she echoed.

'Yes, laurels,' repeated Mr Finchley. 'I ... I hit ... they came in as I left the garage. You see ...'

'You reserve stunts like that for when you're by yourself,' she replied. 'I want to reach Bristol safely.'

'Leave it to me. By the way, am I going in the right direction?'

She nodded. 'Yes. I'll direct you.'

For a while Mr Finchley was decidedly uneasy and the car snaked along the road under his unaccustomed hands. Then he began to get the feel of the machine and within half an hour his confidence – shaken by the laurel bush – returned. Mr Finchley felt exultant. The car sweeping along the dark roads, the growing moon that slipped through the cloud masses and sprang at them from behind houses, the air coming back into his face ... after the purgatory of his imprisonment, all gave him a feeling of conquest. He had given Mr Thornton the slip, and not only that; the escapade had been carried out with a sureness of touch and a deep observance of romantic convention that left nothing more to be wished. What more could he ask? Here he was fleeing from a gang of dangerous rogues – did three constitute a gang, he wondered? – in one of their own cars and by his side sat a lovely – the gloom of the car and the backwash of light from the headlamps was kind to her – girl. What an extraordinary girl she was. Bursting into his room and rescuing him, moving about in the dark like a thief and then whistling like a man ... and yet she was a woman, but how different from Mrs Patten! He asked her gruffly if she did not think so.

'Romantic!' she replied scoffingly. 'It isn't my idea of romance. Too much of a rush.'

'What are you called?' she asked suddenly.

Mr Finchley told her.

'My name is Jane,' she proffered; 'Jane Myers. How did you come to be mixed up with them?'

'That's a long story, Miss Myers—'

'You're a funny old stick, aren't you,' she laughed. 'Why

41

don't you call me Jane? This isn't eighteen ninety-three. I'm glad it is a long story. We have a long way to go. Bristol's about a hundred and fifty miles from here, so we shall want something to pass the time away.'

Her impetuosity amused Mr Finchley. 'Sorry, Miss Jane.'

'That's better. Though,' she added, 'if you'd been a Romeo I might not have said that...'

'Romeo?'

'You know, a sheik, handsome Leslie. A girl must look after herself. That's why I told Jackson where to get off! But I saw that you were a gentleman... Let's hear your story.'

Mr Finchley told her what had happened to him since he had left the office on Saturday morning.

He had just finished his story when the car's lights picked out a crossroad and a finger-post rooted like a white coral arm. They emerged from a side-turning on to a concrete road and he saw the word Oxford on the post.

They passed through Oxford as the east was beginning to pale. Mr Finchley had always wanted to visit Oxford. But now, they tore along the High, past the grey tower of Magdalen College raised high above the quiet poplars and slow mist-laved Cher, and unobservingly by the twisted pillars of St Mary's. This was no time for sightseeing.

An hour later the car rattled out of Faringdon into the clear light of the morning. Mr Finchley switched off his lights and noticed that Jane, who had been talking unceasingly about nothing at all ever since he had finished his story, had fallen silent. He glanced across at her and found that she was asleep.

'Poor child. Probably tired out,' he murmured.

The road dipped to the plain and away in the distance Mr Finchley caught the broad outline of the Berkshires. Very carefully he brought the car to a standstill on a pocket of the road and eased himself out of the driving seat.

'You'd better have your sleep in comfort, my girl,' he said, half to himself and half to Jane, as he made her comfortable in the car with a rug: 'while I go and have a smoke.'

The girl protested sleepily, but feeling the warmth of the

rug around her she relaxed and, almost before Mr Finchley had finished wrapping the rug about her feet, she was asleep again.

SIX

How Deceit is not to be Condoned by Kisses

THE light of morning came spouting over the bare shoulders of the downs, tipping the long ridge with golden lines and throwing great pools of black and grey shadown across the plain. Slowly the broad scarp-faces quickened into a green life that caught at the wavering light and held it fast to the breast of the earth. The sun tipped the edge of the hills in a blazing tiara and every copse and thicket, each barn and cottage, sprang into a bold relief; white wall vivid against chestnut green, and a church clock, black and gold against the grey of the stones.

A blackbird volleyed from a nearby briar brake, shaking the dew from the tall cow-parsley. Mr Finchley felt the young sun warm upon his hand and he carefully knocked his pipe out. It was the first time he had ever seen the sun come over the hills. It was the first time he had listened to the morning concert of the birds. This, he said to himself half regretfully, is what happens every morning. The sun advancing, the thrushes breaking their snails on the slate slab at the gate's side, the iconoclastic crows scraping the furrow under the scarecrow's frayed legs, and the White Horse turning from grey to white on the flank of the hills ... all this happened while he was sleeping. Why had he never known this? He slipped off his gate and walked back through the field, the wet grass making the turn-ups of his trousers heavy with moisture and soaking over his shoes. If he had gone to Margate, he mused, he would have missed this.

A hatred of the towns, of the houses and dark streets, the dusty avenue trees and alley cats, the garish vans and hard lights, the stink and the noise of people and machines swept over him. Margate ... would he find beauty at Margate?...

The air was too rich and the morning too close about him with its rapture to allow Mr Finchley to be morbid any longer and he refused to argue with himself. A spray of honeysuckle wrapped about with purple vetch drew cool fingers over his face and he stopped to pick a cluster of flowers.

Jane was awake when he returned.

'I hope you slept well?' he asked.

'Thank you,' she replied. 'It was nice of you to stop. You don't think we are being followed then?'

'No. At least, I hope not!'

'So do I. But what have you been doing while I slept?'

Mr Finchley laughed.

'Watching the sunrise and thinking,' he said, handing her the spray of honeysuckle.

'Oh! Thank you!' She buried her nose in the blooms and then pinned them into her coat so that they lay quietly against her black collar. 'Thinking? What about?'

'The sun.'

'The sun? What do you mean?' she asked.

Mr Finchley was climbing into the car as he replied and his face was hidden from her.

'Well, you see, I've never watched the sunrise before, and ... it was all so wonderful that ... well, it started me think-ing ... about things.'

The car jerked forward again on the last lap of its journey.

They reached Bristol at ten o'clock and Jane, who knew the town, guided him to a car park outside a hotel.

'Bristol!' Mr Finchley declared with mock triumph. 'And I think before we do anything else we'll both get a wash and have some breakfast. We can settle our respective plans over the food – what do you say?' He was himself again.

'That suits me,' Jane agreed. They crossed the road to the hotel.

As they ate, Jane explained to Mr Finchley what she was going to do.

'My people are rather strict,' she said, 'and, if you don't mind, I think the best thing for me to do is to catch a bus home and say I've come back by train. Otherwise, if I turned up in a car with a strange man and told them that I had travelled all night with him – there'd be hell's own rumpus! Sorry to put it like that, but that's their attitude. You understand, don't you?'

'Of course, I do. You must naturally do whatever you think best,' agreed Mr Finchley over his sausages. 'Why should I object? Had it not been for you I should still be in that horrible room '

'And,' she cut in, 'if it hadn't been for you I might be having a rough time explaining things to Jackson! So we're quits!'

Mr Finchley nodded.

'What about Thornton? Are you going to say anything to the police?'

Jane laughed and shook her head.

'What's the use? They'll have got clear by now. The police couldn't catch 'em. We should only be asking for a lot of trouble in explaining things to the police. And then' – her eyes were serious – 'my people would learn about my escapade!'

'Perhaps you're right. After all the Bentley has been returned and my first holiday hasn't been absolutely ruined by my adventure. Yes' – the more Mr Finchley thought of it, the more certain he was – 'I think we should be wise in saying nothing. Let bygones be bygones. While I was waiting for you just now, I wired to Margate about my rooms to see if they've still kept them for me and I shall probably get a reply in an hour. Then, it's home for you, and Margate for me.'

'Good!' Jane breathed loudly. 'It's the nearest I've ever been to coming a cropper. You don't know how much I owe you.' She glanced sideways at Mr Finchley with a sly look in her eyes, but he was busy with his knife.

The day continued with the fine promise of its dawn.

Outside the sun was throwing bright dapples across the green of a little park and a couple of grey-headed daws fluttered in the lower branches of an elm which stood at the edge of the green. Occasionally a blue and white bus came whirring up over the slope of the hill from the city and rumbled by the hotel. Sitting at their table in the window, Mr Finchley felt completely at ease with himself. The past was the past and the last few days were a long way behind him and to be easily forgotten. He finished his meal and lit a pipe.

Jane glanced across at him and had he not been so immersed in his own thoughts, he might have noticed that she was regarding him with a look almost of friendly regret.

'Do you mind,' she said, 'if I leave you for a moment to phone my people?'

'Do!' Mr Finchley came to earth.

Jane gathered up her handbag and left him. He watched her cross the room, threading a swaying way between the islands of tables.

A nice girl, he told himself. The kind of girl who would make some lucky man a good wife one day. She had courage and knew what she wanted and wanted it enough to see that she got it. If he were not a sworn bachelor and forty-five ... but really, he thought, the reflection in the window might easily have been that of a man about forty.

He re-lighted his pipe and hummed to himself a little tune which he had made up. He hummed it through two or three times before he discovered the tune to be of a well-known hymn and that a hirsute gentleman at the opposite table was staring at him over his fish and beard in a curious fashion.

Mr Finchley stopped humming. A little perplexed he shook his head genially towards the man and said: 'Nice morning.' The pipe between his lips, which he had been too lazy and comfortable to remove, transmuted the phrase until it became: 'Nomorrann.'

The other started guiltily and his suspended knife and fork swooped towards the fish.

Mr Finchley did not mind. He rubbed the top of his tonsure with his warm hand and looked around to see whether

Jane was returning. Instead of Jane a waiter was coming across to his table. 'Mr Finchley, sir?'

'That's right,' answered Mr Finchley.

The waiter handed him a telegram and an envelope embossed with the name of the hotel.

'Thank you.' He put the telegram in his pocket – he knew it must be from Margate – and stared at the white envelope. It was addressed to him in a thin handwriting, the loops of the h's and l's leaning backwards as though they were top-heavy.

For a moment his heart gave him a nasty twinge – perhaps Thornton had followed him; but the next second he knew that it could not be so. The writing was clearly that of a woman.

He turned the letter over several times before he opened it. The note was a few hurried lines on hotel paper and read:

DEAR FINCHY, – I hope you won't think hardly of your little Jane, but I've decided that the best thing to do is to pop off and avoid any further complications. You're a nice old thing, but you must learn not to believe all a woman says. I'm a good liar. Cheerio and thanks for the buggy ride. What are you going to do with the car?

JANE

There were two short rows of kisses underneath the message.

'Well, well! I'll be . . .' Mr Finchley put the note down and frowned at the fish-eating gentleman as though he had been the prime mover in the new turn of events. 'The little baggage! Leaving me like that . . . and the car, too! Bother, I hadn't thought of that!' During their discussion neither of them had given a thought to the question of the disposal of the Austin Seven. At least, Mr Finchley had not, and if Jane had, she had said nothing. What, Mr Finchley argued with himself, did she mean by saying that she was a good liar? Did she mean she was not a servant? Then what could she be? . . . For a while he did not understand. Then he began to see light. The picture he formed of the new Jane was not so pleasing. Women, he remarked unoriginally to the

47

cruet-stand, were the very devils. He was disappointed and hurt. The rows of kisses at the foot of the note caught his eye. The saucy minx! She had hoodwinked him completely. He, a wily old solicitor's clerk, caught by a slip of a girl. Maid . . . he might have known all along that her voice and bearing were not those of a maid. What a fool he had been . . .

Mr Finchley took his bill and left the hotel. He was worried.

He decided that the disposal of the car was an affair that required some thought if it were to be done without going to the police with the whole story. He walked slowly down the slope of the hill towards the centre of the city. A narrow arm of dirty water, which he guessed must be an offshoot of the Avon, came right up into the heart of the city and disappeared under a dark, balustraded archway. Mr Finchley sat on the flat top of the balustrade to think. Behind him lay the muddy water of the docks with black and yellow fruit boxes tilting at their anchorages by the wharfsides. A couple of boys were sculling a boat from the stern with one oar and gathering floating pieces of wood from the water. Before him rows of trams with strange names, Knowle, Fishponds, Durdham Downs, waited at a terminus and occasionally moved off like decrepit argosies with a dipping of trolley arms. Behind the trams, Mr Finchley caught a glimpse of a small square crowded with trees and statues. Rising over the square like a massive ice pinnacle was the square tower of a newspaper building; a glory of clean lines, dazzling façades and wide windows. A clock at the top of the building showed him that it was half past eleven. From the docks and river came the cries of the boys salvaging wood and the hoot of a siren as a ship made its way up the gorge of the Avon on the tide, and all about him sounded the roar and clang of the trams, the snarl and screech of cars and the cry of the newsboys with their morning editions. It was difficult to think consistently with such a babble going on. Mr Finchley rubbed his chin in thought and discovered that he wanted a shave. He would have one and try to decide the question of the car while the barber was shaving him.

48

But the lather and loquacity of the saloon beat him and he arrived back at the car park with the problem still undecided.

He stood with his foot on the running-board of the car lost in thought. This was really a difficult question. He was anxious to avoid bringing the police into the affair; that would only result in lengthy complications. He could, of course, drive the car into the country and leave it, or even manoeuvre it into a river. He could give it away or abandon it in the car park. But all these solutions appeared to lack stability and neatness. He was a tidy man and to leave a car lying about a main road or cul-de-sac or blocking up a river ... well, it was not done and all the clerk in him was opposed to the idea.

'Excuse me, sir!'

A policeman was standing by him.

'Certainly,' said Mr Finchley, absent-mindedly, and he lost himself in thought again. It really seemed as though, after all, there was nothing to do but to tell the police about the whole affair ... then he had arranged with Jane ... She might be involved if he did that. Still, she had left him without ... Oh, damn the whole affair!

'Excuse me, sir. Is this your car?'

Mr Finchley looked up sharply and discovered that the policeman was still with him.

'What's the matter?' he asked. 'What do you want?'

There was a hard glint in the man's eyes and his chin jutted over the strap of his helmet viciously.

'Is this your car?' The question was repeated.

Mr Finchley saw that to delay an answer would only incense the policeman.

'No, it isn't my car,' he answered truthfully enough.

The constable was evidently surprised by the reply. He became suddenly suspicious.

'Oh, I'm sorry! I thought it was your car. From the way you were leaning across it I thought it must be yours!'

'Well, it isn't mine!' Mr Finchley replied.

The policeman did not appear to be satisfied with Mr Finchley's denial.

'I'm sorry to bother you, sir, but if it isn't yours perhaps you know who the owner is?'

Mr Finchley told the lie bravely. He decided that it was impossible to make a clean breast of things now that he had plunged so far.

'No! No! I don't!' he answered.

The policeman was satisfied. He waved a big hand, and forgave everything.

'That's all I wanted to know, sir. You see, the licence in that holder is six months old and it'll mean a nice little fine for the owner when I catch him.'

'Good gracious! So it is!' Mr Finchley faced this fresh complexity with jocularity. 'That's a bit of bad luck for him. Perhaps he's on holiday, too! A nice start-off that would be, eh?'

'Holidays! You're on holiday?' The policeman had plenty of time to spare. 'May I ask where you're going?' he questioned good-naturedly.

'Mar ...' Mr Finchley stopped himself in time. An inspiration seized him as he remembered a poster he had seen in the barber's shop. 'I'm going over to Blagdon. You know the lake . . . may get a spot of fishing.'

'Blagdon . . . Nice spot,' said the policeman, who had apparently not noted Mr Finchley's indecision.

'Yes, Blagdon,' repeated Mr Finchley, who was anxious to get away from the man before any fresh trouble arose. 'Well, I must be going! Goodbye!'

'Good morning, sir. Sorry to have given you any trouble.' The policeman smiled and moved away.

SEVEN

How Bathing and a Black Eye invoke a Decision

MR FINCHLEY sat down on a seat by a bus stop at the foot of the hill. Phew! That had been a near one! He was not accustomed to telling lies with such facility. It was with almost a feeling of admiration for himself that he discovered his new ability. He might be stout and bald; but when it came to a tight squeeze, he could still keep his wits about him and – he chuckled – get the better of the law. He wished that Wally or Jane could have been with him to see and commend. He was taking a risk, though. Unless he soon got to Margate and free of the troublesome implications and mistakes which had accrued after his silly promise to Wally, he might not get a holiday.

The day was getting hotter. He wished that he could leave his waistcoat somewhere. He pulled out his handkerchief to wipe his face, and, as he did so, out of the corner of his eye he saw two figures hurrying down the hill. One was the tall policeman and the other he recognized as that of the car-park keeper. The keeper was trotting along at the side of the policeman like a little dog, and talking excitedly. Mr Finchley could not hear him; but he could see his excited gestures.

He realized without a doubt what had happened. The policeman had done what he should have done in the first place if he had been an intelligent policeman – consulted the attendant about the owner of the car. And the attendant, thought Mr Finchley, had described him. He could almost hear him saying, 'Short man, grey suit and soft hat.'

A silly panic seized him. In a few minutes they would be upon him. If he started to run away they would see him. If he stopped where he was they could not miss him.

The conductor of the bus by the pavement clanged the starting bell and the driver leaned forward in his seat over the gearhandle. The sound of the bell awakened Mr Finchley to action. He was not going to have his holiday spoiled! The first real holiday of his life – to be messed up with questions and explanations, and perhaps a night or two in a cell before everything was put right!

He jumped up. The bus moved forward. A board on its side flashed at him like a flame. In large black letters he saw the magical words Blagdon. Bristol to Blagdon. He acted almost before he realized it.

He leaped across the pavement, a passing couple gave him

the cover he needed from the policeman and the keeper, and gripped the handrail of the bus. The arm of the conductor swept about his waist and he was lifted bodily into the vehicle. The momentum of his leap and the conductor's arm sent him sprawling along the gangway, to collapse like a wet sack over the back of a seat.

'Steady there! Steady on, guv'ner!' The conductor's arm eased him into a seat.

'Thank you! Thank you!' panted Mr Finchley. 'It was very important that I should not miss this bus!' He glanced back through the rear window. The two figures had reached the bottom of the hill and were looking around for him.

'You want to get up earlier next time, guv'ner,' smiled the conductor. 'Where for?' He held up his clutch of tickets interrogatively.

'Single to Blagdon, please,' replied Mr Finchley.

He bought his ticket and breathed deeply. At his age it was disconcerting to have to move so swiftly. The bus swung through streets, past public-houses, parks, under railway bridges, threading in and out of the slower traffic . . . Slowly the houses began to drop away and walls gave place to hedges. There were only two other people in the bus. Mr Finchley took out his pipe and lighted it. After such a narrow escape there was only one thing to restore his composure. He smoked contentedly, and in half an hour – the bus was well into the country now – his uneasiness had disappeared, and he was in such a state that, had he someone to whom to recount his adventures, he could have laughed at the whole chronicle of incidents. He wondered whether he should move back to the conductor and tell him the story. The man's friendly face tempted him. In the end he decided that it would be wiser to say nothing.

So Mr Finchley smoked and kept his thoughts to himself, and the bus bore him westwards through the narrow lanes, whipping the dust from the trailing bedstraws and setting the stiff stems of the yarrows quivering, into a country that was as unknown to him as Tibet, and which held for him all the adventures and beauties which it generally denies to those who go deliberately in search of them.

'Blagdon, sir!' The conductor's voice roused him.

Blagdon is a small village on the side of the Mendips. The houses cling to the steep main road to save themselves from slipping down the sharp slope and falling into the untidily shaped lake that wanders about the valley below. The first thing of which Mr Finchley was aware as he jumped down from the bus was the lake. Crossing the road from the bus station he looked over the wall and there it was below him shining like a steel mirror in the heat of the noonday sun.

He decided to visit the lake.

He wanted to be at the brink, to move his hands through it and, perhaps, to bathe in it.

The road fell quickly from the village to the lake and crossed its far end along the top of a stone dam. Mr Finchley went down through a small copse of firs, and came out on the edge of the lake.

'By golly! This is a great place,' he said aloud. His only answer was the *flop* of a lazy trout rising under the alders away on his left.

It was hot, and the sight of the sand glinting coolly under water and the bright pebbles winking invitingly to him through the green fired him with the desire to bathe. The cool water called to his burning body, but he was afraid. He presented himself with a long list of excuses for not bathing.

He cherished the unnatural contention of civilization that it was wrong to bathe without a costume. But the water called to him potently, and his collar gripped him like a warm pad about his neck.

Why shouldn't he bathe? And having asked himself the question he could find no adequate objection save in his own cowardice. Was he afraid? The debate within himself lasted five minutes. He looked about for a spot to undress and, a few minutes later, stepped from the rear of a blackthorn as naked as the day of his birth. To any observer the pallid white of his flesh might have proved a discordant element in the harmonies of blue and gold and brown. Mr Finchley was not worrying about observers. His little bay was practically

53

hidden from all except the hills opposite, and they were too far away to give him concern. The still water was warm and, after trying it with his foot tentatively, Mr Finchley launched himself with a splash that sent the foam cresting from his breast.

For the next fifteen minutes Mr Finchley enjoyed himself. He puffed about with a graceless breast-stroke; he lay upon his back and kicked his heels in the air; he did clumsy porpoise dives and came to the surface to spout a jet of water at the sky. He laughed as the silver drops rained down upon his face and made him splutter. And when he had tired of swimming he came ashore and lay on the small beach with his shirt over his thighs, sunbathing. The sun and the water, the air and the freedom from other people soaked into Mr Finchley like wine. He was a different man. He felt fit, he felt happy and he expressed his happiness in songs as he dressed. He sang *Sally* while he struggled with his shirt and tie (the song wavered a little as he inspected his shirt which was very dirty); he tiptoed through the tulips into his trousers; he travestied the *Spring Song* as he tugged at his socks, and he was forced to abandon *Men of Harlech* as he bent to fasten his shoes. As he straightened up and slipped on his jacket he heard footsteps on the beach and a man came round the side of the blackthorn. He stopped in front of Mr Finchley and eyed him with a truculent expression. He was a fattish, middle-aged man dressed in a long ragged raincoat from under which a khaki tunic showed. His face was tanned with sun and dirt and a straggling moustache joined forces half-heartedly with a three day growth of beard.

'You bin baving?' the man asked sharply.

Mr Finchley smiled genially.

'Yes. It's glorious in. Why' – the man's appearance prompted the thrust – 'don't you try it?'

'Say! None of yer lip, cocky! It's me duty to tell you that you bin baving in private water. I could 'ave you summoned.'

'Dear, dear!' Mr Finchley refused to be suppressed. His heart was still full of song. 'That would be a bad end to such a fine day.'

'Bad end! That's what you'll be getting. Wajjer mean by baving in this lake for?' he demanded loudly, and thrust his beard close to Mr Finchley's face.

'Mean?' queried Mr Finchley. 'Mean? Nothing except that I wanted to. Anyway who are you to ask such a question? Anyone would think the lake belonged to you.'

'So it does. I'm the keeper!' retorted the other.

Mr Finchley's arms dropped to his sides in astonishment. He stared at the man for a moment, and then he broke into a roar of laughter.

'And I suppose that's your uniform?' He pointed to the tunic.

The man grimaced angrlly. 'That's enough from you. You'd better come along with me. You bin trespassin' and I'll have you summoned.'

At this Mr Finchley stopped laughing and addressed the tramp seriously.

'Listen, old man, you know you're telling a whopper. You're no more a keeper than I am. And if it comes to trespassing – what are you doing?'

'I don't admit that! I said I was the keeper and I am,' the tramp asserted dogmatically; 'but since you don't want no fuss made, I'll tell yer what I'll do. You give me ten bob and I won't do or say anything! Unnerstan – do ner say nothin'!'

He caught Mr Finchley by the lapel of his jacket, and a cajoling look formed a leer above his beard.

'Ten shillings!' cried Mr Finchley, surprised by the sudden demand. 'You won't get anything from me, my man; and if you don't sheer off I'll soon make you!' He was not going to be browbeaten.

'Oh, you won't! Won't you?' said the tramp slowly. 'Well if yer won't give it to me I'll take it, cocky! 'Ow about that?'

Mr Finchley did not reply. He was eyeing the man up and down. The tramp was bigger than he, but he was fat and slow. If it really came to a fight Mr Finchley thought that the chances were even.

'Come on, cocky! Do I get the ready or do I give yer a kybosh for the trouble o' takin' it?'

'You get nothing from me! And if you try it I'll . . . I'll . . .'
Mr Finchley searched for a warlike expression; 'I'll punch
you!'

The tramp laughed nastily.

'What, a maggot like you? Why, I've eaten men like
you!'

Mr Finchley refused to believe it.

'You get nothing from me!' he repeated, and moved back a
pace.

'Well, don't say I didn't give yer a chance. I counts three
and if I don't get the cash – I takes it!'

'Try it then and see,' said Mr Finchley, screwing up his
fingers.

'One!' began the tramp. 'I warned yer! Two – you better
'and it over, cocky! Three – right, this is where I gets it for
myself!' .

With this remark the tramp stepped forward. Mr Finchley
did not wait for him. His right fist struck the tramp's nose
hard.

Taken in the middle of his stride the man staggered and
roared with pain.

'Aoh! You bloody little bastard!'

His arms swung wide like the vanes of a helicopter and a
fist hit Mr Finchley in the eye. The pain of the blow maddened him, and he rushed furiously at the tramp. He pum-
melled wildly at the fat body with both fists. The tramp
grunted and hit Mr Finchley in the eye again. Mr Finchley
went as berserk as it was possible for him to go. Ever since
Saturday morning and his meeting with Wally he had been
ripening towards this moment. Any other time the tramp
might have succeeded. This was his unlucky day. Mr Finchley became a savage, a whirling tornado of fists and legs.
He leaped at the tramp and butted him with his head, and,
before the tramp could recover, he planted two vicious blows
upon his stomach. He danced round the unfortunate man
like a grasshopper and hit hard with both hands as he had
never done before.

The tramp for three minutes stood up to the attack. Then,
as Mr Finchley plunged the bald patch of his head into the

folds of the other's raincoat, the tramp gasped weakly, clapped his hand to his stomach and collapsed backward over the edge of the lake into the water.

'And I hope that's taught you a lesson!' said Mr Finchley severely as the man's head broke water. The tramp dragged himself out. He was beaten, and he took his beating philosophically.

'All right, cocky. Why didn't yer say yer was the Boy Wonder?'

He took off his coat and squeezed the water from it. Silently, he stripped himself of three jackets, two pairs of trousers and a shirt and wrung out each in turn. He dressed slowly in his wet clothes and turned to go. He was a different figure from the man who had fought with Mr Finchley. A pathetic, ludicrous collection of wet rags and tangled hair. Mr Finchley was sorry for him. He had, perhaps, been a little severe with the fellow.

'Here!' He spoke as the tramp started to shuffle off towards the road. 'Take this and get yourself a clean shirt!'

He handed the man a couple of half-crowns. The tramp looked from the coins to Mr Finchley and decided that though Mr Finchley might be mad the money was good. He pocketed it, saying: 'There's lots of curious people in this world, but this is the first time I've met one who's curious in your way, cocky!'

Mr Finchley watched him cross the field and disappear behind the trees.

He lit his pipe and sat down. The fight had exhausted him and his eye was hurting. He pressed the flesh tenderly and knew that he was going to develop a black eye.

'What a life!' he murmured to himself. 'What a life!'

A wood-pigeon answered him from the trees. Across the valley came the barking of a dog mixed with the soft note of a car climbing the hill. A yellow wagtail see-sawed on the stones at the lake's edge.

Mr Finchley sat smoking. And as he smoked he frowned and twisted his face into uncouth expressions. He was discovering a lot of unpleasant things about himself and the life he was forced to lead. Give a boy a motor-cycle and he never returns to his push-bike willingly. A woman falls in love and marvels that she never had the good sense to do it earlier. A man flies over St Paul's in an aeroplane and the dome loses for ever its old grandeur of unassailability. Mr Finchley had lived nearly four days of laughter, anxiety, sunshine and fear. Four days without a daily paper, four days without regular meals or shaves, four days each as different from the other as a Magyar from a Polynesian, and soon he would be returning to the old order of things. And as he smoked he came slowly to see what until now he had never realized; that danger, the wonder of the unexpected, the exhilaration of living and not knowing what one would be doing or where one would next be were the only things that gave colour to life. To drift freely, to move from one thing to another at will ... to be entirely his own master, if only for three weeks, made the memory of the stereotyped routine of his past life a shapeless dream. Within the last four days he had known more excitement and adventure than ever before in his life and, strangely enough, he found himself hoping that such things would continue. If only they could continue ... he mused regretfully. But once he reached Margate, he would be starting a holiday that held no escape ... All his instincts for adventure which had been repressed since he had grown too old to play cowboys-and-indians, all the old yearnings, which he had never had the courage to recognize openly, swept back to him in a flood. A flood that bore him up on its tide and carried him, unresisting, on its crest. He was Edgar Finchley; he was a man. He was no timid clerk. He had mixed with crooks and bested them. He had lazed in the sun and loved its heat on his skin. He had fought with his fists, fought like a wild-cat, and won ... and now he must return to feather beds, to cinemas and pier concerts, to landladies and shilling motor-boat rides?

He knocked his pipe out and rose – a different Mr Finchley. He still suffered from indigestion. He was still bald – though even his tonsure was changing under the sun. He still loved his pipe. Yet he was different. He would not go to

Margate. He remembered the scorn with which Mr Thornton had mouthed the word and he guessed how the crook must have felt.

'No!' he said aloud to the pines; 'I won't go there! This holiday is my own to do as I wish with.'

The pines wrapped themselves deeper in shadow at the outburst but the tall field grasses and the sober sorrels, the waving corn-feverfew and the bright-eyed pimpernels, nodded to him as though they welcomed a friend.

So, Mr Finchley climbed over the gate on to the main road. He made a peculiar figure in his crumpled grey suit, dirty shirt, felt hat on the back of his head and his left eye rapidly eclipsing through varying purple hues to an ugly browny grey. He walked back to Blagdon, and as he climbed the hill he was happy in the thought that he knew what he did not want. Margate would not see him. Exactly what he did intend to do he was not sure, but he trusted to the fates and made his way whistling to Blagdon. He scarcely felt the pain of his eye, and he had forgotten about the Austin.

EIGHT

Of Bicycling

MR FINCHLEY was hungry by the time he had climbed the hill to Blagdon. Halfway up the village street was a thatched cottage with a small sign in its window, proclaiming teas. Farther up the street Mr Finchley could see a baker's shop with tourists' signs and gay swinging boards. For a while he was undecided. He was hungry after his bathe and the fight. Something in the way the reversed S in the cottage tea-sign leaned back in a homely fashion to tickle the A, hinted that the cottage was the better place for him. A home-made sign probably meant home-made cakes. It did.

A pleasantly big woman with warm eyes and a mouth that smiled as she spoke served him and moved, talking, between the room and her kitchen while he ate. She gave him hot scones, so hot that the butter melted into morasses as he spread it. He ate strawberry jam, snow-capped and glaciated with thick cream on new bread, and drank four cups of steaming tea while she talked, partly to herself and partly to him. It was not until the last slice of bread had gone that Mr Finchley thought of his indigestion. He was perturbed, but the woman, seeing that he had finished, broke in upon his thoughts and drove them from him with her slow chatter.

'You've eaten a good tea, sir. That's what I like to see. Fresh air, it is. My boys when they come in from the fields – they keep me runnin', I can tell you. Eat! They eat like horses and as strong!'

'It must be great to lead an open-air life, and to get your appetite straight from the fields!' said Mr Finchley, crossing his legs comfortably, and pulling out his pipe.

'Not so good that it hasn't got something wrong with it. You city folk who only see the country in the summer, wouldn't like it in the winter. Last winter me eldest had to cycle fourteen miles every day to Winford and back to work. It's not so good then. The poor lamb—'

'Yes, there's always something wrong,' agreed Mr Finchley.

'Still, we must be contented, I say, with God's providence and not grumble. If you do the best you can for yourself and others that's all that matters. Not like some said to me when I started doing teas. You give 'em little and charge high, was their advice; but I wouldn't have none of that. I know what my boys would call a good tea and that's what I give other people. What's good for one is good for another.'

She had cleared the table and Mr Finchley rose to go.

'What do I owe you?' he asked.

'That'll be two shillings, sir.'

Mr Finchley would have liked to pay her more, but he could see that to argue with her would have been useless. She followed him to the doorway.

'Goodbye!' Mr Finchley held out his hand. 'And thank you for the best tea I've had for a long time – and the cheapest!' he added.

The woman laughed.

'You're welcome, sir – mind the cycle!' she called to him quickly as he turned. She was too late. In turning, Mr Finchley's legs caught in the pedal of a bicycle which was leaning against one side of the porch. Mr Finchley crashed to the ground and the machine crashed with him. One pedal wrapped itself angularly about his neck, and the greasy chain drew a careful smudge of oil along the side of his nose.

'Bother the machine!' The woman leaned forward, jerked the cycle off Mr Finchley and helped him to his feet. 'I hope it didn't hurt you, sir? The useless thing! It's been a nuisance ever since Jim got a job up at Smeldon's and stopped cycling to Winford. No one wants to buy it and no one uses it, so it rusts on my porch. You're dusty, I'll fetch a brush!' She disappeared into the house for a clothes-brush, leaving Mr Finchley alone in the porch with the cycle.

Rubbing the oil from his nose, Mr Finchley eyed the bicycle. It was a good stout machine. The tyres were good, and the enamel dulled with the weather, while the plating on the bars was flaking.

'This way a little, sir!' She was brushing him down. 'There! That's taken that off!'

An idea had germinated in Mr Finchley's mind. He began to see in the incident the hand of a benign fate.

'Did you say,' he said slowly, when she had finished, 'that you wanted to sell that machine?'

'Jim's been trying for the last six months, but no one wants it. At least, no one wants it at his price. He gave six pounds for it new, and he won't take less than a pound for it, though I've often said it would be better for it to be given away than to rust there, mucking the place up! But he's obstinate.'

Mr Finchley's mind was made up.

'Well, here you are!' He withdrew his hand from his breast-pocket and flourished a pound note under her nose.

'Why, sir—' she began. 'You mustn't think I was askin' you to buy it. Lord preserve us!'

'No, no!' Mr Finchley assured her, waving the note like a banner as he spoke. 'You misunderstand me. I really want to buy it. I want it!'

She laughed, not to be caught.

'No, sir, I thank you for your generosity, but I can't sell it to you like that. Why you hadn't thought of buying it until you fell over it!'

'But that's just why I want to buy it!' insisted Mr Finchley. 'Because I fell over it! In a way, I think that I was meant to buy it! You'll sell it, won't you? Here' – he did not wait for her reply, but pressed the note into her hand – 'take this.' Something, Mr Finchley was inclined to call it fate (the good lady of the tea obviously regarded it as generous stupidity), told him that he must buy it.

'Well, if you are sure . . .'

'Of course, I'm sure. I shouldn't buy it otherwise. Jim only wanted a pound? If you think I ought to make it two . . .' Mr Finchley began to fumble again, but the woman stopped him.

'Now then!' she cried hastily. 'You'd better take the machine away, before you insist on paying double its value and shaming me for a grasping hussy.'

'No one could mistake you for that!' replied Mr Finchley gallantly, and holding the bicycle by the bars he wheeled it slowly down the garden path to the roadway. The woman followed him.

'You know how to ride it, I suppose?' she asked, when they were outside.

'I think so,' answered Mr Finchley. His last memories of push-biking were not pleasant; dust figured prominently in them.

'You're certain?' she asked dubiously.

'Of course,' said Mr Finchley, resenting the suspicion in her voice, 'though you might just hold the saddle while I get on.'

Mr Finchley scrambled awkwardly across the bar and she held the back of the machine while he adjusted himself into the saddle. It was a delicate operation. The road sloped downhill, the saddle was a little too high for Mr Finchley's legs, and her grip on the machine was as good-natured and easy-going as herself.

Mr Finchley wobbled.

'Hold her! Hold her!' he shouted.

'I've got her, sir!'

Mr Finchley felt for the pedals. He found one.

'Which way do you want to go?'

She straightened up a little to ask the question, and her grip slackened. The bicycle began to move slowly downhill, partly supported by her.

'Hey! Hey! I didn't say push!' yelled Mr Finchley, struggling to maintain a balance.

'I can't hold it . . . I can't hold . . .' She ran alongside, with her apron fluttering dangerously near the spinning spokes. Their momentum increased. Mr Finchley's other foot found a pedal and, without quite knowing why, he pedalled. He was surprised to feel the machine leap away under him.

'All right, let her go!' he shouted. 'I can manage!'

'Which way are you going?' the woman panted as she ran alongside. Then the speed was too much for her. She released the machine. The bicycle jerked away from her. She slipped, and throwing herself backwards to break the fall, skidded ungracefully off the crown of the road into the gutter.

'Thank you!' Mr Finchley twisted round, and as he did so, his hat blew off. He did not realize his loss so amazed was he with the scene behind him. Unknown to either him or his friend, a small cluster of folks had collected outside the public-house. He was first aware of a lusty cheer from the onlookers and a voice rising louder than the others:

'Ride 'im, cowboy!' Then he saw the woman. She was sitting up in the gutter with her legs widespread, her arms waving vigorously, while bending down over her a brown mare, harnessed to a baker's van, nuzzled curiously at her hair.

'Goodbye!' Mr Finchley waved one arm. His motion caused the machine to wobble. He turned quickly, and for thirty anxious seconds fought with the erratic equilibrium of the bicycle and his own mounting fear. The wobble died away and Mr Finchley breathed again.

By this time the machine was racing at a good speed downhill. Before him the road forked, one fork turned quickly to the left and the other led straight down over the hill to the lake and so back to Bristol. Mr Finchley decided, or rather a motor which suddenly backed out of a gateway decided for him, that he did not want to go to Bristol. Pulling on his brakes, he eased his cycle up to a speed which would allow him to take the sharp corner. As he swept round the corner he had time to read on the sign – Weston-super-Mare – and remembered advertisements he had seen at Paddington.

For a while the road twisted downhill through private parkland. On his left hung the bare outcrops of Mendip stone, massive blocks and spurs, with their crests hidden in bracken and whortle-bushes. Lower down scrubby oaks and wild cherry trees found a footing, and then came the dark elms, with an occasional ash to paint their funereal tones. The road twisted within its low thorn hedges. Once the shade of a wood closed over him, and the pulsing smell of leaf-mould and ferns filled his nostrils. The shade was as cool and sweet as a carillon, and from somewhere in the dark avenues a finch fluted tenderly to the rhythm of running water.

After he had accustomed himself to the motion and the high saddle, he discovered that he had lost little of his old aptitude, and before half an hour was gone he was swinging through the lanes as though he had been riding for years.

For twelve miles the road moved along in the blue shadow of the Mendips, taking him through tired villages, where whitewashed cottages paled in the long shadows of the trees, and the sweet air of the evening started the birds to song. In the hedges the tall cow-parsley lazed in dusty silence, and the trefoils hid beneath their leaves, mourning for the sun which still flecked the ling patches to a vivid life on the topmost points of the hills. Soon the sun went, and the valley lay wrapt in a growing mist that sprang from the dying heat of the day.

Mr Finchley passed through a small town whose name he did not learn. The streets were narrow and rough, and the houses thrust themselves over the pavements like grey boulders, round whose butts swirled a happy stream. Young girls and boys were talking and laughing on a corner, and sitting on his shop-step an ironmonger was reading with one eye on the paper and the other alternatively on the passing traffic and his dog. The dog was enlivening a dull existence by passing and re-passing across the bows of cars, in a slow and haughty fashion that made the motorists, who were serious, swear, and his owner, who was bored, chuckle.

Mr Finchley, who was happy and singing a little song in tune to the whirr of his tyres, did not see the dog until it jumped yelping from under his front wheel, which had flicked its waving rudder. The sound made him start and he lost control. He headed straight for the closed iron gates of the village school and had a reeling vision of the flaming red torch of a County Library sign. The ironmonger bellowed with laughter at the dog's discomfiture. The front wheel of the bicycle struck the kerbstone and mounted the pavement. With a superb effort, Mr Finchley barely avoided the school gates and ran along the flagstones for a while in a desultory, bell-ringing manner and finally found the road again. He decided that cycling through towns was a serious business and concentrated upon his pedalling for the rest of the journey.

It was dark when he reached the outskirts of Weston-super-Mare, and rather than risk the attention of the police by riding without a light, he walked his machine into the town. He left his bicycle at a garage for the night and on the garageman's recommendation took a room at a small private hotel. He ate a solitary supper and went quickly to bed.

NINE

*How Mr Finchley is nearly throttled and finds
Happiness in a View*

MR FINCHLEY was up early next morning, and walked briskly along the promenade, opening his jacket to let the breeze ruffle his shirt. The smell of salt beat into his nostrils, and the sea wind played about his bare head. Before him the sands curved away in a thin ridge of gold to the distant redoubt of cliff and down. Like a huge beast the far side of the bay sprawled across the sea, so that the tide beat a white tattoo on its flank and glistening spume spouted over its muzzle. The tide was in, and the pier stood up to its knees in water.

Weston-super-Mare was a jolly place that morning. Mr Finchley felt he could have had a very good holiday there. A holiday very like the one he was missing at Margate. Yet the idea of staying on never even occurred to him. He went back to his hotel for a hearty breakfast, paid his bill, and was on his way by ten o'clock. On his back he now carried a rucksack filled with some things he had bought – an open-necked shirt, a cap, a map, a light raincoat, and washing gear.

The town was soon behind him and he cycled slowly, taking his time and stopping to rest at intervals, in a southerly direction. Soon he was passing along the lower slope of the tailing Mendips. Above him rose the gentle hillside white with occasional outcrops of stone and small patches of sheep, while on his left, straddling across the green valley and bridging rean and field and hedge and copse with rigid cables, stretched a row of grey pylons. The road ran through a straggling village and a signpost showed him that he was on the way to Cheddar. Turning a corner by a clump of pines, Mr Finchley saw before him a narrow pass.

On each side of the pass, the hills came tumbling down to the road. Mr Finchley dismounted. The sunlight on the hills and the cool of the shadows cast by shouldering scars across the road made him long to climb to the top of the ridge and see the country from a height. In the pass, the hills made him feel small and they seemed to be annoyed with him. If he climbed their flanks and found the top they might become his friends. A small pathway led into beech woods above which shone the flame of gorse bushes. He laid his cycle on the grass and started up the pathway.

Inside the wood all was quiet and the little-used path was padded with last year's leaves and rotting twigs. It twined in and out of the trees, growing steeper at every step and occasionally Mr Finchley was forced to grasp the smooth silver of the beech trunks to save himself from falling backwards. He sweated with his exertions and was glad that he was wearing an open shirt. Finally the wood ended in a small stone wall which the path crossed by means of a stile fashioned of flat stones. Mr Finchley sat on the wall to rest himself. He was still not at the top of the hill, and from his seat could see nothing but the green and silver of the wood before him, and behind him the steep scarp.

He wiped his forehead with his handkerchief, settled the rucksack on his back more comfortably and took out his pipe to fill it. The bowl primed, he struck a match, but it never reached the bowl. As he held it spurting in his hand, there was a shout and a rush of footsteps from behind him. A hand caught Mr Finchley by the back of the neck, jerking him from the wall to fall heavily into the dry ditch behind him. The pipe went flying from his hand as a large man hurled himself upon him and caught him by the throat.

Mr Finchley opened his mouth to shout but the grip about his neck choked the words. The man increased his grasp and, as he squeezed at Mr Finchley's neck, he snarled like an animal. Mr Finchley was so completely overcome by the suddenness of the assault that for a time he could do no more than gaze stupidly into the eyes of the man who was slowly choking him.

He was a dark-skinned man, wearing an old green felt hat, an open coat of velvet and dark blue trousers, and his eyes were red-rimmed with rage. Mr Finchley had no time to observe more before he felt his breath going. He struggled to free himself, but was held firmly. The grip at his throat that threatened to choke the life from him wrought a mad panic in him. He twisted and clawed, but the stranger only laughed at his efforts and held his neck tighter. Mr Finchley's nails dug the flesh from the lean brown hands, but the man made no movement to release him. Then he kicked and scratched with all his strength. He was being killed and he wanted to live. But resolutely the big stranger hung over him like an eagle, and the red kerchief at his neck came loose to sweep into Mr Finchley's eyes. His head rebelled against the rest of his body and his heart beat a thundering tattoo against his ribs.

Mr Finchley was not to die that morning. At that moment there was a loud scream from the hill above them, and Mr Finchley was dimly aware of a woman bounding down the slope towards them.

'Tawny! Tawny!' she screamed as she came, clearing the clumps of heather like a deer.

The man glanced up at her and his grip on Mr Finchley relaxed a little.

'Mara! I have him! The weasel! He shall die!' he said.

She stopped panting by them and looked down at Mr Finchley.

'Fool!' She turned and gave the man a buffet on the ear which, catching him by surprise, knocked him from Mr Finchley. He was up again in a flash and, while Mr Finchley still lay in the ditch recovering his breath and wondering whether the world had suddenly gone mad about his ears, returned her blow with such force that the woman stumbled and fell to the ground.

'Fool! Is it fool you would call me for killing such a weasel?' he said, and turned towards Mr Finchley.

'Tawny! Tawny! It is not the man!' she cried, rising from the ground and holding him back.

'Not the weasel?' he shouted at her.

'No, no! He was tall and had hair—' She pointed at Mr Finchley's bald head.

'Not him!' Tawny cried and shouted an oath.

'Which way did he go?' He addressed himself to Mr Finchley. But Mr Finchley was still too occupied with his own troubles. He shook his head, and rubbed his throat tenderly, taking in great gasps of air as he did so.

The man evidently took his nod to indicate the pathway. With a cry he leaped the wall and started away through the trees. As he went he cried over his shoulder to Mr Finchley:

'Stay, I will return!'

The woman glanced first at Mr Finchley and then in the direction which Tawny had taken. Mr Finchley fast recovering himself heard her mutter to herself: 'He will kill him.'

68

Then she ran to the wall and climbed over. She, too, as she dropped, called over her shoulder:

'Wait! We come again.'

And they were gone. Mr Finchley heard their cries echo through the wood and gradually fade away.

His first desire when he had composed himself was to fetch a policeman and make a complaint. It was ridiculous, he raged, as he dusted himself down and hunted for his pipe in the dry bracken, that a man could not climb a hillside without being assaulted by a pair of gipsies who, discovering they were throttling the wrong man, just left him gasping in the ditch and went tearing away down the hillside like mad people! He would have something to say about it! Then a thought struck him. Was he to call the police? Police! Mr Finchley muttered the word aloud. He was man enough to look after himself. Hadn't he escaped from Thornton and beaten the fighting tramp? And now because a gipsy caught him by the neck he was afraid and wanted to go to the police? From being angry at the assault, Mr Finchley became almost indignant with himself for entertaining such a dispirited desire . . . fetch the police! As though the police could stop life from doing what it wanted with him. He might just as well try to stem the rush of a mad bull by arguments. He must accept things as they came and make the best of them!

He was about to abandon the search for his pipe when he saw its black stem glinting at him from the foot of a clump of tansies. As he bent to pick it up, he noticed a small bright-coloured object caught up in the flowers. It was a brooch. Mr Finchley picked it up and examined it. It was of gold. The design was of a trout leaping, carrying in its mouth a thin arrow.

He gave the brooch a rub and dropped it absent-mindedly into his pocket. The truth was that Mr Finchley was still unsettled with the abruptness of the recent onslaught. Adventure did not run off his back like water from the gloss of a duck. It left an impression.

Mr Finchley recovered his rucksack from the ditch and set off again up the hill. The two gipsies had called to him to wait, but he was in no mood for waiting. Very probably, he told himself, they would never return, and the morning was too good to be wasted sitting in the lee of a ditch.

As he leaned forward to the slope which grew steeper with every step he took, a pencil fell from his breast pocket. He replaced it and in doing so he felt a thin envelope. He pulled it out, and stared perplexedly at it for a second. It was a red telegram envelope. Where had it come from? He remembered. The waiter had brought it to him together with the note from Jane in the hotel at Bristol. He opened it. It was from the hotel at Margate:

ROOMS NOT AVAILABLE NOW. LUGGAGE RETURNED VICTORIA.

He laughed, screwed the paper into a tight red ball, and tossed it away into the grass to flame in rivalry with the knapweed.

'What do I care?' he asked the wheeling clouds. 'I can do some other thing!' The altitude and wind stirred him to exultation.

In a short time he had reached the top of the ridge. He moved across the springy grass and found a seat beneath a contorted thorn tree that flung a perpetual plume of foliage backwards to the east, in which direction the strong sou-westerlies, coming up the valley and from distant Exmoor, had forced its growth.

Mr Finchley had studied his map and was able to pick out his surroundings a little. Away in the distance, faint and arched as a child's eyebrow, he caught the soft line of Exmoor, and nearer, with smoke rolls from moor fire wreathing off its hogback, the royal line of the Quantocks. Fifty miles of marshland and pastures, fifty miles of fir clumps and oaks; miles rich with peaceful cattle and quiet men, whose spirit and life lay wrapt firmly about the low fields that were flooded in winter, and blazoned with king-cups and trefoils in summer, miles of road and village, town and hamlet, miles of beauty and leisure, where the peace of the reans and the glory of the withies laughed at the contesting roar of the main roads as they had laughed at the cries of the

Danes as they harried the creeks, and the oaths of the Butcher's men as they hounded fugitives from Sedgemoor . . . fifty miles where time measured itself against the growth of elms, that lost their crests in the dazzle of the sun, and where the life of a man was like the noontide odyssey of a may-fly.

Mr Finchley held his hands about his knees and rocked gently. He was happy. Happier than he had been for a long time. The wide valley below him, kindly as the hand of God; the gleam of the sea making wanton quicksilver on his right, and the dusty outline of Glastonbury Tor, standing like a sentinel on his left, with its feet lost in apple garths . . . these were England, the England which he had denied himself for so long.

All through that day, the joy of the hilltop lived vividly in his mind as he cycled haphazardly through the afternoon, across the plain. The day had been too hot and fine to bother with map-reading, and he had followed the road along slow streams, over gentle knolls crowned with hazel copse and orchard, and past occasional white houses with cedar and yew trees dark against their walls.

At seven o'clock he stopped at the Blue Mitre. He had to stop for the road ended abruptly in the stone wall of an apple orchard. He propped his cycle against the wall of the public-house and went inside. The bar was empty. The men, the landlord told him, were haymaking and working late in the fields, and had their beer and cider sent out to them.

'Where y' headin' for?' the man asked genially. 'Bridg-water, perhaps?'

'Yes, Bridgwater,' answered Mr Finchley, lazily.

'You'm a tidy way from there yet,' said the other.

'I've plenty of time,' replied Mr Finchley. He was beginning to feel the strain of cycling, and the fresh air coupled with the strong beer he was drinking made him sleepy. Mr Finchley sat down on the settle outside the house, and placing his back against the wall, and his hands into his pockets, prepared to sleep. As he put his hand into his pocket he felt something prick him. He withdrew his hand quickly and with it the brooch.

71

'Ah! The little brooch . . .'

He would not have admitted it but the beer had made him just a bit fuddled. Silly, riotous thoughts were chasing one another about his head. He held it in his palm for a while, examining it. It was a fine piece of workmanship, and its beauty delighted him. He could almost imagine the water showering back from the fish as it leaped upwards.

'Silly . . . why keep it in my pocket?' he muttered half to himself and half to the brooch. 'Brooches . . . brooches . . . what about brooches? Of course, brooches are to be worn, not put in pocket . . .' And in an awkward manner, because his arms and legs were overcome by a glorious limpness, he pinned the brooch to his coat lapel, and then went to sleep. The landlord's head came round the door. He saw Mr Finchley sleeping and smiled. He turned to someone within the house and said slowly: 'Strong sun or strong beer, no matter which it be, it won't be Bridgwater he'll reach this night!'

TEN

Of a Shop which Keeps Open all Night

MR FINCHLEY had been sleeping for an hour when the sound of voices disturbed him. Half asleep, he listened. Two women were talking. One voice was low and cajoling, the other sharp and decisive.

'Come on, deary, let me show you.'

'I doan want un and that's that!'

'But is it sense to say you don't want what you haven't seen? Now look here – see this!'

'I see un and I doan want un!'

'Gorgeous lady, not want a carpet that came all the way from my people in the country over the sea? And a lovely thing, too. Look closely at the colours. Did you ever see such a beauty?'

'Beauty or no beauty, I doan want un!'

'But think how stately, a real queen ye'll be, sitting at your hearth with this gorgeous thing beneath your feet and the colours, gorgeous colours for a brave lady like you, matching your eyes and hair. And your man, think how he'll be proud to see you sitting before him, like a queen upon a throne before her king. Feel it, lady.'

'It's my man I'm thinkin' of. He won't call me a queen, but a vool for wastin' his money on such stuff . . .'

'Money! Is it money I've been askin' for? Money could not buy such a gorgeous carpet, a kingdom could not buy such a gorgeous carpet if I did not wish it. But with you, gorgeous one, it's different. It's a pity that a brave lady like yourself should be without the carpet, and for you I'll sell it. But not for another creature in this village. Sell it, I'll almost give it to you. Give me five pounds and a carpet that no king could buy, if I would not sell, is yours. Five pounds, gorgeous . . .'

'Five pounds . . . I doan know . . .' The other weakened.

'It is little for such a thing. Tell me, gorgeous, is it a good carpet? Feel it!'

'Yes, it be a good un, and . . .'

'For you, a queen to sit over such a carpet, only four pounds!'

'Four . . . well, I be doing wrong.'

'Wrong . . . can a gorgeous queen do wrong? I'll bring it in and lay it on your hearth with my own hands, while you get the money. There . . .'

Mr Finchley came out of his doze, in time to see the skirts of two women disappear into the cottage which stood next to the Blue Mitre.

He stretched himself, and wondered what was the actual worth of the carpet. He wheeled his cycle into the road, and was about to mount, when the door of the cottage opened and a woman came out. She was dressed in a green skirt, surmounted by a dirty yellow jumper, and her hair was pulled back, black and sleek, across her head and partly covered by a red handkerchief caught under her chin. Under one arm she carried a thin roll of carpets. She came down the garden path, walking with an easy swinging motion of the hips. There was a smile on her lips. Mr Finchley saw that she was

73

young and possessed a rude kind of beauty; a beauty of tanned, dark skin and full lips, against which her teeth shone as she smiled. She reached the gate and saw Mr Finchley. She stopped suddenly, and then, with a cry, she sprang forward and seized him by the arm.

'It is him!' she cried.

Mr Finchley was amazed at her action and shook himself free from her hold.

'Let go,' he said. 'I don't know you!'

'Don't know me!' She was surprised.

'No!'

'Don't know Mara! Don't know Mara, who stopped that fool Tawny from choking you in his madness? And if you don't know Mara, why do you wear Mara's brooch?'

Mr Finchley realized that it was the woman whom he had seen that morning.

'Now do you know, Mara?' she asked.

'Of course, now I do – but . . .'

'Come.' She took him by the arm. 'We will go to Tawny. He wants to see you. Tawny cried "wait". Mara said "wait", but the gorgeous one went away.'

'But I don't want to go to Tawny,' said Mr Finchley. 'I've seen enough of Tawny already. And felt enough . . .' He rubbed his neck, which was still sore.

'No, no!' She shook her head fiercely and drew him up the road. 'You are wrong. Tawny and Mara are sorry for the mistake. They wish to say together that they are sorry. Besides, you wear Mara's brooch and that makes you Mara's friend for ever, and Mara's friends are Tawny's friends.'

'That's all right, then,' replied Mr Finchley. 'You are sorry and, of course, I realize it was a mistake. But I don't want to come with you. As for your brooch – here it is – you are lucky to get it back.'

'Back! No – you must not do that. It is yours now!'

'I don't want it,' said Mr Finchley, 'and I'm not anxious to see Tawny. Here, take it!'

'No!' The vehemence of her reply startled Mr Finchley. 'You must come . . .'

'But I don't—'

'The gorgeous one jokes. Is Mara to go to Tawny and say, "Tonight in the village I met the gorgeous one you choked, and I said Mara she is sorry and Tawny he is sorry. They are both sorry. And the gorgeous one said he understands"? Then Tawny would say – "Why did you not bring back the mistaken one to our place to eat with us, and to sleep and drink? Tawny would say himself that he is sorry." And if I answered, and said I forgot or could not, then I was no true daughter of my people and Tawny would beat me with his stick for my sin.'

Mr Finchley was horrified. 'Do you mean that if I don't come, Tawny will beat you for not bringing me?'

'Why not?' she answered simply. 'Am I not Mara, his wife? If he did not, then he could not love me. Tawny loves Mara, that is why he beats her. That is why he nearly choked you because he thought you were the one who had made love to Mara while she slept. Come, we waste time talking!'

Mr Finchley had to go.

'All right, if you insist. I shouldn't like you to be beaten.'

So, wheeling his cycle with one hand, Mr Finchley set off with Mara at his side. A mile from the village they came to a place where the road forked. In the fork was a small wood set thinly with trees, through which Mr Finchley could see a green caravan with a little lean-to tent against its side. In front of the tent Tawny was tending a small fire. Mr Finchley, following Mara, wheeled his cycle across the pine needles. They came to the small clearing, and Tawny rose to his feet, staring first at Mr Finchley and then at Mara. He did not recognize his victim of the morning.

'Why do you bring the stranger, Mara?' he asked.

'Stranger!' she almost shouted. 'Do you not see, little bat, that it is no stranger but him, and look, he wears Mara's brooch!' She added something quickly in their own gipsy tongue. At her words Tawny started and looked closely at Mr Finchley. Then he stepped forward, and holding out his hand, caught Mr Finchley's in its grasp.

'I am glad you have come,' he said. 'Tawny is sorry for the mistake this morning.'

'That's all right,' replied Mr Finchley, a little relieved to find that Tawny was not such a ferocious individual as he had suspected from that morning's meeting. 'I realize that it was a mistake and I don't bear any malice. If you don't mind, though, I must be going. You see I have a long way to go.'

'Go!' said Tawny. 'Where can you go from here?'

'To find a night's lodging,' answered Mr Finchley.

'Come!' Tawny took him by the arm and led him forward to the caravan. 'Look!' He pointed to the small lean-to tent. 'There is your bed.'

'And here' – Mara appeared at the door of the caravan with a loaf and a pan in her hand – 'is food enough for us all.'

Mr Finchley saw that they were eager to share their food and shelter with him. They wanted to show him that the mistake had indeed been a mistake.

'Very well, since you wish me to, I will,' he said.

'Good,' replied Tawny, and taking Mr Finchley's bicycle he wheeled it into the wood a little way and covered it with bracken to protect it from the night dew.

They accepted Mr Finchley's presence with a finality that produced in him a reassuring confidence. He left his ruck-sack in the tent, where he was to sleep, and followed the big gipsy to a stream. Stripped to the waist, he splashed the water over his bare skin and felt it stinging into his face, which was reddened by the sun.

When they returned Mara had cooked the evening meal, light bread fresh-baked in the embers, fried potatoes, and brown cutlets of fish. Mr Finchley exercised a mild curiosity over the fish. He ate largely, breaking the soft bread and drinking hot tea, tea livened with a slight tang of wood smoke. And when his first appetite had gone, he said:

'What kind of fish is this?'

'Fish?' A flicker of light splayed about Tawny's eyes.

'Yes, this—' Mr Finchley prodded his plate.

'That is not fish, brother,' said Tawny seriously. 'That is snake – viper!'

'Snake!' Mr Finchley started. 'What, fried viper?'

He was acutely conscious of the meat which he had eaten within the last ten minutes.

'Yes, vipers which I trap!' went on Tawny, but the heavy look on his face suddenly became a grin, and he started to roar with laughter, smacking his leg.

'Peace, Tawny!' cried Mara, who had so far been silent. 'Would you frighten him again? Eat the fish, for such it is; eel caught this morning.'

Mr Finchley recovered his composure and finished the fish, not without a look at Tawny, who still continued to regard him slyly.

When they had finished eating, Tawny accepted some of Mr Finchley's tobacco, and they both sat over the fire talking, while Mara moved about inside the van. The night was well upon them and, through the pine branches above, the stars were braving a sky of drifting cloud wracks. They sat for some time and Tawny told how he and Mara cut withies and made baskets to sell to the people of the plain. He also told Mr Finchley how that morning Mara had been sleeping on the hillside, waiting for him to return from certain business he had in the fields lower down the slope, and a man had kissed her as she slept. Mara had held the weasel and called for him, but before he could come the weasel had slipped free, and though they chased him they found only Mr Finchley. But if ever he should find him – Mr Tawny made an expressive gesture into the night, and Mr Finchley knew what he meant.

'And you earn a living by making baskets and pegs and selling carpets?'

'Almost, brother.'

'I've heard it said,' Mr Finchley murmured, watching Tawny from the corner of his eye, 'that gipsies are a bad lot, stealing the farmwife's clothes and chickens, and trapping the game from preserves.'

'The man who said it was a liar and no gipsy.'

'That is as it may be,' answered Mr Finchley, and shortly afterwards, as the night grew colder and the fire lay down on its ashes and whispered, he went to his tent – Tawny and Mara disappeared inside the van.

It was a long time before Mr Finchley slept. He tossed about in the blankets which Mara had thrown to him and listened to the stamping of the horse and the frequent whine of Tawny's dog which was curled under the van. Mr Finchley wondered what Mrs Patten would say if she could see him. He felt at that moment almost tolerantly disposed towards Mrs Patten. Somehow he knew that in future he would be able to handle her ... at least, he would not be so completely quiescent to her moods. It was strange that he should be sleeping in a gipsy encampment, who not five days ago had been stewing in a solicitor's office. It just shows, he said to the ridge of the tent, what joy there is in life if only one had the courage ... It was rather a pleasing thing to discover that he had the courage ... the faith to find these joys ... With this consoling thought in his mind Mr Finchley fell asleep, and forgot the strangeness of his thigh hard against the ground.

When Mr Finchley awoke again, the sun had warmed the canvas of the tent and Mara had been busy for an hour about the fire and van. Tawny was nowhere to be seen, but as Mr Finchley returned from washing he saw him standing by the fireside watching Mara crack small brown eggs dexterously on the edge of her pan.

'Good morning, Tawny.'

'Good morning, brother,' he said, and smiled.

Mr Finchley ate well, without thought of his indigestion, and after breakfast was over, he retired into his tent and packed his gear.

'You are not leaving us?' asked Mara as she saw him come out.

'I must,' answered Mr Finchley. 'I have a long way to go.'

'Where?' asked Tawny.

Mr Finchley pointed westwards.

'Mara would wish that the little bat would stay but if he must go she wishes him well.'

'Thank you,' replied Mr Finchley, 'and you, too, Mr Tawny. You have been very kind to me. Perhaps some time

78

we shall meet again. Here' – he put his hand to his coat lapel – 'is your brooch.'

'No!' Mara jumped back from him. 'It is yours. You found it. To take it back would bring evil. He who finds Mara's brooch must keep it.'

'But it is yours and I don't want it!' urged Mr Finchley.

'No, brother,' interposed Tawny, 'the brooch is yours. You found it. To take it back, as Mara says, would bring evil. Take it and wherever there are our people you will find food and company. Goodbye!'

'Goodbye,' Mr Finchley said, realizing that it was useless to attempt to persuade them to take it back, and wheeled his bicycle towards the road.

Neither of them followed. They sat on the shaft of the van and watched him go, Tawny smoking a clay pipe and Mara standing up with one leg bent across the shaft and a frying-pan hanging from her hand like a buckler.

Mr Finchley waved and mounted his machine. As he cycled away westwards across the flat country he looked back. Behind him the small wood stood like a spearhead and, in a thin ribbon floating over the tall trees, the smoke from their fire drifted and lost itself in the sunshine and wind.

ELEVEN

Of Laziness and Sentiment

It was one o'clock by his watch when Mr Finchley sat down under a hedge in the shade of a huge elm and brought out a packet of sandwiches which a girl at an inn had prepared for him.

He laid the packet on the grass and climbed a gateway into a field through which ran a small stream. Riding had made him thirsty. He flung himself flat on his stomach by the edge of the water and drank. It was not a comfortable procedure, but by the time he had wetted the whole of his face and soiled the knees of his trousers and the elbows of his jacket with mud from the stream's brink, Mr Finchley had quenched his thirst and was conscious of his enormous hunger. He hurried back to his sandwiches. As he climbed the gateway, he saw that a man was sitting on the grass where he had left the packet. Mr Finchley was surprised to see that the sandwiches now lay between the man's legs, which guarded them on two sides with a proprietary stubbornness.

'Hey!' Mr Finchley rushed forward and shouted at the man, who was raising one of the sandwiches to his mouth.

'Hey!' shouted Mr Finchley again. The man took no notice of him and a huge bite from the sandwich.

'You're eating my sandwiches!'

'I'm what?' The man rose and stood over the packet. He was a tall fellow with a large, beaked nose from high over which two beady eyes gleamed down at Mr Finchley.

'You're eating my sandwiches!' repeated Mr Finchley.

'Oh! And who are you?' asked the man, ignoring Mr Finchley's remark.

'Who am I? Why ... why ... I'm Mr Finchley! Yes, Finchley's my name. But that's nothing to do with the sandwiches. I ...'

'And how do I know you're telling the truth? How do I know that your name is really what you say it is? Can you prove it?'

'Of course I can't prove it!' replied Mr Finchley, irritably. 'And I don't want to prove it; I want my sandwiches!' He stepped forward to take them, but the man stopped him.

'Steady, steady there!' he called, catching Mr Finchley by the arm. 'If you can't prove that your name is Finchley, you can't prove that these are your sandwiches – can you?'

'I don't need to prove it – they are mine! I left them there. Mind the way, please! I'm hungry and I've had enough of this nonsense!' Mr Finchley felt that he was in very great danger of losing his temper.

'Not until we've settled this properly. You say the sandwiches are yours because you left them, but you can't prove it. I say the sandwiches are mine because I found them, and I can prove it. Ergo, they are mine!'

'You think so?' questioned Mr Finchley fiercely.

'I do!'

'Well, I'll disprove it for you!'

'How?'

'Like this,' said Mr Finchley. The other was a big man, but Mr Finchley was hungry and the last few days had taught him a lot.

'Like what?'

'This!'

Mr Finchley hit out with his right fist and struck the man on the nose. The blow sent him toppling into the dry ditch at the roadside, where his long awkward legs waved for a few seconds above the dead nettles and then subsided as he rolled over. He rose from the ditch rubbing his beaked nose. Mr Finchley expected him to retaliate, but the man made no movement towards him. He merely continued to rub his nose and sat down on the dry grass.

'You win,' he said, laconically.

'I'm glad of that,' snorted Mr Finchley, a little less belligerently. He took up his sandwiches, made himself comfortable, and commenced his delayed lunch.

'Force,' said the other, eyeing him as he ate rapidly, 'is a stronger argument than logic. Would you be noble enough to allow me to finish the sandwich I started to cat?'

'Hunger,' replied Mr Finchley, dexterously manoeuvring a straying piece of ham into his mouth, '. . . is the strongest force of all. Take it!' He handed the man the sandwich, and watched him eat it. He had the general air of a tramp, but his clothes were a little too presentable; a well-worn, but tidy, brown jacket, and sober grey-flannel trousers gave the lie to a pair of very dusty shoes that bulged around the welts.

'Passivity,' said the stranger, after he had eaten the sandwich, 'is a stronger force than hunger. I am hungry, but, had I fought, you would perhaps have beaten me and I should have had no food. I let you hit me, declining to remonstrate or to strike back. *Palman qui meruit ferat!* I could, if you are not going to eat all those, manage another . . .'

Mr Finchley handed him another. There was more food than he could eat.

'Thank you.'

They were silent as they ate. When the man had finished his sandwich, Mr Finchley pointed to the packet. He took another, and they sat eating like old friends.

'Are you . . . are you on the road?' Mr Finchley asked, after their meal was done. He filled his pipe slowly and waited for the other to reply.

'I am wandering in search of the *lapis philosophorum*. Yes, I am on the road.'

'Lapis . . .?' Mr Finchley's Latin was small.

'The philosopher's stone.'

'I don't understand you,' said Mr Finchley.

'I don't really understand myself,' replied the other, pulling out a cherrywood pipe with a huge bowl and looking fixedly at Mr Finchley's pouch.

'That sounds rather odd.'

'Not at all! It's the happiest state a man can ever be in. If you understand yourself, there is nothing further to be done. You've reached finality, but not to understand yourself is to have a thousand pleasures before you.'

'I think I see what you mean. How does that account for you being on the road?'

'In this way, you see; I had too facile a conscience to live among men. My philosophy is a lazy one and the lazy philosopher, if he lives in a city, becomes a crook. I dislike criminals so I took to the road.' As he said this he tapped his pipe on his heel and looked at Mr Finchley.

'Have a fill, and tell me about it!' smiled Mr Finchley, who was uncertain whether he had to deal with a lazy rogue or a harmless idiot.

'Thank you! I will, since you appear to be interested. Yes, I am a lazy man. I have been lazy since the day I ceased to be a *helluo librorum*. Books are scourges. Had I never read other than Defoe and Debrett I should be a happy man with a wife and a seat at a university. As it is I am a happier man, and the only seat I have is a patched one.' He rolled over and exhibited the worn backside of his trousers.

'Books convince one of the futility of endeavour. I finished reading at twenty-two, and, having discovered the futility of all endeavour, I left Oxford and took to the road. Since then I have wandered about England, the Continent, and, once, America, pursuing my philosophy of passivity and laziness. I have had a very happy time. I do not know whether my parents still live. I do not care. Sometimes even, I forget my own name. Once I forgot it for a whole week and that was the happiest week of my life.'

'But how do you live?' inquired Mr Finchley.

'I eat and drink and sleep and silly women, thinking me *non compos mentis* and anxious for me to leave the door, give me their husbands' clothes.'

'You don't work?'

'Work?' The man took his pipe from his mouth and laughed aloud. 'Work! Why should I work? I eat and drink – what more?'

'But how can you eat and drink, if you don't work?'

'How? Why by just taking things, or waiting for people to give them to me. Haven't you supplied me with a meal and tobacco?'

'That's true, but doesn't that ever become dangerous?'

'It does, but generally my laziness saves me.'

'Saves you – how?' asked Mr Finchley.

'In many ways. I will tell you of one. Yesterday, I was on the hills back there . . .' He flourished with his hand in the direction of the Mendips. 'Under a tree I came upon a woman sleeping. Now, my laziness does not prevent me from appreciating beauty. And she was a very beautiful woman. *Simplex munditiis* . . . a gipsy woman. She slept and her lips were parted. Lips were meant to be kissed so I kissed them for her. She woke with a scream and I ran as she called to her husband. I did not run far. I was tired; I was too lazy. So I climbed a tree, a small tree, and had they looked as they passed they must have seen me, but their eyes were filled with anger and they rushed by . . . Had I continued running from them they must have caught me, for the man was fleet-footed.'

'You were lucky to escape,' said Mr Finchley, thinking of Tawny's grip about his throat.

'I am always lucky. But I don't call it luck. It's just laziness

83

and an easy conscience. Morality, civic and sexual, is some-thing which exists not for me. *Necessitas non habet legem!* Are you going, Mr Finchley?' He rose to his feet as Mr Finchley stood up.

Mr Finchley laughed. 'I am. Much as I should like to pro-long our conversation – or rather your monologue on the philosophy of laziness – I do not want to stop here all day.'

'To talk one need not be still. I will come your way and we will talk as we walk.'

'I think not,' answered Mr Finchley as he walked to the gateway with the other following him. 'You see I am not walking. I have a cycle!' As he spoke he lifted the machine from the hedge where the long summer grasses had hidden it from sight.

'A bicycle!' exclaimed the stranger. 'What memories! Do you know the last time that Ignatius de Wieder rode a bicycle?'

'De Wieder?' queried Mr Finchley. 'I don't know the man.'

'Oh, you do. That's my name. I've just remembered it. The bicycle brought it back to me. The last time I rode one was when I left Oxford ... down Cornmarket and past places where an undergraduate can get discreetly drunk, and up St Giles' Street with the elms like tipsy soldiers, or maybe it was I who was tipsy ... You almost make me regret that I decided to become a lazy man, Mr Finchley. Those mem-ories ...'

The man spoke with an expression of sincerity that seemed to soften the hardness of the lines that dropped in two scars on either side of his nose. Mr Finchley guessed that perhaps his story of voluntarily seeking this life was his own version of a sadder affair. Mr Finchley was ready to be sorry for a failure, and the sight of the man bravely disguising failure found a response within him. He wished there was something he could do for him. The man was a rogue perhaps, and he had insulted Mara, but ... well, he was human and Mr Finchley's heart was soft.

'I say, Ignatius' – and the name did not even sound lu-dicrous – 'is there anything I can do? I mean if it's money ...' Mr Finchley put his hand in his pocket.

The man shook his head strangely.

'No ... no ... it's not money I want. Would you do me a favour?' he asked suddenly.

'What?'

'This; the sight of that bicycle brings a lot back to me. Would you mind if I just rode it up the road a little way and back ... for the sake of those days? I know it's a sentimental request, but lazy men are prone to sentiment.'

'Why, of course, you may,' cried Mr Finchley, eager to please him.

'Thank you.'

Mr Finchley watched him mount. He was not very sure of his balance at first, then the machine steadied and he pedalled along the road slowly. Fifty yards away the road looped round a knoll and was lost to sight. As he neared the bend, Ignatius de Wieder turned and waved to Mr Finchley. Mr Finchley waved back. The cycle and man disappeared behind the knoll. Mr Finchley sat on the grass and waited for him to return. It was three o'clock by his watch. The sun was striking across the fields like a hot iron and the road, a blazing whiteness, danced and shimmered in the heat. Patiently Mr Finchley waited for the return of Ignatius. The minutes slipped into the heat; half an hour passed by and Mr Finchley began to realize that the other did not intend to return. His feelings broke loose. He recalled all the bad language of his youth and was unashamed. He danced angrily on the turf. He kicked his rucksack about the road in a passion, and swore that he would never trust another man. And after he had blasphemed everything within sight, including himself, he felt a little better. Realizing the futility of waiting, he started to walk in the direction which the other had taken. For an hour Mr Finchley was in such a state of annoyance that he wished himself safely at Margate. But only for an hour, and by that time he was sane again; sane and inclined to laugh at the rascality of Ignatius; though he promised himself that if he ever got near enough to that gentleman he would satisfy both himself and Tawny.

TWELVE

How a Top-hat Plays a Large Part

THE hills sweep round in a narrowing curve. Long woods of fir stream up their flanks and mask the valleys in darkness where slow streams go wandering by deep banks to find the sunshine of the plains. And at the far end of the hill lies a gap, and in the gap is a village, that was a village when the sabre-tooth roamed the hills. It is no more than a collection of whitewashed houses, thrown about a large green, where geese wander in hissing squadrons, and a donkey divides his time uncertainly between thistles and small boys who wear corduroys and hobnailed boots.

Today the geese do not wander. They are penned carefully in the yard of the George and the donkey kicks the boards of his stall restlessly. Today the whole village lives in a furious, laughing, joking, running, shouting, sweating, eating, drinking, betting, leaping whirl of action. Today, the landlord of the George sells more beer than is normally drunk in a fortnight, and mixed with the curious speech of the countrymen is the short, debased vowel of the Cockney. Today the village green is no longer green, and the sedge-rimmed pond swims mottled with paper under the drooping sun. The air is tortured by the sound of dance music, the screech of steam whistle, and the scream of mechanical organs. White booths face the main road, stalls and hoop-la rinks shout across the crowd where yesterday the geese hissed. Today the fair is in the village and the sun shines to greet the holiday.

The shadow of the hill was already lying across one corner of the fair when Mr Finchley left the George, where he had arrived after a three hours' walk, and made his way towards the green. The sideways and alleys of the fair were crowded. Folk had come from the surrounding villages and even from so far away as Taunton and Langport, and in the yard of the George were cars with mud caked thick about their axle-trees, gigs, traps and ancient motor-cycle combinations. Mr Finchley was taken into the pulsing crowd and lost. The swarm of people took him up and down. He saw the fat lady smirking under a feather boa, and was torn away in time to avoid the showman's invitation: 'Here, pinch her, mister, and see fer yerself! She's yuman! She's real!' He laughed at the dismal clown who tried to devour the sword-swallower's steel because the doctor said he needed iron. Everywhere was noise and laughter.

He watched farmers' sons shoot coloured balls from fountains. Crack! Crack! The rifles barked and the youths in their checks betted stolidly and the showman took their money. And in his car a tall man boomed a drum, while a sallow youth from Birmingham, dressed in chaps and a dirty sombrero, spun a rope and jumped in and out of the tilting circle.

'This way! This way! The only true rough-riders now tourin' the country. Four real cowboys all the way from Arizona. Come on, lads! This way! Knife-throwin'. Shootin' and rope-spinnin'. See the Coyote Kid 'imself in the great spectacular drama "The Man the Law Wanted"! Come on! Tickets sixpence each. The next show now about to commence ...'

The Coyote Kid ceased spinning his rope, winked at a girl in the crowd and disappeared behind the flap of the marquee. The crowd surged forward. It spun Mr Finchley by the shoulders, and when he recovered himself, the rush had ceased and he had been cast aside from the main current of people and was standing free at the far end of the fair. In front of him was a small, square tent with a large notice painted over its canvas:

MADAME STELLA MARIS.
LONDON, VIENNA, PARIS
AND ROYALTY.
WHAT IS YOUR HOROSCOPE? DO YOU KNOW YOUR
LUCKY DAY
PHRENOLOGY — THE SCIENCE OF THE FUTURE.
CONSULT ME AND KNOW YOUR FATE.

Underneath the notice was a large chart of a man's skull.

Mr Finchley examined the chart for a while and then turned away to find his way back into the fair. As he turned he bumped into a short, miserable-looking man who was leaning against a cradle of wooden balls, that stood outside a stall.

'Sorry,' said Mr Finchley, stepping backwards.

'That's all right, mate,' replied the man, who was in shirt sleeves, and wearing a large green cap that dwarfed his glum face. 'Don't mind me. No one ever minds me. Step on me face. Kick me in the stomach. I don't mind. It's all part of the gime!'

He said this in a melancholy voice that gave Mr Finchley the impression that were it not for the energy required to lie down and die, he would have done so on the spot.

Mr Finchley laughed.

'You don't sound very happy,' he said.

''Appy!' moaned the other. 'How d'yer expect me to be 'appy when I got ter stand 'ere watchin' the other guys tike the cash, just cos yer pal does the dirty on yer.'

'What happened to your pal?' asked Mr Finchley.

'We quarrelled and 'e's gone. 'E even wanted to tike the topper, but I stopped that.'

'The topper?'

'Yes, the topper! He wore a top-hat and walked up and down behind that wire screen' – here he pointed to a screen made of wire-netting at the far end of the stall – 'while I sold the balls for the lads to chuck at 'is 'at! Three for tuppence and a packet of fags if yer knocks 'is hat off.'

'Um, that's unfortunate for you,' sympathized Mr Finchley. 'Couldn't you get anyone else?'

'How? Not none of the village folk, and all the rest of the chaps have their own work to do. If 'e hadn't left me! 'E was a good pal. I've knowd 'im some nights wear the topper wivaht it once being knocked off!'

'Indeed!'

'Yes. But he was too fond of his . . .' He tipped one elbow meaningly. 'And if there's one thing Shorty Walters won't 'ave it's drinkin' in business hours. It don't pay.'

'Quite right, too. I'm sorry to hear of your misfortune, though.'

' 'Ere, harf a mo', mite!' The face of Shorty lost a little of its gloom. 'I got an idea!'

'An idea?' Mr Finchley echoed.

'Yes, a dodge fer gettin' me aht of this 'ere predicalment, and fer gettin' you a nice bit of ready to buy yerself a pair of shoes.' He pointed to Mr Finchley's dusty and despairing shoes.

'I'm afraid I don't understand what you are talking about,' said Mr Finchley. 'It's true that my shoes are wearing out but I've done quite a lot of walking lately and . . .'

'I knows, mite, I knows,' cut in the other, quickly, 'and yer don't want no charity. I ain't offerin' it – am I?'

'I didn't say that . . .' Mr Finchley was amazed at the happy metamorphosis which had taken hold of the other's face. He was beaming.

'I knows, I knows. We ain't goin' to argue abaht it. Come on, you pop in behind that net and we'll soon 'ave the lads biffing at yer topper.'

He darted to the back of the stall and was at Mr Finchley's side again before that gentleman had time to remonstrate. In his hand Shorty held a faded top-hat. There were several dents in the sides and the crown was engaged in divorce proceedings with the rest of the hat; otherwise it was quite a serviceable hat. Shorty rubbed it on his sleeve.

'There y'are!' He thrust the hat into Mr Finchley's hand.

'But what on earth are you giving me this for,' said Mr Finchley. 'Do you expect me to wear it and walk about behind that screen while people throw those at me?' He pointed with innocent horror to the cradle of hard wooden balls.

'Yer doin' fine, mite! Yer gettin' me meanin'! Oh, yer a wonder! An' I thought I was goin' to have a thin day. You'll draw 'em. You got the figure! You got the class! But take a tip from me—' He leaned towards Mr Finchley, though there was no one near. 'Don't lift yer head above the screen. It ain't safe. Some on 'em holds the balls behind their backs and waits. Just keep the topper showin'! Remember, you ain't a tip-topper like me pal that was. But you got the style. Come on!' He seized Mr Finchley by the arm.

Mr Finchley gasped. Become a guy in a third-rate side-show! He, Edgar Finchley, solicitor's clerk! He looked down at his clothes. Did he look so disreputable? Did he look so very much like a tramp? A little perhaps; but even Shorty had discerned his traces of class and style. Even Shorty had enough sense to see that he was not wholly . . .

'I'm sorry, Mr Walters,' Mr Finchley said; 'but what you propose is impossible. I don't want a job like that. I'm not a tramp, though my clothes are perhaps misleading.'

He handed the topper back to Shorty. Shorty was not dismayed.

'Now then, now then! Who said anything abaht tramps? I knows a gentleman when I sees one. But we all gits a bit of 'ard luck, don't we?'

Mr Finchley shook his head firmly.

'You still don't understand. I don't want any job at all! I'm not in need of a job. I'm not down on my luck. I'm on holiday . . .'

Poor Shorty's face reverted to its depressing gloom.

'Well, if you ain't the bleedin' limit. Jist as I was thinkin' me luck 'ad turned yer begins to mike it clear that yer don't want to help me. I'll jist starve on this green. It'll be a quiet place to die in. Fancy raisin' a feller's hopes like that . . .'

Shorty assumed an attitude of total dejection. His clothes hung from him dispiritedly; his hands lay limp at his sides, and his green hat shuffled ingloriously to one side.

Mr Finchley was sorry for Shorty. But it wasn't the sort of thing a man in his position did!

'No, Shorty . . . I can't help you.' As Mr Finchley turned on his heel, he heard the voice within shout loudly: 'Coward! You're afraid!'

Something happened to Mr Finchley. Afraid? He was finding it difficult lately to stand that taunt. He swung round with a growing determination. In two swift strides he reached Shorty.

'Give that to me!' he said, snatching the topper from the

other's loose fingers. Ramming the hat upon his head and pushing his cap into his pocket, Mr Finchley darted to the end of the stall shouting to Shorty as he went: 'Go on! Call them on. I've changed my mind. Afraid!'

Shorty wasted no time. Almost before Mr Finchley was safely ensconced behind his netting he was shouting:

'This way! This way! Three balls for tuppence!'

His voice roared out over the crowd which up to now had passed him by, and caused heads to turn.

'This way! Dahn with the aristocracy! Every time yer 'its the topper off a packet of fags! Come an' tike a pot at the Park Line Percy!'

And they came.

Within three minutes thirty wooden balls had whistled by Mr Finchley's head, and one rebounded off the canvas behind him, to raise a respectable bruise on his calf. But he did not mind. As he walked up and down his heart sang; and the laughing youths who hurled their balls at his head knew not that Mr Finchley's heart was happy.

'H'yar, sir! Three fer tuppence!' Shorty called to a huge labourer, whose red face shone above a collar that had been clean and white two hours since. 'Knock 'is hat off and yer gets a packet of fags!'

'Knock un off. Reckon 'e'll have to hold un on to stop me! Give us six balls, mister.'

'That's the spirit!' cried Shorty, as the man took his stance at the stall.

Mr Finchley lifted his hat jauntily to the crowd that stared at him as though he were a wild animal. The labourer's arm flew forward and a ball sung against the netting below Mr Finchley's neck.

'Bad luck, sir!'

Mr Finchley lifted his hat derisively and continued walking. Another ball raised a wind above his head. The crowd roared.

'I'll have un in a minute, the beauty!'

'Come on! Tike a pot at Percy's topper and dahn with the aristocracy!'

Three times the man slung a ball at him and each time

Mr Finchley's doubts about the strength of the netting grew, but his topper remained intact. But the labourer was wily. The first of his last two balls missed the hat, and as Mr Finchley raised his hat, he was amazed to find the topper struck violently from his hand. It went spinning away to the back of the stall. The labourer had been ready for him.

'That's the ticket!' cried Shorty. 'Step up, sir, and take yer fags. If I'd known yer was comin' I'd 'ave brought me special cigars!'

'I knew'd I'd gettun!' grinned the man as he took the cigarettes.

Mr Finchley was not caught again so easily. He proved an able dodger. In the next two hours his hat only touched the ground six times. Shorty was enraptured. In the intervals between handing out his balls he shouted his delighted approval. Every time a ball missed him narrowly, Mr Finchley raised his hat in polite derision and the throwing became a challenge between the thrower and himself.

He attracted a constant crowd. Darkness came and Shorty stood like a squat Colossus between naphtha flares.

Mr Finchley must have walked at least four miles behind the netting. The noise of steam organ and rifle cracks was still loud, but the night was passing and people were drifting back to their houses and the inn. Only the bucks of the village and the schoolboys, loath to leave so much pleasure and novelty, still wandered aimlessly about, chaffing the girls and filling the gondolas and cakewalks.

Mr Finchley fell into a reverie as he walked. He wondered what people, the people he knew, would say to all his. He wondered himself if he were not going just a little too far; but he crushed the thought instantly. He was on holiday and could do as he pleased. Still, Mrs Patten would, if she ever came to know, make good capital out of it. He laughed quietly as he bent to pick up the top-hat which had been knocked from his head. No one would ever know. That was the beauty of such adventures. He straightened up with the hat in his hand. He saw Shorty handing a packet of cigarettes to the lucky marksman, and he saw something else. From the passing crowd two beady eyes above a strong hooked nose winked at the stall. A furious desire leaped him. He dashed from behind the netting.

'Here, Shorty!' he shouted. 'Take this. I'm going!'

' 'Ere! 'ere! What's bleedy well bit yer, mite?' cried Shorty, juggling with the falling topper. 'Where yer going?'

'I'm going to catch Ignatius!' cried Mr Finchley over his shoulder, forcing his way through the crowd. He had easily recognized the lean, wolfish look, and the tall, sloping shoulders of his friend of the morning.

'Icknashus? Icknashus . . .' Shorty scratched his scalp. 'Can't say I knows the gent. Sounds more like a rice hoss to me . . .'

Mr Finchley disappeared in the direction taken by Ignatius. Progress was not easy, although the crowd had thinned. For a time he kept Ignatius in view, then a jam held him up for a second and he lost sight of him. He darted quickly by the chair-o-planes, scanning the crowd as he went, but Ignatius had disappeared. He went quickly round the green. There was no sign of his man anywhere.

Mr Finchley had enjoyed more exercise that day than London usually vouchsafed to him in a year. He was too tired to return to Shorty and enter into lengthy explanations. Wearily, he entered the George. He declined the landlord's offer of supper, bathed, and went to bed. In five minutes he was sleeping soundly. Twenty yards away, where he had settled himself an hour before, Ignatius slept the sleep of the lazy unjust, in the hayloft of the George; and the cycle lifted its tarnishing handlebars to the moon in the garden of a cowhand's cottage five miles away. Ignatius had a pretty judgement of the cash value of sentiment.

THIRTEEN

Which Proves that a Footpath may be a Short-cut, but a Short-cut is not always a Footpath

THE next morning, while he was having his breakfast, the landlord of the George handed Mr Finchley a note, saying: 'This is for you, sir. One of the men from the fair left it early this morning before he went away.'

'For me?' asked Mr Finchley, glancing at the envelope, which bore no name. 'Are you sure?'

'Yes, sir. Seeing that you're the only man in the house that is – beggin' your pardon, sir, I'm sure – bald and wearin' a light grey suit.'

Mr Finchley ignored the description, and opened the envelope. It was from Shorty and contained, besides a message scribbled on the back of a handbill, a ten-shilling note.

DEAR SIR, – I was sorry about Icknashus and you jumping the rails like that when all was set for a good thing. I don't grumble. The takings was good, and I have the honour to enclose herewith an amount which will suitably close our score. If ever you was to think about the top-hat game, I could do with a steady pal. Shorty Walters, Amusements Proprietor, the Worlds Fair is the name.

Thanking you for the honour, and hoping as how you finds that Icknashus.

SHORTY

Mr Finchley laughed.

'Thank you,' he said to the landlord, who had been trying to look over his shoulder. 'It was for me.'

He fingered the ten-shilling note. He could not reject it now. It was rather a pleasant thought, however, that the money should have been fairly earned by him. If ever, Mr Finchley contemplated the remote possibility, he lost his job as a clerk he knew where to get another one. The feeling of the note between his fingers reminded him of the thrill he had experienced twenty-eight years ago when Bardwell had paid him his first week's wages ... that too had been ten shillings – but not a note. He had thought that the pleasure of earning was lost to him for ever, but Shorty had disproved it. He had earned every penny. Had he not three bruises on his calves to show that it had been no child's labour?

In a reminiscent mood, he paid his bill and made his way into the courtyard of the inn. The day was far from fine. Heavy masses of clouds climbed up into the sky from the western horizon, and the wind spilled cold gusts about his ears.

Buttoning his coat about his neck, he started down the road. There was no sound but the steady fall of the rain on the road, the crunch of Mr Finchley's shoes, and the gentle drip, drip of the leaves. He pulled his cap low over his eyes and soon the warmth of the coat and the exercise of walking fired him with a soft glow. He was in a shallow valley-like depression, and it was difficult to see the surrounding country. Willow trees and an occasional elm or beech lined the roadway while on either side lay flat fields of beet, rape and clover. After an hour's steady plodding he saw a muddy stile by the road marked to Taunton. He debated whether he should take the path or stick to the firmer going of the road. He finally took to the path. It might be muddier, but it was sure to be less monotonous than the flat road. In half an hour he had regretted his decision. Like most footpaths which profess to be short-cuts, this path was a thing of moods. Mr Finchley's first indication of its temperamental qualities came when it led him blithely to the edge of a wide rean and left him facing six feet of muddy water and be-draggled weeds. Across the rean lay a mouldy, moss-green plank that cracked just too late to precipitate him into the water with the sticklebacks that fought beneath the weeds, and then he was confronted by a field of tall grass which awaited the mowing-machine. A hundred yards of tall, wet grasses, moving slowly in the faint wind which was rising, stretched before him. Here and there a poppy lazed in bloody beauty and trailing convolvulus made sheaths of the coarse knot-grasses around the hedges. On the far side of the field were three gates and the path might lead to any of them. If he had been a countryman, Mr Finchley would have known that the right thing to do when one comes to a field of mowing-grass ready for the cutter is to walk around the hedges. He looked to see the path heading across the field towards one of the gates; but there was no sign of it. Summer growths had obscured it. There was instead a tiny track, close against the hog-weeds and knot-grasses of the hedge, which Mr Finchley did not see. He made the plunge. Thrusting his way through the grass which wetted his trousers and sent runnels of water squelching in his shoes, he worked his way towards the gate on the extreme right. When he reached it he was wet and breathless with pushing aside the grasses. He had no thought for his wet feet. His one aim was to reach the main road. He had long since realized the futility of worry over wet feet when at any moment he might slip into a rean.

He climbed the gate and was relieved to find a path leading from it. He trekked on for a mile before he began to wonder whether he had struck the wrong path. After forcing his way through two hedges he was certain that he had, but it was too late to return. He was travelling in the right direction. He gritted his teeth and went onwards. He was possessed of a fierce determination that forced him forward. By now he was hungry, it was long past lunchtime. The rain stopped and he took off his coat, but he was wet through to his shirt. The path disappeared completely; still Mr Finchley went on, forcing a way where necessary. Little thorns stuck themselves into his cap and frequently into his face. The turn-ups of his trousers collected a granary of grass seeds and buttercup petals. The wind found a new life to drive the clouds from the watery sky. A weak sun nodded to him occasionally over the top of a bank of cloud drift and, somewhere in a hazel thicket as he climbed what must have been his fiftieth gate, a blackbird screeched like an electric train. The noise startled him and he slipped on the wet earth, saving himself by digging his hands deep into welcoming, soft mud.

Mr Finchley lost his temper. He swore. But he went on. Wiping the mud off his hands with wet grass he headed across the field. He was halfway across it when he heard a sound behind him. It might almost have been a sigh, a sigh accompanied by a sodden, rhythmic thunder. He turned. A young bull was prancing over the grass towards him. Its head was lowered, its glistening shoulders moved, like pistons, up and down, and as it came it tossed a pair of short wicked horns. Mr Finchley neither shouted nor screamed. He saved his breath – and ran. He ran in a terrible, panting silence, and behind him, gaining a little at each stride, charged the frolicking bull, which had not enjoyed itself so much for months. Stumbling and leaping over the hillocks and mounds left by moles, Mr Finchley raced away from the animal. His rucksack thumped the small of his back as he ran. The snorting sounded closer. He glanced behind and saw that he could never reach the gateway on the opposite side of the field. He swerved desperately towards the other and nearer side of the field. There was no hedge, only a dark line that marked a ditch. Mr Finchley prayed that it might be a narrow one, narrow enough for him to jump and wide enough to stop the bull.

The bull skidded on the wet grass as he swerved and the skid gained Mr Finchley three yards. Then the beast was charging in his rear again with happy gruntings and sighings that reached his ears transmuted into fearful bellowings and roars. He looked round again and saw that he had a flimsy chance. The ditch rushed towards him. He saw with horror that, although it was wide enough to stop the bull, it was hardly narrow enough for him to jump over. The lumbering bull behind presented no alternative.

With all the strength at his command, Mr Finchley leaped forward into the air. The water leaped up, but with an effort he threw himself forward and landed with a *plop!* in the black mud at the far side of the ditch. The force of his landing threw him face downwards on the bank and from that position he wriggled slowly to the top of the ditch. Behind him, he left one shoe stuck fast in the mud. On the other bank, the bull, whose leaping abilities were inferior to

Mr Finchley's, nosed at the grass as though it had been grazing peacefully for hours and had never seen Mr Finchley. The sight of the complacent bull nuzzling the grass made Mr Finchley wonder whether the last two minutes had been a dream. But the bull suddenly threw up its heels and frolicked away to the far side of the field to show him that he had not dreamed.

As he watched the bull, a voice sounded in his ear:

'Well jumped, well jumped; but if you sit on my fish much longer they will be uneatable!'

Mr Finchley turned. Sitting a little higher up the bank was a small man. Indeed, the man was so small that for a moment Mr Finchley wondered if he were not staring at some earthly troglodyte come to laugh at his discomfiture. Dwarf or no, the fellow was evidently enjoying Mr Finchley's embarrassment. Mr Finchley lifted himself from the grass to discover that he had been sitting on three roaches which the other had taken from the ditch with the rod he held in his hand.

'I beg your pardon,' said Mr Finchley.

The dwarf bent down and put the fish into the large pockets of his thick, black serge jacket.

'I'm afraid I was too exhausted to look where I sat. You saw what happened?'

'I saw,' replied the other, carefully disjointing his rod. Mr Finchley observed, as he packed the rod into a canvas case, that the man was hunchbacked. He wore no hat and his head was covered by a mass of close, curly black hair, so that he had the appearance of an Ethiopian; but the face beneath the black mass was pale and, now that he was no longer laughing, divided by severe lines. His shoulders were broad and massive, carrying his deformity with ease, but below the chest his body was thin and wasted and supported by two thin legs. He finished his packing and said:

'Yes, I saw, I saw! I saw that a frightened man will do things that his normal self draws back from. You were frightened – weren't you?' he asked, coming close under Mr Finchley's face and twisting his black head back until it almost touched his hump.

'I certainly was!' admitted Mr Finchley unashamedly. 'I think I had a very good reason to be!'

'I like you for that! I like you for that!' The hunchback caught his arm in a friendly manner.

'Why, what's this?' he cried as he felt the damp cloth. 'You're wet through. You must come with me and I'll dry your things. Come, come! You shall eat the fish while your clothes dry.'

'Oh, no! No, thank you, Mr . . . whatever your name is?'

'Humpy, call me! Humpy, call me – they all do and find it funny!' the hunchback snarled in an excess of quick animus. Then, seeing the look on Mr Finchley's face, his manner changed completely. 'Forget it! Forget it! I am cruel to myself to forget the cruelty of others. Call me Ernst. It is a good name, though not truly my own.'

'Ernst, then,' said Mr Finchley. 'I won't trouble you. I shall soon reach some house or inn where I can dry my clothes. It is very kind of you to offer.'

'I will not allow it. Taurus sent you to me, and you will be my guest while I dry those things and you eat my fish with me. You were meant to come with me. All this day I have spoken to no man and now the desire for company has come – or perhaps you do not wish to be seen with a wretched little hunchback, eh?' Ernst caught him again by the arm and sneered.

'If that is how you feel then I will not come!' replied Mr Finchley quickly, and broke away from Ernst's grip.

'You are right; you are right. That is not what I think. That is what my hump thinks. You will come, will you? If you do, Ernst will play his fiddle for you . . .' He took Mr Finchley's arm again, pathetically.

'All right, I'll come and eat your fish. But if you act like that again I shall go.' He felt as though he were reprimanding a naughty child.

'Good! I knew you would come. Shall I tell you why?'

'Why?' echoed Mr Finchley.

'Yes, why! You will come because you wear Mara's brooch; and Ernst once wore Mara's brooch – though that was long enough ago.'

99

'Mara's brooch?' said Mr Finchley. 'You mean this?' He fingered the gold brooch which he had continued to wear, from some queer fancy, ever since he had left the gipsies.

'Mara's brooch, yes. All those who wear Mara's brooch are brothers, and now you wear Mara's brooch and are my brother. Had I not seen the brooch when you jumped the rean and sat on my fish, I should have beaten you about the head with my stick. I did not know Mara and her man were in the country. Now come, you are wet, and as we walk you shall tell me how you came by the brooch . . .'

'You know Mara, then?' questioned Mr Finchley, as he retrieved his shoe and followed Ernst across the field.

'Ay, I know Mara; though I have not seen her for ten years. Tell me how you came by the brooch?'

Ernst was walking at a rapid pace as he spoke, and Mr Finchley had difficulty in keeping company with him. He started to tell the story of his meeting with Mara and her man, Tawny, and the curious way in which he had come into possession of the brooch. As Mr Finchley talked, Ernst made his way across the fields in the direction of a low ridge crowned by a beech copse.

FOURTEEN

Of Fish and Wisdom

BY the time Mr Finchley had finished his story, they had reached the foot of the knoll. In a sheltered dell on the eastern slope, there was a small, brightly painted caravan with a white horse tethered to one side of it and, in the open space before the caravan, a fire burned low.

'Here we are,' said Ernst, leading the way into the van. 'Now I'll rouse the fire while you take off those wet clothes. Here – you can wear this while they are drying!' He passed Mr Finchley a huge greatcoat with lapels like a whale's fins and skirts like sails, a red woollen blanket and a shirt.

The caravan was furnished very differently from Tawny's.

Along one side was a bunk, over which hung three small cupboards for crockery, cooking gear and food. At the far end was an iron stove with a crooked pipe that thrust itself through the roof. Opposite the bunk was a table that, during the daytime, folded flat against the wall. By the table stood a small organ, and hanging on the wall from a silk sling was a fiddle, very old and brown. The wall between the window and the doorway was covered by bookshelves that held, Mr Finchley approximated, nearly four hundred volumes. Over the bookshelves was an oleograph of a gentleman with a high cravat and long side-whiskers.

Ernst suddenly appeared at the door.

'Drink,' he said, and handed him a cup of hot milk.

Mr Finchley took it and drank.

'Soon,' said Ernst, watching him drink, 'your clothes will be dry. Until then, perhaps, you are tired and would like to sleep?' He pointed to the empty bunk and then went out. Looking through the window, Mr Finchley saw him climb up the side of the knoll until he disappeared into the belt of trees. He glanced at his watch. It was four o'clock. He had had no lunch and it seemed as though Ernst had forgotten all about the fish. He went to the bunk and lay down. Perhaps he could sleep and forget his hunger.

Ernst returned an hour later. Mr Finchley was sleeping soundly. The hunchback smiled down at the figure on the bunk. He turned to one of the cupboards, took some things from it and left the van. Very soon there was the sound of frying and the smell of cooking, blown by the wind, entered the van.

The rain clouds had gone, the evening was alive with the smell of the earth, and the air was fresh and fragrant with the scent of grass. The trees stood bright-washed and the sky paled away into delicate shades of blue, clear as a hedge-sparrow's egg, above the dell, and fading to the fineness of wood smoke in the east.

The fish was cooked and Ernst called to Mr Finchley, who did not at first hear him. The hunchback thrust his broad shoulders through the doorway and shook his guest by the foot.

'Wake, wake! There is food, and bread which I have fetched!'

Mr Finchley was awake in an instant and hungry.

'Are my clothes dry?' he asked.

'Here.' Ernst appeared at the doorway again and handed him his suit. It was not dry as Mrs Patten understood that word, but Mr Finchley's life at that moment held no place for finesse. He was hungry and he dressed quickly.

Ernst was waiting for him beside the fire. As he approached, the hunchback nodded to a large flat stone by the fireside.

'Take your place, and eat fish that comes from the stream yonder, and bread baked of good wheat. I have neither wine nor sauce for you, but a hungry man needs no sauce, other than a good appetite. Eat!'

Mr Finchley watched the hunchback dividing the crisply fried roach, and washing down his bread with water from a tin mug at his side. He was beginning to appreciate that men who live in the open do not eat as a matter of form, but when they are hungry, and then the only thing that matters is the food, not tablecloths of damask or ivory-handled fish knives. Mr Finchley followed Ernst's example and ate. There was plenty of fish and the bread was still warm.

When they had finished eating Mr Finchley pulled out his pipe and filled it.

'Do you smoke?' He held the pouch towards Ernst.

'I have a better solace,' said Ernst. He watched his companion enter the caravan, to reappear with the old fiddle in his hand. Without a word, Ernst piled more fuel on the fire, to protect them against the fresh evening air that filled the dell at the dropping of the sun behind the knoll, and sat himself upon the shaft of the cart with the fire between him and Mr Finchley.

Mr Finchley smoked and watched Ernst. The other held the fiddle loosely. His eye caught that of Mr Finchley. He smiled and raised the fiddle.

Across the dip of the dell sounded a thin treble note, a note that deepened and swelled slowly. Ernst's head swung for-

ward and his eyes were lidded. His arm swept across the
fiddle. He played a slow, melancholy strain that rose and fell,
like a reed-warbler chattering and weeping to itself in the
dark sedges. The melody grew. Now and then a savage trill
of pleasure would break through the sad strains, but mostly
the tune was low and uneasy with a hidden sorrow. The
hollow was gradually filled with the music. It swirled about
the craggy thorn trees and lost itself in the vagrant smoke
swathes of the fire. It wakened a queer emotion in Mr Finchley. He was unhappy because he knew Ernst was unhappy
and would always be so. Life had cast Ernst in a grotesque
mould, and always Ernst was revenging himself upon life by
sneering at it, and hating those who made him conscious of
his deformity. Mr Finchley wanted to jump up and sit beside
the man, to put his arm around his shoulders and tell him
that he had a friend.

Ernst stopped playing suddenly and laughed. His laugh
surprised Mr Finchley.

'Well, what do you think of my tune?'

'It's a sad one, don't you think so?'

'Perhaps you are right. But 'tis played by a sad man. Don't
you know the player?' he shouted suddenly. 'It's Humpy, the
hunchback! Humpy, at whom the little boys laugh and
throw mud in the street, because he is not as their fathers
are. Now do you know why it is sad?' His anger was gone as
quickly at it came.

'Wouldn't it be better for you to try to forget yourself in
merry tunes?'

Ernst laughed.

'Oh, the little man, who runs from bulls because he is
frightened, is a philosopher then? Very well, I am glad you
are so. I will play a gay tune such as makes the girls dance
and men love their drink the more. Listen!'

He played again. His bow chased and harried the strings
and the notes tumbled after one another through the evening, and set the valley dancing with their merriment. Ernst
rose and finished the reel, with a few prancing steps that
took him to Mr Finchley's side.

'There!'

Mr Finchley smiled.

'That was better. That's the kind of tune that would make anyone happy.'

'No tune could make me happy. But' – Ernst saw the shadow on Mr Finchley's face – 'we will forget that. Kick the fire and I will tell you a story.'

Mr Finchley kicked the fire obediently. He liked the sound of Ernst's soft voice, and there were less pleasant ways of spending a summer evening than by the side of a clear fire in a green dell.

'This is the story of a hunchback who was the son of noble parents. But noble parents are not always the best parents and his were disappointed in him. They could trace in him no likeness to either of them and his hump filled them with horror. They brought him up as the son of a noble and accustomed him to the ways of the rich, but of his deformity they said nothing to him. It is not necessary to speak to show hatred!

'The hunchback was well aware of their hatred, and when an aunt, who had never seen his hump, out of compassion left him her fortune, he decided to leave his home that was no home and his parents, who were no parents. They said no word against his going, but they did not bid him to stay. So he left home, and buying a little caravan – very much the same as the one there' – Ernst tossed his head so that his thick black hair shook, in the direction of his van – 'the hunchback wandered about the countryside, living his own life and making friends with the gipsies, who proved kinder to him than his own people.

'But a hunchback, little brother, is human even as other men, though he may look like a monster and scowl. And this hunchback, passing through a village one day, saw a pretty girl, who did not shrink away from him as others, but looked him full in the eyes and smiled. Seeing her smile, and noting the friendliness in her eyes, the hunchback smiled back, and that evening and for many evenings his caravan stayed in a little wood outside the village. He saw the girl again and smiled and soon he talked with her and they laughed together and one day they told one another of their love.

104

'Strange, isn't it, that a hunchback should love? And stranger still that he should find a pretty girl to love him? You do not answer. That is wise. So, the two would be married ... but two months before the time fixed there came a newcomer to the village. A tall, handsome farmer who had bought a nearby farm. He, too, saw the girl and wished for her. That she was already betrothed did not worry him. He set about his wooing by deriding the poor hunchback and making fun of his deformity before the whole village; and the villagers laughed, as there are always plenty to laugh at another's misfortune when someone gives them the lead.

'At first the girl was angry, but the young farmer was wily and played upon her womanhood. Why should she, a beautiful woman, waste herself upon a poor, miserable hunchback? She rebuked him and told him of her love, but the poison was in her mind. What happened, little brother? Women are only women, and like clouds they chase their own shadows. There was no marriage for the hunchback, he went away on the day that she told him of her love for the farmer and asked his forgiveness. The hunchback gave it, for he still loved her, but before he went the farmer came and spat in the hunchback's face for presuming to woo the girl whom he was to marry. And the hunchback struck him across the mouth with his stick, so that it should always carry a scar, and while the man lay unconscious on the ground he went away.

'Then one day he heard that the girl, now the farmer's wife, was dead – of a broken heart, who can tell? – for the farmer, as soon as he had married her, treated her less than one of his cows. So the hunchback returned in the night to the farm to take his revenge.

'Revenge is the one thing that makes sweet the life of the oppressed. In the night he set fire to the farmer's ricks and byres, and when the man came running from his bed, the hunchback was there to greet him with a sneer. The farmer knew him, and they fought in the light of the blazing farm.

'Now, the hunchback, though deformed, was strong in the arms, and after a while he had the farmer at his mercy.

He picked him up like a child, and holding him struggling above his head, carried him to the white-hot ricks and, laughing, threw him into the largest, where he burned to death, shrieking and leaping like an eel on a grid. As for the hunchback, it is not known what happened to him, for there was none by to see or hear. Some say he threw himself into the flames after the farmer to torment him in his death, others say he disappeared from the countryside and went to another land. I do not know. I know only that it is a terrible story for so sweet an evening.'

'I should think so!' said Mr Finchley emphatically. 'It's an evil story. Don't you know any jolly ones?'

'A hundred, little brother, but not now. I will play for you for a while. Pleasant music; and then we must part for our ways do not lie together for long.'

Ernst took his fiddle and played quietly. He played so that the memory of the story was wiped from Mr Finchley's mind and the peace of the darkening evening came sweeping over him in a wave. He played until Mr Finchley's pipe was cold, and an owl beat its soft way across the dell. The ashes of the untended fire whitened and whispered. The music ceased and Ernst rose.

'Time to go,' he said, and put his hand upon Mr Finchley's shoulder.

'Go where?' asked Mr Finchley. 'Aren't you going to spend the night here?'

'No. When I have been in a place for three days the trees and the grasses and flowers begin to hate me – so I go on. I will give you a ride to the road and then we part.'

He left Mr Finchley and began to harness the horse to the van. Mr Finchley went across and helped him. Ernst did not want help, but Mr Finchley wanted to do something to help him and this seemed the only thing.

'You are a good man,' said Ernst suddenly, peering over the back of the horse. 'I wish there were more so!'

'There are plenty of good people in this world, Ernst,' replied Mr Finchley. 'The trouble is that they don't advertise themselves. I think you are inclined to judge people too hastily. You only look for the bad in them ...' Which remark needed no little temerity on Mr Finchley's part. Ernst was not annoyed. He smiled back.

'Perhaps so, little brother, but I have been so often disappointed that I have learned now to guard against disappointment by seeing all men as evil. When I meet a good man, like you ... well, my heart sings louder and sweeter than the fiddle!'

He laughed merrily and shook the horse's bit.

'Come, we must be going or you will not get to Taunton tonight.'

They drove from the dell out into the warm gloom of a grass-covered lane and so, round the skirt of the knoll on to the main road. Presently they came to a fork road and Ernst stopped the caravan.

'That is your way,' he said. 'Goodbye, and remember Ernst when you pray!'

'Goodbye, Ernst,' said Mr Finchley.

The white horse started forward and Mr Finchley was left standing in the half-light watching the caravan recede from him. He was never to see Ernst again, but he was often to remember the unfortunate hunchback who went twisting through the narrow lanes of England trying to escape a destiny that hung over him as immutable as the Northern Star.

FIFTEEN

Of a Want which was filled

MR FINCHLEY reached Taunton at nine o'clock, and found lodgings in a side-street. The place was kept by a tall, thin-featured woman who wore glasses. Her manner suggested that he might smell, that his feet were probably unclean and his bathing habits irregular. She was particular about her beds. She said so, blinking. Mr Finchley assured her that he was only wanting a bed for one night and that he was not a tramp, but she was not convinced until he took out his wallet and offered to pay for his bed and breakfast in advance. The gesture disarmed her. She expanded. Her lean body bent and swayed benignly and her eyes grew warm and moist with a gentle persuasion.

'Oh! That's all right, sir,' she said. 'You see, we get so many people through and they ain't all what you might call ... well ... well, if you know what I mean – they're not quite ...'

'Up to sample, eh?' laughed Mr Finchley, seeing that he had conquered

'That's it, sir. That's it, completely! Why, you mightn't believe it, sir, but I had one fellow in ... the week before last it was, if I remember right. No! It was last week, because Ada said to me on Friday about her rheumatism and I distinctly remember that it was just as we'd finished ... Yes, that was it – last Friday! We had this man in for the night and would you believe it, sir? The next morning he was gone without so much as a by-your-leave and took with 'im the towel from the room and a little wooden cross what the hubby – he's dead now, sir, but a straighter man never lived, give me.'

'Well, you needn't fear anything like that from me,' said Mr Finchley. 'I'm on holiday and walking for the exercise.'

He escaped into the open air and breathed.

He walked up to the centre of the town, through streets that were crowded with people, who walked regardlessly amongst the traffic of the road, loitered in front of cars and motor-cycles in a lenient manner and stepped recklessly in front of coaches as though the presence of traffic was an affliction best to be ignored. Mr Finchley, who was London-bred and used to the decorum and sanity of traffic regulations and policemen whose nod was a law, could only stand and stare, waiting for the accidents which never happened.

In the centre of the town stood the Town Hall. Mr Finchley assumed that it stood normally. When he saw it the walls were being propped up by youths in navy-blue suits and red pullovers, with now and then a girl in a cheap print frock and a flowering hat to lend a light hand; close to the building was a meeting of Salvation Army folk with a lusty hymn in progress. Their leader edged towards him shaking in his one hand a collection box and in the other a white leaflet. Mr Finchley retreated through the warm night, the shouting crowd and the blaring traffic, to find a quiet public-house and a long drink.

He found what he wanted in a low bar, that was as sombre as the inside of one of its old puncheons. There was no sign outside, no flashy lure to trap the passer, except the dimmed-gold letters of the proprietor's name. Mr Finchley had his drink and lighted his pipe. Presently, when he was beginning his second glass, for the beer was good enough to warrant more than one glass even to a man of temperate habits (good enough to furnish an excuse for drunkenness, some said), a man came and sat on the settle at his side.

'Stranger in these parts?' he asked after a while.

'I am,' answered Mr Finchley, lowering his glass. 'How did you know that?'

The other laughed. He was not well dressed. His clothes were patched, neatly patched, and his face was sunburnt except where it was covered by a thick beard that ran down the sides of his cheeks in two spates to meet at his chin's point like the confluence of flood-brown Exmoor torrents.

'I'm not a detective. The people who come to George's place are either regulars or strangers to the town.'

'You are a regular?'

'Not quite. I'm what you might call a regular-stranger. That is, I come whenever I'm in the town. About six times a year. Just enough to justify my calling George by his first name when I ask for my beer. That's what gave you away.'

'Where do you come from?'

'Come from?' laughed his companion. He prefixed all his remarks by a short laugh entailing an upward movement of his head that revealed his dark skin. 'I don't come from any-where. I just wander about the country doing my work.'

The man's words roused Mr Finchley's curiosity. At first he had imagined him to be one of the usual drifters, but his speech and tone held a definiteness and precision that belied his clothes. It was plain that he was no roadman.

'Work? What is your work?'

'Have you ever heard of the Walking Parson?'

'No. Until recently I've lived all my life in London.'

'London!' The man laughed, and this time, as his head tilted back, Mr Finchley had time to see a hard white collar round his neck, which was normally obscured by his beard. 'No, I don't touch London. There's enough of my kind there already. I wander about the country – chiefly Devon and Cornwall, and Somerset – preaching. I haven't a living, I haven't a church, but that doesn't deter me. There are plenty of farmhouses and greens and some villages without churches where I'm welcome. I preach when I can get an audience and I work when I can get work. It's a rough life, but I like it. You may not believe it, but there are some places where, if a man wants to hear the teachings of Christ or to enjoy the benefits of a good sermon, he has to walk ten or twelve miles!'

Mr Finchley expressed his amazement.

'It's true; even in these days of wireless. Not all cottagers can afford a wireless set. I've just come from Porlock way. Do you know Porlock? Over on the edge of the Exmoor Forest. Over there they have a couplet which expresses what I've told you. Listen to it:

> *'Culbone, Oare and Stoke Pero,*
> *Parishes three no parson'll go!*

'That's not strictly true, of course, but there are many places of that kind.'

'Well, I can believe that,' answered Mr Finchley, raising his glass to discover that it was empty. He ordered another for himself and the parson. 'Lately, I've been discovering quite a lot of things for myself. There seems to be a large floating population, especially in the countryside, which never stops in one place long enough to enjoy the privileges of which you speak. And yet . . .' he mused doubtfully, 'they certainly seem happy enough, most of them. Tramps, gipsies and roadmen . . . they worry very little and they work perhaps enough to provide themselves with food and shelter.

Some of them don't even bother about working.' He was thinking of Ignatius.

'You've been meeting people like that?' questioned the parson.

'Yes – why not?' Mr Finchley's mild eyes interrogated the other.

The parson laughed. 'No reason at all. I imagined that you were perhaps a city clerk who had been betrayed by his outfitter into wearing a khaki shirt and deserted by his wife in Taunton while she shopped or called on a relative . . .'

'Not quite,' laughed Mr Finchley. 'I'm a clerk all right, but I'm not married. Worse, I have a housekeeper! I'll tell you some of the things that have happened to me recently, since I left London.'

For the first time Mr Finchley outlined to someone else the trend of incidents which had torn him roughly from London and by degrees shuffled him westwards across the country. He told the parson of Thornton and made him laugh; he lied bravely about Jane and the parson knew he was lying, but said nothing; he described the fight at the lakeside and the other had to order more beer to stay his mirth; he tried to describe Mara and Tawny and their kindness, to tell of Ignatius and his roguery, and Shorty's greening top-hat; and to picture the defiant misery of Ernst – his efforts were clumsy. Words were strange media with Mr Finchley, but he succeeded sufficiently well to show the parson that in his short week of freedom he had done and seen more than is ordinarily granted to most men. His companion listened to him attentively. Now and then he asked a question, but mostly he was silent. As Mr Finchley neared the completion of his story, a slow twinkle leaped to life in the preacher's eyes, a twinkle that was devilish until his white collar showed beneath his beard and canonized the devilry to merriment.

'That's a holiday!' he said simply, when Mr Finchley had finished.

'I should say it is,' breathed Mr Finchley, finding himself a little warm with much talk of beer. Now that the memory of his acts spread over the actual facts themselves like a palimpsest, he was proud of his actions. There were few men . . .

The parson cut in upon his thoughts.

'Yes, that is a holiday, indeed. In part I envy you. I've been on the road for a good many years, but you have been more fortunate than I. But there is one thing wrong. Yes,' he said, and shook his head gravely, and the twinkle disappeared – not died – from his eyes, 'there is one thing wrong.'

'Wrong!' queried Mr Finchley. 'What do you mean? I ought to have notified the police or anything like that?'

'Oh, no! Not that!' The parson laughed, and the twinkle was stronger than ever. 'Not wrong that way.'

'How, then?'

'When I say wrong, I mean in the sense that you have been doing all this under false pretences. You remember during the war how famous generals and princes and kings used to go right up into the front-line trenches and visit the soldiers? And how the newspapers used to puff about kings who were willing to share the hardships of their soldiers and generals who lived under the same conditions as the tommies? Well, we all know that it wasn't so. The position of the tommy penned in his trenches for days on end was a far more dangerous one than that of the great man who walked down the trenches during the quiet time – the War Office had probably arranged things with the other side. He became a tommy under false pretences. And that's what you've been doing, Mr Finchley. You said Finchley, didn't you?'

'Yes. But I don't understand . . .' Mr Finchley was puzzled and ready to be annoyed.

'Don't you? Well, I'll explain further. You've done all these things – particularly wandering about the countryside – in the wrong atmosphere. You met these people and enjoyed their company. They were living as you found them because they had to, or wanted to. They were living – not holidaying. None of them, perhaps, had more than a half a crown in his pocket; and they lived, some under the shadow of game, poaching and other laws, in fear of detection – and one under the shadow of a sick soul. You met them and derived pleasure from their company, and they thought you were as they were. A wanderer and forced to do it. I'll wager – although I'm a parson – that you've probably had five or ten pounds in your pocket all the time, so that if you were too tired to sleep comfortably under a hedge, or it should rain hard, you could walk into a hotel! Do you call that roughing it? Do you think you can ever reach the real heart of these folks unless you approach them from their own plane? You must be penniless and ready to work for your food before you can understand the spirit which keeps these people wandering and living. To appreciate their love of the countryside, of this England, you have to see it as they do, as the country which gives them food, shelter and friendship. They love the high road because it leads them somewhere, they greet the birds and the flowers as comrades, because by them they tell the seasons and the weather – and you've been eavesdropping!'

Mr Finchley believed he had been insulted. What right this man to sit in front of him and say such things? What right . . . that was a thought. Perhaps he had every right. He said nothing for a minute while he weighed the parson's words. Perhaps he did have a right. He was one of the people for whom he spoke. He was one with Shorty Walters and Ignatius, with the tramp at Blagdon and Tawny; only his business was God's Word and not top-hats. He rested his chin in his hands and his eyes searched the stone floor. Had Mr Finchley looked up he might have seen that his companion was watching him eagerly, and about his mouth was wrinkled a smile; the smile of a man who knew his fellows better than he knew himself; a man who loved his fellows enough to spur them to tests of Arthurian chivalry and Rabelaisian adventures so they might discover the good in themselves for themselves.

The parson rose and stood over Mr Finchley.

'I'd never thought of it that way,' Mr Finchley admitted.

'Oh, that's only an opinion. I was not criticizing. To live the real tramper's life needs courage; money can't buy courage – the kind of courage which laughs at rain and hunger.

113

These folk have little money; but they live – perhaps too dangerously for most of us to wish to emulate their ways . . . Few people would have the guts to do it—'

Mr Finchley was an earnest man; he hated shams. The parson's words moved him strangely. They formed a challenge to him; a challenge to prove his cowardice or manhood. Then he thought of roaming the roads, penniless, and discovered that he was still very much Edgar Finchley, Esquire, with the dust of Nassington Avenue thick in the corners of his pockets.

Was he afraid? Was he . . . ? He walked back to his lodging, thinking. He undressed slowly, thinking. He lay on his bed for a while, still thinking, and then slept to dream a dream in which he was a wandering troubadour singing his songs under the oriel windows of Rapunzels and being entertained in the rush-paved halls of black-armoured knights.

He awoke, and the sun was warming his counterpane, while from a laburnum tree by the window a blackbird, which had wandered from the Quantocks, filled the morning with a vibrant beauty of sound. The sun and the song decided for Mr Finchley. A man could face anything with such a sun for a friend, and with such song for comfort.

He dressed and counted his money. After paying for his lodging he had exactly forty-six pounds, ten shillings and sixpence. He packed his gear and made his way to the General Post Office. He purchased a money-order, put it into a registered envelope, and mailed it to himself at the Exeter Post Office.

Mr Finchley stepped out into the sunshine, one and sixpence in his pocket, gladness in his heart and good tobacco in his pipe. At that moment he wanted no more.

He walked out along the Exeter road, but it was not intended that Mr Finchley should travel very far in that direction on this day. The road was wide, dusty and unpleasant, and shortly after leaving the town it began to rise.

Halfway up the rise, Mr Finchley came upon a garage, a long wooden shack, with room for twenty cars, fronted by a rubble patch and defended by three chromatic petrol pumps. On the standard of one of the pumps hung a sign. Mr Finchley stopped and read it and knew at once that it was intended for him.

MAN WANTED

That was all, but it was enough. He thought of the parson, he thought of Shorty and Tawny ... and he thought of the eighteenpence in his pocket and the food he would soon be wanting. Eighteenpence would not go far.

He dived into the wooden shed and squeezed his way between cars, in varying stages of collapse and overhaul, towards a small, half-glass cubicle at the end of the shed. As he approached, a man lurched through the doorway and faced him. He was a short, fat man with a neck that creased over the collar-band of his shirt, hiding the band and its layer of dirt. His clothes would never wear out for they were well protected by a stout epidermis of dirt, grease and a green substance which Mr Finchley guessed was paint.

'Coming, sir! Coming, sir!' the fat man rumbled, and spun towards Mr Finchley like a top.

'What is it you want?' he asked. 'Petrol? How many gallons? Sorry I didn't hear your car draw up – that's the trouble. I'm shorthanded till my mechanic gets back this evening. How many gallons did you say?' he repeated, though Mr Finchley had neither said nor done anything, but gaze in amazement at the mountain of flesh which heaved before him.

'I don't want petrol. I haven't a car,' he said timidly. 'I want ...'

'Don't want petrol?'

The man's manner changed, as the surface of a glass dulls beneath a hot breath. 'Then what do you want?' He shot the words out.

Mr Finchley hesitated.

'Well, what is it? What is it? Can't you speak?' shouted the other in an exasperated tone.

'I came in about your sign,' Mr Finchley managed to stutter. He would have stepped backwards out of the garage and

115

away from the man had it not been for a car which was directly behind him, preventing his retreat.

'Well, what about the sign? It's a good one, ain't it?'

'Yes, I suppose it . . . it . . . is.'

'Huh!'

The snort raised the dust from the concrete floor of the garage, and sent it rocketing to the roof and walls, to settle lazily on the advertisements for Flincher tyres and Speedo-Spark Plugs.

'Well, it's good of you to come in and tell me so! It ought to be good. I done it myself, but that ain't no reason why every bandy-legged little runt that passes by should come in and tell me so, and waste my time! Ain't I shorthanded as it is? Ain't it holiday-time and crowds of people on the roads in cars, and me with no petrol hand to serve 'em? And can I do two ruddy jobs at once?' He hurled these questions at Mr Finchley, and with each one stepped a pace forward menacingly, until he had him with his back pressed hard against the car. He stopped shouting and Mr Finchley managed to say:

'You're mistaken I'm not criticizing your sign. I've come about the job. It says you want a man.'

'So it does, so it does!' roared the other. 'But how does that affect you? I want a man who can handle a petrol pump . . .'

Mr Finchley waited while the other recovered. The man's bad temper intimidated him, but he still clung to his original idea of getting a job.

'I could do the job, if you show me how to work the pumps.'

The fat man scratched his head wearily and sighed: 'All right, if you want the job. I don't suppose I shall get anyone else. Six shillings for the day is all I'll pay – don't begin to argue or I shall have a fit! – and I'm finished with you at eight o'clock when my mechanic returns from Bristol.'

Mr Finchley had not dreamed of arguing. Six shillings would be enough to keep him for two days.

'That suits me,' he said and smiled. Probably, this fellow only needed to be humoured. Any man who was shorthanded on the Saturday before Bank Holiday could be excused a bad temper.

'Suiting you ain't the object!' bellowed the garageman, whose name Mr Finchley discovered from a notice on the shed was McGrath. 'Suiting me's the thing I'm worried about. Come on, I'll show you how to work the pump – and the devil help you if you waste much of my petrol!'

Mr McGrath led the way to the petrol pumps and initiated Mr Finchley into the art of supplying fuel. It was very simple – McGrath said so. He said so many times. In fact, he spent ten of his valuable minutes impressing Mr Finchley with the simplicity of supplying petrol to a car.

'D you get that?' he bellowed at last.

'Yes, why yes, I think so.'

'Of course y'do! Of course, it's easy! A child could work a pump – but by Hades if you waste any petrol I'll rip your liver up and feed it to the fowls!'

'Oh, no doubt, I shall manage,' answered Mr Finchley.

He was beginning to see that McGrath was the type of man who bullied and stormed at people – and was surprised when they accused him of losing his temper.

McGrath showed him the oil drums and where the tyre-pump was kept.

'You'll have to look after that as well,' he said, and pointed to a dirty sign – FREE AIR. 'Some lousy scum make a point of never buying petrol unless they want their tyres pumped up! And watch the change!' With this last admonition, McGrath disappeared into the darkness of his shed and presently Mr Finchley heard the sound of tapping coming from that direction.

He was glad that McGrath had disappeared and left him alone with his free air and the dingy pumps. He placed his rucksack in the shade of the fence and sat down on the edge of the pumps to wait for customers.

'This,' said Mr Finchley, to his dusty feet, 'is an easy way of earning six shillings.'

He had become so far acclimatized to his new mode of living, that the fact that he was on holiday and expecting to take a rest from work, did not intrude upon his thoughts.

London and the office lay a long way behind him ... The sun was shining and hot upon his face. He was no longer the pale, slightly pompous, little man who had been hurried off in the Bentley. His skin was browned and, above the bridge of the nose, peeling a little; his suit was worn into comfortable creases and the khaki shirt no longer very clean.

A car came bowling up the rise and stopped by the pump.

'Petrol?' Mr Finchley inquired, jumping to his feet.

The driver of the car was a young girl. She smiled prettily at Mr Finchley.

'No, thank you. I wonder if you would be good enough to direct me to Bradford-on-Tone. It's a small village about here. Would you?'

Mr Finchley longed to help her.

'Certainly,' he replied. 'I should be delighted. Only, I don't know where it is. I'm a stranger about here.'

'What a pity,' she replied. 'Never mind.' She was about to let out her clutch when he stopped her with a gesture.

'Wait. I'll go and ask the owner. He'll know. Don't go, I shan't be a second.'

Mr Finchley skipped about and ran into the garage. Coming from the strong sunlight into the gloom, he was blinded for a moment. He groped his way forward.

'Eh! what the hell's happening?'

There was a seismic upheaval beneath him and a roar burst from the ground. Mr Finchley looked down and found that he was standing on one of a pair of legs that protruded from the underside of a car. He jumped off the leg hurriedly, as he recognized the blue overalls to contain McGrath.

'Sorry!' Mr Finchley stooped and shouted under the car. 'There's someone outside wants to know the way to Bradford.'

'What?' The shout made the panels of the car rattle.

'Bradford!' shouted Mr Finchley. 'The way to Bradford.'

The legs went limp and he heard McGrath moan weakly. The legs commenced to wriggle, and slowly the fat body came into sight until McGrath was sitting on the concrete, staring up at Mr Finchley with the light of despair and exasperation in his eyes. He shook his head. 'I was born unlucky. Do you know' – he was addressing Mr Finchley in a voice which, for him, was a whisper – 'that I have to dismantle the driving shaft of this travelling pantechnicon by four o'clock, and have it ready for the doctor by tomorrow morning? Do you know that? Well! And do you know that it's the Bank Holiday weekend, and I'm going to be as busy as hell with push-cyclists who want new valve rubber, and "please kin I borrow a spanner at the same time?" You do know all this? You do know that the average garageman only rests when he is finally packed between two stout pitch-pine boards? You do? Good! Then' – his voice soared up the octaves to a screech – 'for the love of old Harry don't come worrying me about people who want to borrow Bradshaws! This is a garage, man – not a ruddy Free Library! Now scat!'

Having delivered himself of this oration, McGrath began to disappear into his oily burrow. Mr Finchley caught him by the sleeve.

'Hey, Mr McGrath – you've made a mistake!'

'Mistake?' McGrath's oily face wrinkled.

'Yes—' Mr Finchley prepared for another explosion. 'I didn't say Bradshaw. I said Bradford. There's a young lady outside wants to know the way to Bradford-on-Tone.'

'What a man! What a man!' McGrath ran his grubby fingers through the scant hair that his years of petrol, lubricating oil and exasperation had left him. 'Why didn't you say so at first? What kind of a woman?'

Mr Finchley was surprised by this last question.

'Young and pretty, I think . . .'

'You think! What do you mean? Do you have to think when you see a woman before you can tell whether she's young and pretty? Look out, I'd better see what's the matter, I suppose.'

And he heaved himself aloft and waddled from the garage with Mr Finchley trailing behind; and that was where Mr Finchley stopped. No sooner did McGrath see the girl than his entire manner changed. Mr Finchley could hardly credit the evidence of his own eyes. The garageman expanded; he smiled, he beamed, and his face was big and jovial with friendliness.

'You want to know the way to Bradford, miss?' he asked, and laid one foot on the running-board.

'If you would be good enough to tell me, please,' the girl answered. Mr Finchley guessed that she had smiled, but McGrath's huge form blocked his view.

'Why, certainly. You carry on up the road for about a mile' – McGrath had one arm on the door as though he had known her for years – 'then take the first turning on the right. Better watch out – there's a pretty tough hill beyond the turning. Is that what you wanted?'

'Thank you very much indeed. It's awfully kind of you to trouble.' Mr Finchley guessed she was smiling again.

'No trouble. Always ready to oblige a lady,' laughed McGrath, and added, as she slipped in the clutch, 'and especially a pretty one. Goodbye!' He waved and she was gone up the road, smiling.

He turned back to the pumps. The smile on his face flashed away as he saw Mr Finchley standing and watching.

'Well, what are you hanging about for?' he cried. 'Doesn't take two people to give a simple direction – does it? Why don't you get on with your work?'

Mr Finchley was too astonished to be angry. He felt if only McGrath would give him an opportunity to work himself into a steady wrath he would be satisfied, but the impetuous mountain of flesh swept over him irresistibly. It was as much as he could do to reply, weakly:

'Work – but what is there for me to do? I'm here to serve petrol.'

McGrath laughed, and in a voice that could have withered all living things within a radius of ten yards.

'Petrol! Here, take this leather and polish the pumps up! And when you've done that, sweep the concrete, and when you've done that you'll find a pot of paint and a brush inside the garage – paint the free-air sign, paint any sign, paint anything, paint yourself and the whole garage – only do

something, and leave me alone or I shall go mad, mad ...
mad!'

He stumped away mouthing, and Mr Finchley was left
holding a chamois leather, wondering whether to laugh or to
throw a stone at the rear of McGrath's fat neck. He could
not find a stone handy so he started to whistle and polish the
pumps. Edgar Finchley, Esquire, solicitor's clerk, would have
been indignant and outraged; but Mr Finchley was growing
wiser as his face tanned under the sun.

He cleaned the pumps. He served petrol to five cars during
the morning, and between times he swept the concrete. At
one o'clock McGrath left him in charge of the garage while
he went to lunch. While he was gone, Mr Finchley smoked
and commissioned a small boy to fetch him a pork-pie and a
bottle of milk from a nearby shop.

McGrath returned, and Mr Finchley started to paint the
free-air sign with lovely black paint. He found that painting
gave him a glorious, dreamy feeling. The silky pull of the
brush on smooth board, and the glossy sheen of the paint
filled him with an exhilaration which Leonardo da Vinci
might have envied.

He was frequently interrupted in his work. Two petrols
and an oil while he was doing the F. The R brought a motor-
cyclist to borrow an adjustable spanner, which Mr Finchley
filched from the garage, not daring to disturb McGrath, who
was still worrying the innards of the car. Water for a charabanc radiator and six petrols during the first E. He thought
he never should finish the last E – ten petrols, an oil, one
water and a sniffing lavender-seller with a fish-tail
moustache. Then the weekend rush from city and town to
village and moor had commenced. He was kept busy from
three until six serving at the pumps, and by that time had
earned his six shillings.

Just after six o'clock the mechanic returned.

'All right, mister,' he said. 'You're fired now. I'll take on.
The boss'll be out in a minute.'

Mr Finchley was relieved. He had had enough work for
one day. His arms ached with lifting the petrol pipes and
carrying oil. His legs ached with running about from car to

garage. But he did not regret his day; he had enjoyed it – except for McGrath's periodical sallies from the maw of the doctor's car to curse him for various things – and, he told himself with a bit of luck he might have put the crown to a noble effort by painting the word AIR. Still, he had done FREE. He eyed his masterpiece and his breast swelled a little with pride. There at least was something he could point to and say was well done, whatever McGrath might say about his petrol-serving abilities!

'Thank you. Going to keep fine over the holiday, I think,' he added in a friendly spirit.

'Better for me if it rains – less work!' returned the weary lad laconically, and was silent.

Mr Finchley recovered his rucksack and waited for McGrath.

McGrath was not long in coming.

'Well. I suppose you're waiting to be paid, eh?' he snorted. 'To be paid for a day of leisure! It's a pity you tramps don't stick to regular jobs and learn how to do 'em properly! Here am I going to pay you for doing nothing all day ... nothing!'

Mr Finchley was firm.

'You can hardly say that with any truth, you know. I've taken over four pounds at the pumps for you. Is that doing nothing?'

'Of course, it's doing nothing!' returned McGrath. 'A child could do it. The pump does the work – not you. Six shillings, I said; I must have been crazy. Five shillings for a day of leisure! Five shillings for nothing at all, simply nothing ...'

Mr Finchley thought it better to interrupt him.

'You're joking, Mr McGrath,' he said. 'And even if working the pumps is not hard labour – which I certainly do not admit – look at the yard – haven't I swept that? And look at that sign' – he pointed proudly to the FREE AIR board – 'what about that? Did you ever get it painted so well? If I'd had time I should have finished it!'

McGrath looked at the sign – one half of which shone with

new paint and almost obfuscated the other half with its brilliancy.

'Paint!' he yelled. 'D'you call that painting – mussing my sign up with your daubing! Why, I've got a two-year-old boy at home who, blindfolded, could do better with his little finger and a bottle of ink.'

The crude injustice of this assertion shook Mr Finchley. He had reached the climax of his endurance. All day the man had insulted him, and he had said nothing; but when the man sneered at his painting and belittled his work, then Mr Finchley knew that his hour had come. He didn't care very much now whether he got five or six shillings, he did not care whether he got anything at all. He only knew one thing. He wanted to tell McGrath exactly what he thought of him. He had often wanted to do the same with his old employer, Bardwell, before he had died. In him surged a vicious desire to tell McGrath exactly what he thought about him, his personal habits, and the way he treated his employees – a desire that lies close to the hearts of most workers.

Mr Finchley was inspired in a way which comes to man only once in a lifetime.

'Listen, Mr McGrath,' he said quietly, 'I don't care whether you pay me five shillings, or six shillings, or nothing. In fact, I don't care what you do! I only know that I have never met such a noisy, blustering, bad-tempered, unjust and bigoted fool as you. The extent of your blustering and bad temper is only equalled by the size of your big body that could do with exercise, and which I feel tempted to kick. I've worked for you for a day and I've decided that I don't like you. I don't like your face. I don't like your manner. I don't like your dirty habits, or your loud voice. I wonder how I've managed to spend so many hours in your company. Your bad manners and vulgarity smell. And' – Mr Finchley stepped forward menacingly, his choler completely overcoming him – 'it won't help you to goggle there. I'm not afraid of you. If you try to lay hands on me, I'll punch your fat nose. I've decided that I do want my six – six I said – shillings! Now what have you got to say?'

Mr Finchley breathed heavily. He could hardly believe that it was himself speaking. But if Mr Finchley was surprised, McGrath was even more so. He stared open-mouthed at the defiant Mr Finchley. His hands moved weakly over his coat lapels; Mr Finchley's words had struck home. That someone should tell him the truth about himself had been due to McGrath for a long time.

'I . . . I'll wring your dirty little neck . . .' he began, but Mr Finchley stopped him.

'Oh, no you won't. You'll pay me my money – quickly – or I'll have to decide between thrashing you myself or calling a policeman to get the law to do it for me! Now then, come on! Which is it?'

Mr Finchley squared himself to McGrath and hoped desperately that the other would not accept the challenge. His hope was rewarded. McGrath capitulated.

'All right,' he replied meekly. 'Maybe, I have been a bit tough with you. I'm sorry. Honest. I've been worried. And perhaps' – the pleasant look which he had given the girl in the car began to illumine his face – 'I've deserved what you said. Yes, by Harry, I think you are right. I've been near to losing my temper lately. I should have controlled myself. By thunder! I'm glad that you gave me the licking you did!'

It was Mr Finchley's turn to be astonished. McGrath was beaming. He was pleased.

'I'm glad you look at it like that.'

'Glad!' bellowed McGrath, now almost his usual self. 'Of course, I am. All along I've wanted someone to square up to me and tell me what a lousy, unwashed scavenger I was, but the weak-kneed runts about here didn't have the guts! You're a man after my own heart, by Harry! After my own heart! Here, take your six shillings. You've earned every one of 'em! What a day! What a man! Here, take it!'

He thrust the money into Mr Finchley's hands, eager for him to have it. Mr Finchley took it.

'Cheerio, Mr McGrath. We part friends, then?'

'We do! You're my best friend!' cried the other, and patted Mr Finchley on the back as he left the garage. A hundred yards up the road, Mr Finchley turned and looked back at the garage. McGrath had turned to his mechanic, who had been a dumbstruck spectator of the whole affair, and was resuscitating him to activity. The sound of his bellowing voice reached faintly to Mr Finchley, who walked on with laughter in his heart.

SIXTEEN

How Cleopatra and Joan of Arc take part in a Great Burning

MR FINCHLEY was tired and decided to rest himself beside a stream before starting off to find a night's lodgings. He had left the noisy main road for a lane that threaded itself towards a low line of hills on top of which was perched a tall monument. With his back against an oak and his pipe drawing coolly, he sat contentedly; staring at the huge garlic stems that hung green curtains about the water to catch at the moving straws and leaves which floated by in ragged armadas. Peace hung about the spot with heavy fingers and, in the hedge across the road, a goldfinch swung upon a briar and tilted its tail against the sun that moved reddening to the west.

The stream sang its song to the sedges and sky; copper-winged flies and slow blue-backed beetles danced and crawled among the yellow fleabane and starry feverfew; the finch swung like a gilded toy on a Christmas tree, and the oak hung its green leaves to the sun until they were burnished to a dull copper that glowed and set the lane leaping with flashing fires. Mr Finchley slept.

He had not been sleeping long when the leaves of the trees above his head began to shake, a foot appeared and dangled within a few inches of Mr Finchley's head. The foot hung in this position for some moments, as though the owner were trying to decide how he should next proceed. The branch above Mr Finchley's head was the lowest of the tree; the others on the far side of the trunk were too high from which to jump with safety. The owner of the foot had apparently realized this. Presently another foot joined the first. They hung, motionless, very close to Mr Finchley's bald head. The leaves began to rustle again and, at the same time, the legs started to swing with a clumsy pendulum-like motion above Mr Finchley. Their movement sent little whirls of air over his head and ruffled the crisp ring of his tonsure. Mr Finchley did not stir. The legs continued their swinging until they attained their maximum sweep, and then dived forward. Luck was against the unknown. As he swung forward some part of his coat caught in the tree and he fell with ponderous accuracy into Mr Finchley's limp hands, which were guarding his respiring abdomen.

Mr Finchley's reaction was magnificent. He yelled loudly and did three things before the yell had died away. He wakened, rolled swiftly over, and seized by the throat the man who had fallen upon him.

'What does this mean?' he shouted fiercely. 'What does it mean?'

The shock had sent his nerves dancing, so that he was neither conscious of his loud voice nor of his sudden anger.

'Eh, tell me! I'll teach you ... Why don't you answer?' He sat astride of his captive. The man lay passive beneath him and, at Mr Finchley's last bellowing question, he raised his hands to his throat and tapped at Mr Finchley's grip. Mr Finchley, with a sudden diminution of his anger, saw that it was useless to ask for an explanation while he was successfully blocking the only passage by which it could come.

He released his grip, murmuring: 'Didn't mean to hold you so tightly, but you frightened me. What's the idea?'

The other sat up before replying and felt his throat, and Mr Finchley had an opportunity to observe him. He was not a big man. He was, if anything, shorter than Mr Finchley, and his general appearance was disconcerting. He wore an old pair of pin-striped trousers that were frayed round the turnups to a hoary growth which matched his untidy beard. A once smartly cut morning coat hung about his thin body in creases that held long furrows of dust, and at a distance, where it had rolled when he had jumped, was a disreputable top-hat – more worn and shabby than Shorty Walter's. A greasy cravat, that time had pulled and worn until now it looked like a hempen halter, clung closely about his neck. Altogether, he looked as though he had just stepped from a moth infested cupboard instead of having fallen from the green heart of an oak tree.

He replied to Mr Finchley.

'I'm sorry, sir. Extremely sorry, to have wakened you in this extraordinary fashion, and I realize, sir, that an explanation is due from me.'

'I think so, too,' replied Mr Finchley. 'I was never more surprised in all my life.'

'You will, I am sure, forgive me when I explain. You see, sir, it is my habit – one of many years I can assure you – to sequester myself in the peace of this oak tree and to remain there for many hours, alone with my thoughts. I am a man, sir, of many thoughts.' He spoke in a slow, studied voice that held a hint of pomposity.

'I must have been immersed in contemplation when you first arrived and when, in the course of time, I had come to the end of my excogitations and made to descend from my leafy bower, then, sir, I was for the first time aware of your presence on the sward beneath me. Knowing that sleep is the time of peace for many, and having, therefore, a disinclination to awaken you from your slumbers, I essayed to avoid your sleeping body by vaulting from the lower limb of the tree. Unfortunately – and with the unhappy results which we have both experienced – I lost my footing at the penultimate moment. I tender you my apologies, sir.' He finished speaking and reached for his top-hat. Without brushing the dust from it, he placed it on his head at a sober angle.

'I understand exactly,' replied Mr Finchley, who was actually very far from understanding who this queer person might be who wore morning clothes in the fashion of 1914 and spoke with the fastidiousness of a student of Roget. 'These accidents will happen, and sometimes they aren't always unfortunate.'

'As to that, sir, it is a matter to which, in the time at my disposal, I have given very careful thought. A great many of the historical events which have shaken the world and disrupted whole kingdoms, at first appear to have been actuated by accidents. Ratiocination, or a belief in the intervention of providence in the works of man, proves conclusively, I venture to suggest, that what we call accidents are not such! Napoleon was stayed from a probably successful invasion of England by the accident of bad weather and contrary winds, and Cesare Borgia lost Italy for himself owing to the accident of his almost fatal illness coinciding with the death of Pope Alexander the Sixth, which prevented him from effectively influencing the election of the new pope in his own interests.'

He continued to cite examples of accidents which had directed the course of the world's history into stormier or more peaceful paths. Mr Finchley watched him as he talked. His new companion was a middle-aged man. About fifty, thought Mr Finchley, and he wondered why this man with his ragged beard and eyes that burned with a quiet steadfastness in their deep sockets should wear such shabby clothes. His accent spoke of leisure and culture.

The man stopped speaking and stood up. Mr Finchley rose as well.

'I am obliged to you for your little talk,' said Mr Finchley. 'It has been interesting and certainly opens a fresh view to me.' The other regarded him solemnly.

'It appears, sir, that you are in the way of being a moral and practical philosopher. I seldom meet such in these days. My name is Woodall, and yours?'

'Finchley. I am on holiday . . . walking.'

'Ah, Finchley.' He paused for a moment. Then he went on: 'I wonder, sir, whether you would do me the honour of becoming my guest at dinner tonight? I shall be alone, and after that, if you care to stop, there is a bed at your disposal.'

As he eyed the elegant, fustian scarecrow before him, Mr Finchley was distressed and assumed that Mr Woodall was mad. A spare bed for him, and yet Mr Woodall looked as though he passed most of his nights under a hedge!

'You hesitate to reply, sir? Perhaps you would rather not?'

'Oh, no! I should be delighted,' agreed Mr Finchley, nervously. Without allowing him time to consider the possible effects of his action, Mr Woodall bowed sharply, and taking him by the arm, walked slowly down the lane and began to talk again of historical coincidences. Mr Finchley followed, rucksack in hand, and as his companion continued to talk easily, he recovered his composure and even laughed quietly to himself.

The lane turned sharply and Mr Finchley saw that they were in front of a tall pair of lodge gates. To one side of the gates, and obscured by thick laurel bushes and banks of rhododendrons, stood a grey-stone lodge.

'Here we are,' said Mr Woodall, and flourished his arm sedately to the gates, on each side of which two mutilated stone griffins peered over the tops of their illegible shields.

'Do you live here?' Mr Finchley asked, although he felt that it was an impudent question.

'I do,' came the reply. They approached the gates and a man came running out. The huge gates swung open to let them through, though it would have been a simple matter to have entered through the small wicket-gate.

The gate-keeper touched his cap to Mr Woodall and closed the gates behind them.

The drive led from the gates down a long twisting avenue of beech trees. Through the trees, Mr Finchley glimpsed a small, but well-kept, park with sheep and horses grazing. In one corner of the park stood a black clump of elms with noisy rooks swinging high on their crests. Across the still evening air came the sound of cawing, mixed with the plaintive cry of the sheep. A turn in the drive showed him a long white country house in the Queen Anne style, faced by green lawns and spotless gravel spaces.

Since passing the gate, Mr Woodall had been silent, but now as a tall liveried footman opened the door, he said:

'Take Mr Finchley, Jordan, and show him his room and tell Mrs Lawson to serve dinner for two.'

'Yes, sir,' replied the footman, who was too well-trained to show his surprise. Before Mr Finchley had time to look around, the footman had deprived him of his rucksack and cap and, after giving him a long stare, the kind of stare which stamps the words 'I don't believe it' over its wearer's countenance, he led the way up the broad staircase at the end of the hall and showed Mr Finchley his room. He tidied himself and washed the grime from his hands and face. He had been tempted to take a bath while he was in the magnificent bathroom, but feared that he might be called to dinner before he had finished.

The dinner was very simple, and served by a silent woman, dressed in housekeeper's black relieved by a small white apron and white cuffs. She was an old woman, and, like Jordan, she was surprised at Mr Finchley's presence, although she controlled herself in a more able fashion. Mr Finchley, as the evening progressed, began to understand that Mr Woodall was a man who laboured under a peculiarity of temperament. While Mr Finchley ate enormously of the good food that was placed before him, Mr Woodall contented himself with a strict vegetarian diet. He broke the silence of the table to explain to Mr Finchley his views on food and meat-eating.

After dinner was done and the housekeeper had left the room, they moved to a position before the wide windows that overlooked the drive and the green lawns. Mr Finchley filled his pipe from Mr Woodall's pouch and they both smoked in silence for a while, letting the peace of the cool evening sink into them.

The silence did not last long. Mr Woodall had not invited Mr Finchley for the pleasure of his company, but more for the opportunity it would give him to talk to an appreciative listener; and Mr Finchley was the best listener in the world.

'I expect,' said Mr Woodall, 'that you are not a little puzzled and perplexed as to the manner of man with whom you have broken bread?' He looked across at Mr Finchley.

It was an embarrassing moment, but he rose to it gamely.

'Curiosity is one of those things which in childhood I was

taught to control,' replied Mr Finchley. 'Of course, I don't understand why you, a wealthy man – by the look of all this' – he waved his hand – 'should choose to wear clothes that are old and torn and to live in a puritanical style; but if you wish to do so you no doubt have a good reason and that is enough . . .'

'A very excellent attitude, sir. I see that I was not mistaken in my primary estimation of your qualities. You are a man, sir, after my own heart—' (Where, mused Mr Finchley, had he heard someone say that before?)

'The control of the emotions and the body is one of man's greatest difficulties, and gives rise to his failings in the normal undertakings of life. It is not enough to become a Spartan in bodily habits. Men must be Spartans in mind. I think you will agree with me, sir? I am a peculiar man,' he said it with a hint of pride; 'but my idiosyncrasies have been forced upon me. Once, I was young and eager for the manifold pleasures of existence. I had hopes and loves; and now I find that I have only dreams and doubts. I have suffered much, but I have learned more than I should other-wise have done. It is only at night, when the darkness comes and shuts me in with my thoughts, that I doubt the wisdom of my step.'

Mr Finchley nodded comfortingly. He was not quite clear what Mr Woodall was trying to explain, but he could see that here was a warrior turned prophet, grieving as he saw his sword rusty on the wall and his divinations go un-heeded.

While he had been speaking, Jordan entered the room with a small tray holding a decanter and glasses. He set the tray down on a table at Mr Woodall's side and withdrew.

'It is my custom at this time to take port. Will you have a glass?'

'I should be very glad to join you,' said Mr Finchley, and watched him fill the glasses.

Mr Woodall lifted his glass. 'Here's to your very good health, sir.'

Mr Finchley smiled and drank. It was good port.

Mr Woodall, finishing his port, rose to his feet and

standing with his back to the window said, with a suddenness that startled Mr Finchley, 'I have written a book, sir!'

'A book!' returned Mr Finchley. Had he said that he had murdered his mother, Mr Finchley's tone would have been the same.

'Yes, a book. A book in which I have summed up the result of my years of cogitation.'

'Do you mean that it has been published?'

'No, I have considered that it is wiser to defer its publication until after my death. When I die there is a provision in my will for its publication. I have called it "Ruminations on the Fallacy of Endeavour and the Futility of Existence". It has taken me a long time, but now that it is done I find much solace in it. There is a chapter dealing with practically every aspect of man's mental and physical life. I believe that it will prove a valuable contribution to the more thoughtful side of literature. Another glass of port, Mr Finchley?'

He filled the glass and handed it to Mr Finchley. He stood with the decanter in his hand, as though in doubt, then he poured himself another glass, saying: 'It is not my custom to take more than one glass, but tonight is a special occasion. Do you know that for twenty years no person other than myself or my servants has set foot within these walls?'

The wine had wakened Mr Finchley a little and he lifted his glass.

'That, Mr Woodall, is a compliment to me which I value. I drink to you and to the memory of your ancestor who laid down this port. It is the best I have ever tasted!'

'There is no better in England,' answered Mr Woodall, and for the first time he laughed, a brittle, dry gasp that seemed to be wrenched from him.

'There was a time when I could have sung the praises of wine, until wine itself robbed me of my tongue . . . With your permission, Mr Finchley, I will read you a little of my book. I have never before read it to anyone and I shall appreciate this opportunity to observe its effect upon one who is so obviously a man of deliberation and reflection.'

He left the room for a while, to reappear with a thick,

bulging leather case in his hand. This he opened. Mr Finchley saw that it contained a fat pile of paper, neatly fastened and bound. Taking the pile to the window, Mr Woodall turned the pages for a while.

'Here we have the chapter on women,' he said. 'Perhaps the most cogent chapter of the book and an exposition of great force and wisdom. It is the result of many days of thought . . . and deals with a subject that has brought into my life a great happiness and a great sorrow.'

He began to read in his slow tones, and Mr Finchley listened in a happy state. If you have done a hard day's work under a strong sun and then walked six miles the effect of two glasses of port, when the port is good, is such to marvel at. If Lucifer had been standing in front of him, reading a thesis on the prevalence of the seven deadly sins among the inhabitants of Camberwell, Mr Finchley would have regarded him with the same bland feeling of benevolence and good humour as he now regarded Mr Woodall.

It was doleful stuff. Mr Finchley soon saw that Mr Woodall did not like women. Women, Mr Woodall had written, were responsible for the introduction of sin and misery into the world. He proved this by a facile discursion into the history of the lives of famous women, ranging from Clytemnestra to Cleopatra and from Mrs Fitzherbert to Boadicea. There was no misery that could not be traced back to a woman. The world was a bad place, but it was made a thousand times fouler by the women who crept across its surface like lice. There were pages of the tirade. The further Mr Woodall went into the subject the more insistent and hoarse his voice became. When his voice grew too hoarse for Mr Finchley to hear what he was saying with any certainty, then – contrary to his usual custom, as he carefully explained each time – Mr Woodall eased his throat with port. The chapter was a long one and before he was at the end of it the decanter had been lifted six times, and each time he had insisted that Mr Finchley should join him. The last page finished with a magnificent burst of rhetoric and abuse.

' "There is no evil too great for her, there is no misery

which in some way does not spring from hateful women-kind; and her charge upon man's thoughts, and her calamitous insistence upon his love, have brought him to a state almost akin to that of a lice-ridden dog. Nietzsche said, 'When you go to meet a woman – take a whip!' I say never go to meet a woman; but if it be your misfortune to encounter one, scourge her with hot brands and cast her out from the society which suffers at her intrusion . . ."'

Mr Woodall finished, panting with his effort. His face was unnaturally flushed and his hands shook as he held the weighty mass of paper.

Mr Finchley was alarmed at his outburst, and ventured to say as much.

'Don't you think you've gone a bit too far?'

'Too far!' expostulated Mr Woodall, at the same time ringing a small hand-bell. 'There is no thing too evil for woman to do and, justly so, there is no ignominy too great for man to impose upon her! Jordan, bring a bottle of the '47 brandy!'

The footman gaped; Mr Finchley sat up in his chair, dropping his pipe.

'Why do you stand staring at me, Jordan?' Mr Woodall cried in his sharp voice. 'Bring the brandy!' And then to Mr Finchley: 'An occasion such as this needs celebration. Think, sir. This is the first time that any part of that manuscript has ever been committed to the outer world. The work which has been drawn from me at the price of my anguished soul. For the first time I have shared my secret convictions with another, and for the first time in years this house sees a guest of my own choice!'

If the port had affected Mr Finchley, he saw that it had affected Mr Woodall more. Jordan returned with a bottle that shone against the lights in the room. Mr Woodall handed Mr Finchley a huge brandy glass. In the bottom swirled a pool of amber liquid.

'Drink!' cried Mr Woodall, in an excited voice. 'Drink, to the eternal damnation of women!'

Now, Mr Finchley liked women. He was a bachelor, it is true, but that only enhanced his admiration for women. He did not hate them at all – only Mrs Patten, and not her consistently. The whole of his incurable longing for romance revolted at Mr Woodall's blasphemous toast. He looked across at the man and his mind was occupied with many thoughts. He might want to throw the brandy in Mr Woodall's face and tell him what a maudlin, prejudiced, bigoted old fool he was. A shrewd caution whispered to him that the safe thing to do was to maintain his silence and leave well alone. He drank. He drank the whole of his unaccustomed brandy at one draught. The liquor stung his throat like fire and jerked his neck muscles forward, making him cough and splutter. He doubled up in a paroxysm of coughing, and dropped his glass to the small table.

Mr Woodall cackled. The port had mellowed his laughter a little, but his laugh was still no more than a cackle.

'It is plain, sir, that good brandy comes amiss to you. Brandy, such as this, that was maturing at the fall of Sebastopol, must be treated with respect. In heaven's name, Jordan, what are you doing there – gaping at me?' He roared his question at Jordan, who all this time had been hovering uneasily in the background.

'I beg your pardon, sir. I thought, perhaps, you might want me.'

'Go! Go!' He waved an impatient hand.

The brandy proved their undoing. Mr Finchley ceased his coughing and shook his head. Mr Woodall wavered up and down in his chair. Mr Woodall wavered up and down so much that Mr Finchley ventured to assure himself of his host's well-being.

'I trust, Mr Woodall, that you are in good health?'

At this question, the other squinted over the top of his brandy bowl, rose and bowed.

'I return the solicitation, sir. I am in the best of spirits. Damme! The best of spirits! Pray take a little more brandy!'

He handed Mr Finchley his bowl. He was too weak to refuse.

The influence of the brandy rose within them and infused them with memories. The air between them was warm with friendship and confidences. Mr Finchley told Mr Woodall of his travels, and painted them with an imagination that would have shamed Rabelais; and Mr Woodall returned his confidence with a shower of compliments upon his understanding and sympathy.

Ten minutes later, Jordan peered round the corner of the door and was confronted by a sight which, for the rest of his life, he was never to forget. To serve in the house of a recluse and eccentric for ten years is preparation for many things; but even Jordan was to be excused his astonishment.

Mr Finchley was standing by the fireplace with his hands placed jauntily on his hips, in the manner of a ballerina. Before him, deep in a chair, his owlish face afire with admiration and joy, was Mr Woodall. Mr Finchley was executing a wild dance, kicking out his legs in unsteady movements and singing.

He stopped for breath.

'Bravo! Damme! Bravo!' cried Mr Woodall, and clambered from his chair. 'Now . . . I'll show you one I saw at the Alhambra years ago . . . oh, years and years and years ago! A performance of great distinction for its high artistic values.'

He commenced to march up and down the great room with uncertain strides, and as he marched he swung over his shoulder a pike that he had awkwardly unhitched from the wall.

'This is how it went . . .'

He started to sing *Soldiers of the Queen*, and Mr Finchley, recognizing the tune, beat a loud time on the table-top with the port decanter. Together they trolled the words of the song. Mr Woodall made an unsteady circumambulation of the room with his pike. As the song finished, he saw Jordan staring round the door. With a loud 'Halloo!' he flourished his pike and charged the door. Jordan disappeared hastily and the pike stuck quivering in the doorway.

'Damme!' cried Mr Woodall. 'Can't a man take his wine without the scullions making a holiday? Can he? Answer me that, Finch?'

'Don't ask me, Woody! Don't ask me,' hiccuped Mr Finchley; 's'matter for the high courts . . .'

They both burst into silly laughter and clung to one another's shoulders for support.

They had mixed their drinks well.

In the great hall stood a knot of wondering servants, headed by Mrs Lawson. From behind the closed door came bursts of laughter and occasional scraps of song.

'The house has been like a morgue long enough,' grinned Jordan. 'It's good to hear it—'

'Jordan! That's enough!' snapped Mrs Lawson. 'I'm sure I don't know what's come over the master, but it's his affair ...' From the way in which she said it, however, it was plain that she felt it was her affair.

'His affair or not,' continued the grinning footman, 'it makes me kind of lonely to see others getting drunk and me havin' to watch. Just fancy – tight as owls on the liquor they've taken!'

'Now come on, all of you: clear off!' Mrs Lawson bustled them away like chicken.

'You know, Woody,' said Mr Finchley, as they lay on their backs with the brandy bottle wedged between them, and gazed at the rosette of plaster on the ceiling, 'I think you're wrong. You've been making a mistake all these years.'

'Sir, don't reproach me with my faults. I know I was wrong. For years I've kept that brandy in the cellar. Years! Think of that, Finch! And I might have had it up and used it to help me in my work. Tonight my brain is clear and active. My head is full of thoughts. I'll write another chapter before I go to bed.'

'No, not that! Not the brandy ...' Mr Finchley's brain was buzzing; but he was determined to say what was in his mind. 'Woody, ol' man, you're all wrong about women. They aren't what you think they are, s'true! I know' – he winked – 'I know. They are the prettiest, daintiest little creatures that ever walked the earth, I love 'em. Yes, I love 'em! Do you deny it?'

'No, I don't deny it. I love 'em too. What are you talking about?'

Mr Finchley was silent for a while. Then his eyes sparkled with the germ of an idea.

'Woody, ol' boy, I got an idea.'

'Damme! Then why keep it to yourself, sir? Is this' – Mr Woodall raised himself to Mr Finchley's level and adjusted his stringy cravat – 'the way to treat a friend?'

'Woody, thish – I mean this – is my idea. Let's burn that old book. It's a blasphemy. Let's burn it and dance round the flames.'

'By gad, sir, that's a splendid notion. A notion that comes from an inspired mind. After all the paper didn't cost much and I can afford it. We'll burn it!'

They staggered enthusiastically to their feet and seized the manuscript. With a whoop of joy Mr Woodall flung the bundle into the fireplace, where it hit the iron and burst like a bomb into a flurry of white fragments.

In a few moments it was flaring in shooting flames up the chimney.

'Halloo, sir!' cried Mr Woodall. 'There go my excogitations on a noble theme. Bring the brandy, Finch! Bring the brandy, man! No Woodall leaves a bottle unemptied . . .'

And while the flames licked and spurted round the edges of the quarto folios, they finished the bottle, singing and telling each other what fine fellows they were. By midnight there was no brandy in the bottle and only a pile of greying ashes marked the death of a masterpiece. The ashes fluttered in the draught as the door of the room opened slightly to show Jordan's goggling countenance. Mr Finchley was lying on the floor, snoring and nursing a cushion, while, from the window-seat, answered the snores of Mr Woodall, who had wrapped himself in a bearskin.

SEVENTEEN

Where Happy Men are Aristocrats, Battles but Thunderstorms, and Kings may go Unshaven

MR FINCHLEY awoke possessed by a headache and a dry tongue. The room in which he lay was strange. The bed was unfamiliar and he knew that should he take the trouble to arise and look from the window the view would be strange to him. During the last twenty-four hours he had been living in a strange world and sharing queer company. Now it was Sunday morning – he could hear a bell tolling outside – and it was time for him to revert to his normal self. What had happened? He tried to recast in his mind the events of the past hours. His flagging head could help him but little. He remembered Mr Woodall's reading and a great drinking of port. And after that? Ah, Jordan with brandy. Beyond this point he could remember nothing. He had a vague feeling that things had not progressed so decorously as they should have done. Just why he should think so he could not tell. He lay in bed pondering over the question.

The door opened quietly and Jordan entered carrying a tray.

'Good morning, sir.'

'Good morning,' answered Mr Finchley, sitting up in bed. The movement sent a twinge of pain shooting through his head. He groaned and held his forehead.

Jordan smiled compassionately.

'I thought, perhaps, sir, you might feel the need of this . . .' He handed Mr Finchley a tumbler from the tray and watched him drink. Mr Finchley never knew what the liquid was. He was conscious only of its potency. It went rolling down his throat, burning, and set fire to the pit of his stomach. He tried to forget the fire, and addressed the silent Jordan.

'Tell me,' he said, 'what happened last night?'

'Happened, sir?' An air of incredulity slid like a mask over Jordan's face.

'Yes – happened! What happened last night?'

'Nothing, sir. You dined with the master – and later went to bed.'

'I . . . did I go to bed by myself?' Mr Finchley stuttered. 'Do you mean that . . . I don't remember coming up here'

Jordan helped him. 'Well, sir, you didn't exactly go by yourself.'

'Do you mean' – Mr Finchley's fears were taking definite shape as the easing drink and Jordan's words drove the depression from his brain and brought clarity to him – 'that I was so . . . er . . . so . . . gone that I had to be put to bed?'

'That is so, sir.'

'Good gracious!' gasped Mr Finchley. 'What a disgrace! Did Mr Woodall . . . I mean . . . what did he do?'

Jordan saw that Mr Finchley's recollection of the past evening was faulty enough to warrant his dispensing with the civilities of a well-bred servant and explaining things as one man to another.

'The master, sir? He was – begging your pardon sir – as far gone as yourself. We had a very troublesome time with him, sir. He said he'd walk upstairs by himself – and he did, though it took him half an hour and we had to pick him up and face him in the right direction four times. Very obstinate he was, sir, and talking beautifully all the time! It's the first time he's been like that for twenty years. I almost hope, sir, that this is only the beginning. Perhaps now he'll see what a fool – beggin' your leave, sir – he's been all these years and leave off his foolish habits.' Jordan stopped to observe the effect of his words on Mr Finchley. Mr Finchley was watching him, and his face was round and pale with horror. His headache had vanished. A deep sense of shame and mortification at his own conduct overcame him.

'I expect, sir, you already know Mr Woodall's sad story?'

Mr Finchley shook his head weakly.

'If you would wish me, sir, I will tell you.'

Mr Finchley nodded mechanically. Perched up in the bed he stared at Jordan. He might have been a sparrow facing the cold glitter of a serpent's eye. He was conscious of a great wrong which he had committed. The abuse of hospitality.

'For twenty years,' began Jordan, 'he's worn the same old suit and lived the life of a hermit, keeping himself aloof from the outer world. What for? All for the sake of a woman. Church et la fam, as the French say, though there was too little church about this and a great deal of fam.' Jordan, warming to his subject, relapsed into a familiar style which Mr Finchley was too worried to notice.

'Women – what woman's worth wearing the same suit for twenty years, I say? Twenty years ago it was, and the master was going to marry her. Almost married her, you might say, seeing as he'd got as far as the church and was waitin' for her to come. She was a rare beauty, there's no denying it, and she liked him in a way, I think, but it was more of a family arrangement than a love affair. Though the love weren't lacking on his side. She never turned up, sir. He waited at the church, but she never came and even her people didn't know what had happened. She just disappeared clean off the face of the earth. Not that I don't believe there wasn't a lot more in it than that. There was a lover knockin' around in the background somewhere. I think, they just fooled 'em up to the last moment and then they ran off together . . .'

Jordan ran on and drew in a crude way a picture of a younger Mr Woodall, dressed in his smartly-cut coat and well-creased trousers . . . waiting in the church with an impatience that grew as the minutes passed and no bride appeared . . . Mr Finchley saw him, a more youthful, more impatient and fiery Woodall, as he faced the ignominy and strain. He had shouted, Jordan said, a dreadful oath in the church that startled the priest into protest and the choirboys to interest.

'That's the simple truth, sir. They had to take him by force from the place. He was like a madman. And when he came to himself he sacked every married man on the estate so that he should never be troubled by the sight of women. He kept Mrs Lawson because she had been his nurse. And ever since that day he's kept his oath, worn the same suit and cursed every woman he met. I don't believe he's ever been farther than two hundred yards from the lodge gate since that day . . .'

Mr Finchley understood the terrible thing which he had done. His whole being revolted against the horror of his actions. He could not stand the shame of it. The very room in which he lay reproached him for his betrayal of Mr Woodall's hospitality. He had come into the house as a guest and in return . . .

He jumped from the bed.

'Nothing the matter, sir, I hope?' Jordan inquired.

'No . . . no, nothing. If Mr Woodall asks for me, tell him I'm still asleep.'

'Very good, sir,' said Jordan, and withdrew, wondering.

Mr Finchley washed and dressed himself in record time. When he was ready, he stole from the room and down the wide stairway. It was not until he was out in the fresh air and feeling the sun upon his face that he stopped to look back upon his actions. He was forced to confess to himself that he was ashamed; bitterly ashamed of himself. The thought of facing Mr Woodall, with the black memory of the preceding night lying between them, was more than he could stand.

So, Mr Finchley ran away. And in this, perhaps, he proved himself more wise than he thought. Where another man might have proven his good breeding by apologies, Mr Finchley exercised his good nature and frail humanity by deserting. He was a very lonely and chastened man for the next three hours. Even when the sun had blazed its way well into the heavens, and slanting through the knot-glassed window of an inn on the Blackdowns, found him drinking his cider and thoughtfully chewing bread and cheese, the vision of Mr Woodall's severe-cut face and sunken eyes occasioned him pangs of self-loathing.

After he had finished his lunch, he went out into the sunshine again, walking aimlessly. He was too troubled to worry about his direction. Gradually, however, the rhythm of his walking drove his mood from him and he was slowly conscious of his surroundings.

He was on the crest of a long ridge of hills, the Blackdowns. On one side the land swept down into the peaceful Taunton valley and on the other stretched away in hills and rounded slopes, until the green faded into the sky, forming a broken edge of land that cut against the blue and hinted of the sea. It was a glorious day; hot and sultry with no breath of air stirring. Momentary murmurs of thunder rolled faintly up from the west, to shake the pollen from the king-cups. The vague thunder disturbed Mr Finchley, but he soon forgot it in the splendour of the day. All that morning, and part of the afternoon, he had moved in a querulous dream. Now his ill-humours were gone, and before him, like a magic carpet, spread a valley as fair and fertile as an arcadian vision, and beneath his feet as he walked spread a marvellous pattern of soft turf and tremulous flowers. He had long since deserted the road. Leisurely, he made his way along the sweep of the hills. Sometimes he came to wide patches of bracken, brown and crackling under his feet, that stained the green seas of the hills like floating masses of seaweed. Goldfinches flirted in the thistle-growths. The cool shade of copses claimed him from the sun. He came to a dip in the hills, where a small stream broke its way from a bank of fern and tall hog-weed. The water slipped across the flat-tened grass stems and spread out to a quagmire of lush cress and trailing white bedstraw that shone in wanton stars upon the cress. Here Mr Finchley found a quiet place and lay down to rest.

He was tired now that he had set himself down. He had slept the sleep of the drunkard the previous night and his body ached, as that morning his soul had ached, with a curious weariness. His rucksack for a pillow he lazed by the waterside, listening to the tale that the stream told to the stones, and to the low murmur of the insects as they swung between the grasses. A princely tortoise-shell butterfly flat-tened its wings upon a slate and lay breathing gently as a sleeping maid. Mr Finchley stretched out his hand and touched the slender antennae. The creature rose into the air with a flashing of gorgeous wings and was gone. He was alone in a friendly and beautiful solitude ... he drew a deep breath and took to himself the freedom and riotous glory of the place.

Never before had he known such joy. London ... for years

he had been denied all this. London ... for years his cramped limbs had ached for the feel of smooth turf and long straight stretches of uplands. How far away seemed Nassington Avenue and all the shrieking, discordant elements that made up his life. Here he was alone and happy; alone and answerable to himself for his every action. He saw that the pleasures of life lie in the simple things of nature ... He had never known these joyous, yet familiar, things, and for the first time Mr Finchley praised the mad moment which had torn him away from conventions and himself, to find the beauty of this new life which had always been so close to him.

He lighted his pipe and smoked peacefully. There he was: an untidy, bald-headed, short man, of a nondescript appearance. There was nothing about his appearance to suggest that he was happier than most men. He lay and smoked his pipe and watched the smoke-rings mount into the sky, and in his heart was a gladness that would have made him hesitate to change places with a king. He was in need of a shave, his clothes were dusty, and his shirt collar showed growing black marks. The stiff bracken had torn down one of his trouser turn-ups, and the other hung half down, exposing a collection of grass seeds. His face was reddened with the sun, from which his cloth cap had but inadequately sheltered him. He was happier – except for the now less frequent thoughts of Mr Woodall – than any king, for within the last week he had entered into his own kingdom ...

Immersed in his thoughts Mr Finchley went to sleep. The butterfly returned to its stone, and the stream continued its chatter, heedless of Mr Finchley's heavy breathing.

Mr Finchley slept for three hours and when he awoke the day had changed. The thunder in the west was sending up its army, and the bright sky was battalioned with heavy heaps of black cloud that piled upon one another, as though they intended by sheer weight to crush the green land below into subjection.

'Well, I don't like the look of that,' Mr Finchley murmured to himself as he picked up his pipe and rucksack.

Climbing out of the valley he made his way through the bracken to the ridge top and the road.

He had come to the end of the ridge and before him, reminding him of Cleopatra's Needle, was a tall monument thrusting up from the bare top of the hill. He found a spot beneath a tree and consulted his map. It took him a long time to trace his route after leaving Mr Woodall's house. He discovered that the monument was the one which he had seen from the main road – Wellington Monument, in memory of the brave duke. Before him the plain was peppered with patches of red roofs and houses that were town and village, each cluster standing like a nucleus in an immensity of green. A drop of rain struck him sharply on the back of the hand. He looked up. The sky was blue-grey with thunderclouds. The air was stilled, and from a twisted fir tree across the heath a wren began to pipe petulantly. A fierce streak of lightning whipped across the sky, and simultaneously the heavens broke into a crashing peal of thunder that shook the ground, and down came the rain in a wicked bastinado that beat the grass stalks flat and drummed viciously against the fleshy laurel leaves. Mr Finchley waited beneath the tree, but the rain showed no signs of stopping. The clouds lowered themselves, muttering, until they were spread in a depressing grey blanket overhead, so close, it seemed to Mr Finchley, that he might almost have tossed a stone into their midst. He glanced at his watch. It was half past seven. He decided to brave the rain. He left the shelter of his tree, which had long ceased to be shelter and was rewarding his patient faith by dripping lugubriously upon him, and hurried down the road. The unpleasant rubbing of his wet mackintosh irritated him, and the rain clung to his eyelashes in fans that coloured his vision with a shifting iridescence. He could feel the water trickling from his coat on to his trousers. He tried – without success – to prevent this by taking shorter strides. By the time his trousers hung about his legs like sacks he had passed all caring and was actually beginning to enjoy himself.

Would it have been a holiday, he asked himself, if he had

145

experienced only fine weather? No, certainly not. He would show them. His shoes crunched on the wet roadway and the rub of his mac now sang a little song. He laughed and blew at the water which collected into dewdrops at the end of his nose. By the time he was on the outskirts of the town for which he was heading he was almost in a merry mood. The thought that he could encounter the worst weather with a cheerfulness equal to sunny days filled him with elation. He was no fine-weather man. In the centre of the town, alone in the rain, a policeman stood directing the traffic. The rain had driven away the usual knot of Sunday evening loafers, which gathered outside the Assembly Rooms. The lowering rain clouds had brought darkness an hour before its time and the street lamps were alight.

Mr Finchley approached the policeman.

'Can you tell me where I can get a good night's lodging, Constable?' he asked.

The policeman looked at him curiously before answering. His face was hidden under the peak of his helmet.

'A good night's lodging?' he said in a broad voice. 'I don't suppose you've got enough to buy a bed at the Swan, have you?' He nodded across the road to the broad doorway of an old-fashioned hostelry. Mr Finchley followed his nod and felt the coins in his pocket. He had exactly four shillings and he was over thirty miles from Exeter.

'Hardly the place for me,' he laughed. 'I'm not a million-aire . . .'

'Well, I wasn't sure of you for the minute,' answered the policeman. 'It pays to be careful these days. Some million-aires dress like tramps, you know. You'd better come with me. I'm just going off duty. I'll show you a place.'

'That's very kind of you,' replied Mr Finchley. The police-man, shaking his cape free of rain, started down a side-turning with Mr Finchley at his side.

They walked in silence. The policeman, Mr Finchley thought, was probably thinking of a hot supper and his wait-ing wife. It must be good to have a wife waiting at home when one returned, tired and hungry . . .

They had not gone very far when the policeman stopped at

a small brown door and pressed a bell. After a few minutes, a man, a short stocky man in a blue suit and collarless shirt, appeared.

'Gentleman wants a night's lodgin's, George,' said the policeman. There was a note of irony in his voice, which puzzled Mr Finchley. The policeman left them. The stocky man addressed him:

'Come on, mate, if you don't want to stop out in the rain all night!'

He held the door wide and Mr Finchley passed through it.

The man showed him into a little office and, opening a book, said, 'What's your name?'

'Name?' Mr Finchley was surprised at the question. 'Mr Finchley; why?' He took off his mackintosh as he spoke.

'Full name, mate. You can forget the mister part here.'

The curtness of the man's voice roused Mr Finchley. In his hurry to rid himself of his wet clothes he had paid but little heed to the man. Now, however, he dropped his coat and turned smartly towards him.

'That's hardly the way to address me,' he replied.

The man stared at him, stupefied by the remark. Then he spoke: 'Of all the darned nerve! You're a cool one, mate. What do you think this place is – the Ritz?'

'Hardly that,' laughed Mr Finchley, gladly taking the man's joke as an apology, 'but even the keeper of a lodging-house ought to try to keep his custom by exercising politeness, you know!'

'Lodging-house!' roared the other. 'You're barmy, mate. There ain't no such place in this town. This is the poor–law institution – the casual ward. Oh, don't try and be surprised! I suppose in a jiffy you'll be saying you're Lord Astor on a walking tour? Go on! Say it!'

Mr Finchley did not reply. He had scarcely heard these last remarks.

Casual wards, poor-law institutions; but the policeman...? He looked round the little office quickly, and saw what he would have seen before had he not been so occupied with ridding himself of his wet clothes ... cardboard regulations hung to the walls and there were shelves heavy with files and ledgers. A black-and-white notice confronted him, shrieking ... Gloucester and Somerset Joint Vagrancy Committee – Closure of the following wards ... Mr Finchley fought hard to maintain his composure.

'You mean that I'm in a casual ward?' he asked, weakly.

'Pretty nearly,' replied the man. 'You will be as soon as I've entered your name and particulars, and led you across the yard. Why? Ain't got any objections, 'ave yer? You can't sleep under a hedge tonight, mate. Now come on, don't hang me about. Yer late already. If you're coming in, say so, if yer ain't – there's the door and a pleasant night to you, I says. Though, I wouldn't wish a dog of mine out on such a night!'

The first shock of the revelation numbed Mr Finchley's mind. He recovered himself slowly, and, while the porter was talking, he did some thinking. He had very little money. To find a night's lodgings in some cheap hotel would seriously deplete his small funds; and the porter had said that there were no cheap lodging-houses in the town. He heard the rain beating on the thin roof ...

'Come on, mate. Which is it?'

Mr Finchley looked up.

'Really, you know ... it's a bit of a ...'

'Aw, come on! Make up yer mind! You needn't be scared of the place if it's a doss you want. What's there to be afraid of? I know some of the wards up country may be a bit bad, but we does you proud here! There's nothing to be afraid of.' He laughed reassuringly.

The word 'afraid' stimulated Mr Finchley. At various times within the last seven days, he had been faced with the word, until now it was almost a taunt. He remembered his creed. To take things as they came. That was the way to enjoy a holiday. But to spend a night in a casual ward was hardly a nice act. What would Mrs Patten and Sprake and ...

He stopped himself in time ... damn them! Fate, luck, something had led him to the place, he told himself, just to see whether he would be afraid. To the porter's amazement, he chuckled suddenly and stepped forward.

'It seems as though there's nothing else to do. I can't wander about on a night like this! Edgar Finchley, the name is.'

'Well, I'm glad you've made up yer mind,' grumbled the other as he made the entry in his book. He asked several other questions, some of which Mr Finchley could not answer, and the answers to some the porter refused to believe, although he had, in deference to Mr Finchley's protestations, to enter them.

'Don't know the name of the place you slept at last night, don't yer?'

'I'm afraid I don't,' answered Mr Finchley, cheerfully. He was feeling rather proud of the manful way in which he had accepted this new complication. 'I only know that the house has a drive to it and is surrounded by a deer park. The owner, I believe, though it is disloyal of me to say so, is a little mad. I left before I could discover its name.' He said this hurriedly: the memory of the preceding night still hurt him. The porter did not believe him.

'Looks to me as if you're a bit mad yourself, mate. Anyhow, give us yer kit. You'll have to leave that in the office until you go out. Now come this way and I'll show you where to take off your clothes and get a bath.'

'Bath!' Mr Finchley exclaimed joyfully. 'Do you really mean that I can have a bath?'

'You can – you've got to by law. But why the joy, mate? Some of your kind has to be thrown in!'

'Thrown in!' Mr Finchley could hardly believe it. 'You won't have to do that to me. I want a bath – badly!'

The porter, despite the rain, stopped him in the middle of the courtyard.

'You wants a bath badly,' he intoned solemnly. 'You say that! I knew it – you ain't all there! No sane casual ever admits he wants a bath!'

Shaking his head, he led him into a small wash-house and directed him to undress behind a partition. Mr Finchley heard water running into one of the baths, which lined one side of the room. As he undressed, he looked around him.

The wash-house was very bare, but clean. The walls were painted in two shades of brown. The wood of the partitions, and of the table-top at the far end of the room, was scrubbed to scrupulous whiteness.

'Ready?' called the porter. 'Since yer so eager to have it you'd better get on with it. They generally shout for their supper first. You can have yours in your nightshirt. What do you want? Tea, coffee, cocoa or a bowl of broth?'

'Do I get a choice?'

'Minister of Healf's regulations, Mr Pierpoint Morgan! Yer can 'ave which you want. Which is it?'

'Bowl of broth for me, please,' answered Mr Finchley, still wondering. He had formed a very low opinion of the fashion in which tramps were supposedly treated; an opinion which had occasioned him some trepidation as he entered the wash-house. Things were turning out very differently than he had expected.

The porter showed him the bath and Mr Finchley forgot his worries in the joy of hot water. The bath was as clean as the rest of the place. For ten minutes – he would have made it longer only the porter began to shout – he wallowed and blew in his bath. Had he been alone he would have sung. He jumped out; doused himself under the cold shower and dried upon a rough towel.

'Here y'are – get that on!' The porter thrust a coarse, but clean – so clean that it smelt of scrubbing and disinfectant – nightshirt round the canvas screen to him.

Sitting at the little table Mr Finchley had his broth. The liquid filled him with warmth and good feeling.

The porter watched him with an air of fascination. Here was a strange animal. Like most men of his class, when he could not understand one of his fellows he immediately assumed that the deficiency lay in the other. He knew that he was normal enough, therefore Mr Finchley must be mad.

Mr Finchley, Edgar Finchley, Esquire, of London, was mad. Perhaps he was. Mr Finchley, himself, would have admitted without argument that could the Edgar Finchley of Saturday, July the twenty-ninth, have known what Mr Finchley of Sunday, August the sixth, would be doing, he would have said that madness alone could wreak such a change.

When Mr Finchley had finished his supper, the porter led him away into the main building. There were very few lights in the place and Mr Finchley was unable to do more than guess at his surroundings.

They went up a winding stone stairway, that smelled of fresh paint, disinfectant and wet plaster, into a long room. There, in the half-light of some unseen lamp, Mr Finchley saw a row of low truckle beds lying along the floor like coffins. Only three beds were occupied. On these lay oddly twisted and curiously sounding bundles of manhood. The three men slept on, heedless of his coming. Mr Finchley slipped off his shoes – he learned afterwards that had it not been for his late arrival he would have had to undress in the ward – and the porter indicated the bed.

'That's yours, mate.'

He dropped Mr Finchley's clothes in a pile at the head of the low bed and threw him a couple of blankets.

'And don't make a hell of a noise turning in. I don't want them children woke up!' he whispered.

The porter watched him climb on to the bed and pull the blankets around himself. Then he was gone and Mr Finchley was left to the cold darkness. The piquancy of the situation appealed to him and he lay smiling in the darkness for some time. He forgot the hardness of the mattress as he listened to the heavy breathing of the other men; he forgot the awkward clinging nightshirt which adorned his body, as he contemplated the consternation which would seize his friends if they could but see him.

Sleep gradually came to him. He was tired and his body ready for the grim ease of a hard mattress. Very soon he slept and the ward was quiet.

A full moon ballooned into the sky and made the night a painting of hybrid lights. The grey rays slid through the iron bars of the ward windows and streaked the hard concrete floor with strange patterns. The moon threw its beams upon the sleeping men ... and they slept, with weariness upon their faces, except that of Mr Finchley; and he smiled in his sleep.

EIGHTEEN

How the State turns Inn-keeper

THE men in the ward were three very silent and morose men, moving with a quiet sullenness and making no gesture of friendship. Mr Finchley was to learn later that among those who frequent the casual wards and institutions there is very little affection or love. They move from one area to another, along regular routes, like migrating animals. They have few friends, no feelings beyond themselves and soon lose touch with their own identities. They are just beings whom the institution porters chivvy and to whom the housewives give food and drink to bribe them from their doorsteps. Among them there is little spirit of adventure. They pass through the countryside, but see only their own shadows straining the road before them in the morning, and they loathe the red sun in the evening as it sinks low and brings with it the thought of another ward and porters insistent upon baths. This sounds harsh and harsh it is, but it is true. The real troupers and roadmen shun the wards. They love laughter and good company and, if they cannot beg or earn the price of a night's lodgings, they are prepared to steal it. And when the moon is high they walk through the night and sleep with the sun to keep them warm. Even in winter, some prefer a dry ditch where the cold winds have piled brown leaves high, and there they roll themselves up like hedgehogs to forget the slaty skies and chill nor'-easterlies; and there sometimes they begin the long sleep which brings no grey dawn.

They had been wakened early, and the four of them had breakfasted, under the porter's eye, in a small messroom. It was a poor meal. Bread and butter and tea. Mr Finchley had eaten slowly and waited for someone to open conversation; but no word had passed their lips. He was wise enough to see, however, that he could do nothing to break through their reserve and, as he intended to leave the ward that morning, it ceased to worry him. He would soon be free, he thought.

He continued to think so, until the porter stopped him as he rose from the table and with a curt 'good morning' to the three men made for the doorway.

'Eh, where are you going, mister?'

'Going?' queried Mr Finchley, not understanding the man. 'I'm going out, of course.'

'Going out!'

The porter looked at him curiously. Mr Finchley was a source of endless mystery to him. 'Going – going out where?'

'To Exeter, I hope,' replied Mr Finchley, mystified by the man's amazement.

'Not today you ain't, mate!'

'What do you mean – "not today"? I'm leaving this morning! You can't stop me.'

'Mad! Mad!' moaned the porter, and the three tramps smiled wearily.

'Would you mind fetching me my rucksack and personal belongings, please?' Mr Finchley decided that the only way to deal with the man's impertinence was to ignore it.

His words wakened the porter to a realization of his position.

'Now look here, cocky,' he said in a loud voice, 'I don't want to lose me temper with yer, but I shall if you keep on with this fool's game! You know, as well as I do, that you've got to stop here today to do yer job of work and that you get let out tomorrow morning!'

'What?' Mr Finchley replied, thoroughly startled. 'I've got to stop here all day?' As he spoke he knew that it was so. He remembered that he had read somewhere that each tramp had to do a task before he left.

'No, no, Mister Bloomin' Rockyfeller! *You* don't have to do a task! Yer just sits back in your armchair while me and the three angels there plays our harps to you, and the master brings you oranges on a plate, and one of the ward nurses throws rose petals at yer. Oh, you don't have to work! Not 'arf!'

The sally produced a laugh from the three tramps. It was probably the first time they had laughed for years and the sound was discomforting to such a sensitive person as Mr Finchley. He lost his temper.

'Look here, my man!' he stormed. 'I won't stand this! Do you hear? I won't stand it! I don't believe you have any right to keep me here; and what's more I won't stop! I'll see the master of the institution and speak to him about your conduct!'

'Well, here's yer chance,' grinned the porter. Excitement was a thing which seldom came his way. 'Here is the master.'

A short, thick-set man, with his thin hair oiled back over his head, bustled into the room.

'What the devil's all the row in here, Sampson?' he said to the porter in an angry tone. 'Sounds like bedlam! Why haven't these men finished their breakfast and started about their jobs?'

'This fellow says he won't do his job, sir,' answered the porter. 'He reckons we ain't got no right to keep him,' he added maliciously.

'That is so,' put in Mr Finchley. 'I came here for the night – because I was forced to, but I see no reason why I should have to stay all today and work!'

The master glared at him.

'Reason!' he roared. 'Where d'you think you are? This is a casual ward and you've got your task to do and if you don't do it you don't get any food, and – if I get any more nonsense from you – I'll have you arrested for disobeying my orders!'

'But, but . . .' Mr Finchley protested weakly.

'Don't but me. Do as I say or I'll call the police. What right? What right?' he cried. 'I'll show you what right. Ever heard of the Public Assistance, Casual Poor, Order? Ever read articles seven and ten? Here, Sampson, take them out before I lose my temper completely. I don't know what they are coming to these days!'

He stumped out of the room and left Mr Finchley – beaten. Mr Finchley realized that it was useless to argue. Despite his annoyance and anger at the muddle into which he had precipitated himself, his common-sense told him that the master was clearly in the right. His rebellion ended in his halting before a pile of logs which, the porter blithely informed him, he had to saw into convenient sizes during the day.

The porter left him. Mr Finchley picked up the saw and mechanically started his job. The three men were in some other part of the institution doing their tasks. He was alone in his little yard. The rhythm of his movements helped him to think out his position. He saw that the only thing to do was to show a brave face to the world in which he now found himself.

At three o'clock the sun came spurting through the low clouds which had gloomed the day, and with the sun came back Mr Finchley's peace of mind. The affair began to assume its rightful proportions. The clock in the small tower that capped the building boomed three and a thought suddenly occurred to Mr Finchley. It was Bank Holiday! Bank Holiday – and he was spending it in a casual ward, sawing logs!

The humour of the situation overcame him and he dropped his saw and laughed.

The porter on his rounds looked into the yard and saw him – laughing and holding his sides. The man's eyes widened with fright.

'Mad as a hatter, poor fellow,' he commiserated. He was a good fellow and, seeing that Mr Finchley had almost finished the logs, he withdrew and said nothing to the master. He suffered, however, from momentary pains at the responsibility he was incurring by allowing such a lunatic to take to the road on the morrow.

For several minutes Mr Finchley laughed at the absurdity of his position and then, frightened by the thought that someone might come along and decide that he was demented, he controlled his feeling and applied himself to the logs. He sawed and chuckled alternately and, sometimes, he

155

even sawed and chuckled at the same time; but he had to give this up as the chuckling interfered with his sawing and he grazed the skin from his left thumb.

Five o'clock came, and the porter told him that he could finish for the day and complimented him upon his industry. Mr Finchley waited for tea to appear. When it arrived he learned that it was his supper. He sat down with a good grace, the three casuals arranged around him like carven gargoyles, and ate his bread and dripping and drank his cocoa. They sat for a while after their meal and smoked; but no man spoke. Mr Finchley did not mind the silence. He just smoked and thought, and watched the others. They leaned back against their seats and each man's eyes were centred on the drifting plume of smoke from his pipebowl. One of them went to sleep and his pipe dropped with a clatter to the ground. No one moved; the pipe lay on the floor cooling against the grey slate slabs.

Later they removed to the sleeping ward and undressed under the watchful eye of the warder whose duty it was to make sure that no smoking materials were smuggled into the sleeping wards. Smoking in bed is a habit which Public Assistance authorities do not encourage.

Morning came quickly enough and Mr Finchley dressed, happy in the thought that at last he was to free himself of the institution. He had not been miserable there. In his queer way he had enjoyed his stay; but he found that he was longing for the countryside and fresh air, for time to play with and trees in whose shade he could lie and watch the birds and hours slide by.

The master restored to him at the small lodge his rucksack and belongings. When he had entered the ward the porter had taken all his money – four shillings. Now the master handed him back two shillings and elevenpence.

'I don't think this is the correct amount,' said Mr Finchley, counting the money.

'It's all you're going to get!' answered the master.

'But it's over a shilling short . . .'

The man regarded him sympathetically.

'Listen, mister,' he said, 'you've caused a lot of bother and annoyance since you came in, but I don't want to be hard on you. I can see that you're down on your luck and not used to casual wards. If you were younger, maybe, I could do something for you in the way of training for a new job at one of our training centres – but you're too old. They'll only take young uns! Perhaps you don't know that any money handed over by a tramp must be retained by the master of the institution. Retained, kept, hung on to . . . get that! I needn't give you back any of your money. But I am – why? Because I'm man enough to sympathize with your position. All I've done is to deduct the approximate cost of your lodgings. You can't grumble at that! Now clear out and, in the next ward you go to, try and act more like a casual and less like a millionaire – it'll serve you better!'

With this parting advice Mr Finchley found himself in the roadway. He knew better now than to argue with the master. He took his money and went.

A little way up the street he found a barber's shop. He went in to escape the drifting rain, and to have a shave. The barber, already busy with a customer, flourished a soapy brush at a wooden kitchen chair in the corner of the dark little shop. Mr Finchley sat down, and listened to the rich West Country voice of the barber.

At first, he listened to the man's way of talking rather than to what he said, savouring the slow earthy drawl so different from the clipped Cockney speech of the hairdressing saloon he patronized on Haverstock Hill. Then, the gist of what they were saying was borne in on him, and a qualm of horror touched the pit of his stomach.

'Ar,' the barber was saying. 'An' they do zay as he wor an earl, seemingly. But a-wandering around like an old dedecai, in a caravan. Burned to death he was, and the varmer over to Monkton burned too. Turrible thing, sure enough.' He shook his head and thrust out his underlip in appreciation of the tragedy.

'Tes so,' said his client. 'I just read all about it in the *Morning News*.'

His hand trembling, Mr Finchley picked up the *Western*

Morning News, which lay open on a horsehair sofa. A huge black headline leaped out and struck him like a sword.

Wandering Gipsy Earl's Death in Rick-fire

Beneath the headline, the puckish face of Ernst, his hunchbacked Ernst of the caravan, looked up at him from drawn brows! Harlow and the car, everything but the face of Ernst faded from his knowledge. He heard a violin singing in the clear of the evening. A white horse shuffled in the tall shadows of the caravan. He heard Ernst talking . . . 'Revenge is the one thing that makes the life of the oppressed sweet to live for . . .'

He quickly read the article. It told him little more. There had been a rick-fire at a village near Taunton and the bodies of two men had been recovered. A wandering white horse, drawing an empty caravan, had been found near the spot, and subsequently the bodies had been identified; Ernst's from his hunchback, and the other, a well-known farmer, by the scar on his face. More the paper did not say. It recounted the story of Ernst's life and parentage. Although, had he wished, he might have lived in luxury he preferred to lead a simple wandering life. The tragedy was described as an accident – just that; no hint of anything else.

Mr Finchley let the barber shave him, his thoughts far away, recalling the hours he had passed with Ernst. He knew that Ernst was decent and human. Yet he had taken this terrible revenge, and then thrown himself into the flames. Had that dreadful last act been a final gesture of defiance to a world that had proved unjust? Or . . . and this gave Mr Finchley more comfort . . . had he been overcome by his deed and taken his own life as a punishment?

Deep in his thoughts, Mr Finchley paid the wondering barber who had never shaved so silent a customer, and following the signposts, set out on the road to Exeter.

Twenty miles is a long hard way for a man not used to exercise. But Mr Finchley felt the need for the steady grind that liberates the thoughts. Doggedly he tramped along, welcoming any physical distress that came to ease the pain he knew at Ernst's terrible death.

By the time he reached Exeter he felt more composed. Whatever Ernst had done he knew him for a good man. Perhaps the tragic gipsy earl now rested in enduring peace.

In Exeter a tired but calm Mr Finchley found the Post Office and collected his money. With surprise he realized it was early evening, and that he was very hungry. He ate his tea in a huge restaurant shaped like a well, surrounded by crowded tables of cheerful, chattering people. The proximity of his fellow beings, the sound of laughter, and the warm tea and good food, all conspired to bring Mr Finchley to his normal self.

NINETEEN

Of Art and Beer

HE left the restaurant and wandered down the narrow main street with his rucksack over his shoulder. Outwardly he was still the same Mr Finchley; sunburnt, his suit wrinkled and worn, and his cloth cap slanted at a ridiculous angle on his head; but in his heart he was changed. He had changed a little each day since leaving London. An expansion was taking place in his mind. Each day he had to accommodate some fresh imposition, some new revelation, and he was finding that to do this called for a growing tolerance. Mr Finchley knew that it was a strange and wonderful world; how strange and wonderful he was but beginning to discover for himself.

He opened his map and leaned in the angle made by two walls. He turned his thoughts to the future. He was in Exeter, further than that he had no plans. The breeze whipped at the open sheet in his hands and tore it from his grasp. He jumped forward and trapped the map with his foot. He picked it up and dusted the dirt from the leaves. A name caught his eyes. Princetown. Princetown, Dartmoor, convicts and heather; bell-mouthed hounds and long stretches of moors . . .

He would go to Princetown. He lost no time about it. A policeman directed him and, his heart growing lighter every moment, he swung down the hill towards the river and soon left the narrow streets behind him.

It was nearly five o'clock when Mr Finchley left Exeter. At six o'clock he was within four miles of Moreton Hampstead. He had not walked all the way. A man driving a horse and trap had seen him sitting in the hedge and had offered him a ride. He took Mr Finchley within four miles of Moreton Hampstead. During the drive Mr Finchley was prevented from viewing the countryside by the tall dusty hedges and red banks, with razor-edged slabs of slate cutting through the earth, which shut the road from the fields and valleys. At the top of a long hill, where a small road debouched into a woody valley, the man left him.

Mr Finchley watched the cart go down the rutty road. After it had disappeared he stood still, taking pleasure in marking its progress by the sound of its squealing skidpan, which the man had fixed to one of the wheels. The last echo of the cart faded into the air. He turned and started along the road. He had not gone five yards when from the high bank on his right there came a crashing of twigs, and a tall, lean man precipitated himself on to the roadway with a loud *whoop!*

Mr Finchley stepped backwards as the newcomer shook himself like a dog and scattered a shower of earth and leaves around him.

'That's better,' the man said, when he had finished. 'I thought that the road lay on the other side.' He brushed the last of the leaves and dirt from himself and fell into stride with Mr Finchley.

'Are you,' said Mr Finchley good-naturedly, 'going my way?'

'On the contrary,' replied the other drily, as he pulled out a meerschaum and hung it over his lower lip, 'you are going my way. I shall appreciate the pleasure of your company.'

'Your way or my way – it doesn't matter which,' agreed Mr Finchley and surveyed this strange individual who had leaped from the hedgeway.

He was a tall man, very tall and, to increase the grotesqueness of his stature, he had upon his head a high-crowned, large-brimmed hat of green felt. For the rest of his costume he wore a bright green shirt and dark blue velvet trousers. The neck of his shirt was drawn close with a tie of similar colour and material as the shirt. He carried no rucksack or coat. His skin was burnt a deep mahogany that told of hot days far away from England. His face was lean and hatchet-shaped and his chin hidden by a young goatee.

Mr Finchley pulled out his pouch and offered it to the man.

'Thank you, no! I seldom smoke when I am walking. I like to suck my pipe, though. It gives me a pleasant feeling.' Although he talked but little, Mr Finchley gradually began to learn who this stranger was. He was an artist, poor – because, as he wryly explained, he was a genius – who had gone into the country to lose himself for a while. He had no money – he said this with joy.

'Not a penny piece! Look!' He turned his trousers pockets inside out. 'I don't need any. Once I knew what it was to have plenty of money, but now – I'm poor and my painting has improved. For two weeks I've fed and slept and paid for my bread and bed by my art. Think of it! I'm the first man to work out the true equation of life and art.' Mr Finchley's sympathetic silence drew the man into speech. 'In the West End pictures have a value which any fool knows to be false. How false I never knew until recently. Now I know. My pictures are worth bread and bed, and good talk and brown beer – that's all I want. I'm beginning to discover real values and to forget things I once valued. Yesterday, I thought of a dress-shirt and seats at the opera. Today, I've forgotten them altogether.'

'But surely, M—'

'You can call me John!'

'John, then!' laughed Mr Finchley, enjoying himself. 'Surely, you don't pay your way by drawing pictures?'

'I do. I can understand your surprise – you have never seen my pictures! We shall be thirsty soon, and then I shall earn you a drink, and after that, if our paths still lie together, I will earn you bed and food.'

So, they continued along the road, talking. And when they tired of talk, John sucked his empty pipe and Mr Finchley hummed quietly to himself and thought occasionally of Ernst.

Before them the sun was dipping to the moors and painting the hills with crimson. From a telegraph pole a yellow-hammer repeated its ditty, until the noise of a passing car sent it flirting across the fields.

Presently the road divided. Mr Finchley was about to take the right-hand turn, but as John, because he happened to be on that side of the road, swung to the left without hesitation, Mr Finchley followed him. Why he did so, he did not know. Perhaps it was because one road is as good as another when a man's destination is nowhere in particular.

The road dipped between steep banks to where a stream, bridged by two long granite slabs, rushed along the valley bottom in a noisy spate of brown. A few ducks swam in a pond below the bridge, and on a green beyond the stream, village boys were playing cricket with a wicket of coats.

They stopped for a while and watched. The boys paid no attention to the tall, quaintly dressed stranger and the round-faced Mr Finchley. Cricket is cricket, and, whether it is played on a village green or at Lord's, it demands the whole of one's attention. Only the small girl, who had been bribed into acting as scorer, missed a leg-bye as she eyed the vivid green shirt. A woman coming from the end house of the village street looked at them curiously.

They passed to the parlour of the public-house. The Jolly Mariner. He was a jolly mariner; hoisted high on his sign and straddling a rum cask, a pipe in one hand and a tankard in the other. He was fat and beaming, and his bow legs held him as firmly to the cask as they would have done had he been on a slanting deck.

Inside the public-house they met the counterpart of the

162

sign. He was fat and jolly and beaming. In the place of a blue jersey he wore a black-and-white checked waistcoat.

'I wonder,' said John, as they drank their beer, 'whether his legs are bowed?'

The landlord came from behind his bar to talk to them. Mr Finchley smiled into the top of his glass. The man's legs were bowed.

'Nice day, gentlemen!' said the landlord as he sat down.

'A very nice day, indeed,' replied John. He raised his glass significantly and drank deeply.

'You be walkin', I suppose?'

They nodded.

He shook his head over them.

'I can't, fer the life of me, understand it. All this – hikin' they call it! Where's the sense in walkin' unless you've got to get somewhere, and if you've got to get somewhere, what's the good of civilization if you can't take a train or motor?'

He rumbled comfortingly, and moved to the bar to refill their glasses.

There were two other men in the bar, a couple of farm-hands playing darts at the far side of the room. Mr Finchley, remembering his desire to visit Princetown questioned the landlord about that town, and, while they were talking, John, unnoticed by either, unhooked a large cardboard cider advertisement from the wall. Using the blank side of the board, he set to work with his charcoal.

They were still talking when John had finished. He broke in upon their conversation.

'We must be going, my friend! Landlord, I've enjoyed your beer, but I can't pay you in money, because I haven't any. Here – do you think that'll settle the debt? If not, I'll draw one of the wife as well. What do you say?'

He handed the landlord the sheet of cardboard. The land-lord did not understand. He looked at John and Mr Finchley suspiciously, as though they were trying to wrap some mystery about him. Then he glanced at the cardboard. He started. There, staring at him from the white board, were the plump face and merry eyes that confronted him every morning as he shaved. He let out a loud whistle of astonishment. The dart-players came hurrying across the room.

John winked at Mr Finchley.

'Well, I'll be darned if it ain't the livin' likeness!' said one of the farmhands.

'It's ... it's me!' said the landlord suddenly, and turned to John. 'Did you do that while I was talkin'?'

John nodded.

'You'm one of they artistic chaps, then?'

'Guilty,' laughed John. 'Hang it up, landlord, in your parlour. I think it settles our score for today – what do you say?'

'You're welcome to what ye've had,' the man said slowly. 'I only wish the wife was at home, then you could do one of her. 'Tis a miracle to me how you did it ...'

They left him with his dart-players to wonder while they wandered down the country lanes.

Later that evening they entered another inn. The place was crowded with working-men and labourers, enjoying their beer and talking horses, crops, prices, and politics; and high above the noise of all voices came that of the landlord. He was an astute-faced fellow, sarcastic, and had a coarse manner. Mr Finchley did not want to pay for their beer in John's way.

'I think you'd better let me pay for this,' he said as they finished their beer.

'Why, aren't we practically partners? I pay for the beer and you provide the company! I've been with the trees and hedges too long. I need a man to talk to for a while.'

Mr Finchley was silent, determined, however, to pay for the beer if the occasion demanded it.

The whole bar burst into roars of laughter at a bawdy joke which the landlord had delivered aloud, as John made his way to the bar. He was quite frank.

'Landlord, we've enjoyed your beer, but I'm afraid that we have no money to pay for it!'

Here was no jolly mariner. The man had a thin, callous face, strangely vulpine. He was a businessman and equal to the open admission.

164

'Well, what d'you want me to do about it? Give you half-a-crown to help you find a night's lodgings? Beer is beer, and has to be paid for! Why did you have it, if you knew you couldn't pay?'

'I can pay; but not in cash!'

'Not in cash! How?' The men were silent, listening. Mr Finchley sensed the tension in the air and noticed the eager grin of the barman, a huge fellow with broken nails and hands like an ape.

'If you'll pass me down that advertisement for potato crisps I'll show you,' answered John calmly.

Mr Finchley might be apprehensive, but not John. He knew his man. The landlord guessed that this tall stranger who dressed like a punchinello had some cards up his sleeve; besides, the evening was long and there was time enough for rough play. He handed John the advertisement.

John turned it over, and taking out his charcoal began to draw. He leaned against the wall as he did so, in order that none might see what he was doing.

Mr Finchley watched John's skilful hand move across the board. The scene impressed itself upon his mind with a clarity that was to last: the crowded room, hung about with faded pictures and dirty whisky and cigar signs, the low bar with its beer handles like truncheons, the wet-topped tables glistening with spilt beer, the spittoons on the saw-dusted floor and the men, each one straining towards the corner in which John stood, each one eager for fun. The face of the landlord was calm as he waited with a scornful, almost evil patience.

Five minutes passed. John finished his drawing and tossed the cardboard on the counter.

'Does that settle it?' he asked.

The men crowded forward and with them, unable to resist the desire, went Mr Finchley. A low murmur of amazement broke from them.

John had done his work well. From the cardboard the fox-like face of the landlord sneered at them, twisted lips and half-closed eyes. It was not the remarkable likeness alone which drew the crowd's amazement. It was something else;

something that roused even the landlord's interest and startled him from his calmness. From the centre of the man's forehead in the picture sprang a horn. Mr Finchley trembled at the insult.

The landlord spoke. 'Why the horn?'

John smiled, and his face was like a wrinkled map.

'Why do you ask that? I've listened to you for half an hour, and must it be said that I know you better than all these men who come here every night? Why? I will tell you!'

He stepped forward, took the board, and wrote beneath the picture. He threw it in front of the man, so that all could read his words, which ran:

'He's a bit of a devil!'

The audacity of the stranger captured the admiration of the men. They burst into laughter and stamped their feet. Even the landlord smiled.

Mr Finchley's admiration for his companion increased. He had prided himself that he could read his fellows. John did more; he read them at a glance, captured between charcoal lines their very soul and then insulted them with a suavity which rendered his insult a compliment.

They did not drink again that evening. They wandered through the deep hills and steep lanes. Past cottages, shrinking into the bourgeoning dusk, in the shade of tall trees and by the side of unseen streams that sang darkly to the waning moon ... they walked together and smoked one another's tobacco. And as they walked they talked. Mr Finchley found himself telling John of his adventures; and John found in Mr Finchley a man who knew when to be silent, a man who fitted his moods and enjoyed his dry humour. They found a barn, and without question, they dug themselves deep holes into the soft hay.

'Goodnight, John,' Mr Finchley called softly, and wriggled deeper into his hole.

'Goodnight! Pleasant dreams.'

They slept, dreamless. And on the pent-ridge of the barn an owl rested at intervals through the night. Sometimes it hooted mournfully. At the sound, a hunting weasel in the dock-plants of an adjoining field lifted its head and showed a quick row of white teeth. Outside the barn, owl harried field mice, weasel trailed rabbit, and a fox crossed the top of the barnyard on his way to the farm. Inside the barn, the rats and mice skittered in the hay, and a long-legged spider walked with seven-leagued strides across Mr Finchley's face, undisturbed by his gentle breathing.

TWENTY

How, when Men take to Water, Water-boatmen must beware

MR FINCHLEY woke to find the daylight flooding through the open barn door. In the yard a chaffinch was calling incessantly. Mr Finchley discovered that during the night the weight of his body had carried him deep into the straw. He hoisted himself from his crater and looked round for John.

'Hey, lazybones! Time to get up,' he called into the gaping hole at his side.

There was no answer from John. Mr Finchley rolled across the straw and, unable to stop himself, fell into the hole. He landed – not, as he expected, on John, but on receptive hay.

'I wonder where he is?' he murmured, and pulled himself out of the hole. Then he saw the note scribbled on the inside of a torn cigarette carton, pinned to his rucksack.

Good morning!

I have awakened to find the moon high and the night warm. I am no man to sleep while Selene rides. We may meet again – in a Tube train!

JOHN

They might meet again in a Tube train. Mr Finchley almost hoped they would not. He preferred to imagine himself with John, walking through the night with the moon above. Mr Finchley regretted that John had not wakened him . . .

He left the barn and found the road. Although it was still early the sun was warm. Mr Finchley pushed his cap comfortably to the back of his head, lighted his pipe and did five easy miles before breakfasting at a farm.

Walking after breakfast was not so pleasant. The sun grew stronger and the valley, through which the road wound, was oppressively hot. There was no wind and little shade. The cattle lay in drowsy heaps against the hedges, and the very leaves on the trees hung limply against the heat, which threw a shimmering cloak over the countryside . . . Nothing moved but Mr Finchley and the clumsy bumble-bees which banged their way from flower to flower.

He was soon perspiring and thirsty. He came at last to a stile in the hedge and he sat down to rest. To his ears came the sound of running water. Mr Finchley dropped to the ground and made his way across the field to a freshet that trickled down from a hillside into a pool. The place was very still and warm. About the edge of the pool a few thorns and alders formed a screen, and on its sandy bottom minnows scuttled, and a water-boatman oared itself along in a tremendous hurry.

Mr Finchley cupped his hands under the fall and drank the cool water. He decided to have a wash. He could feel bits of straw from his bed tickling his body, and he was anxious to rid himself of the nuisance, chiefly because he had an uneasy feeling that the tickling was not entirely due to straw. There are other animals than rats and mice which hide in hay. He took off his shirt and bent to the water. He caught sight of his reflection in the water and laughed.

'Good morning, Mr Finchley,' he said, playfully. 'Have a good night? Of course you did. Just going to have a wash, I see. Better late than never, eh? Pity you can't have a bath.'

He straightened up at the thought. Why not? He was on holiday, and . . .

'Hullo! Still there, I see,' he called to his reflection again. 'That was a good idea of yours. Half a moment and I'll join you.'

He undressed, and then, standing on the bank above the pool remembered a trick of his schooldays. He drew a breath and jumped into the water. Jumped so that he landed on the surface of the water, backside first, and sent a tidal wave roaring to the sides and washing about the dry stems of the overhanging briars and nettles. He stood up and measured by the wet banks the effects of his plunge. He drew a pleasant satisfaction from the fact that the pond showed a dark, wet line three inches above its normal surface. Mr Finchley proceeded to enjoy himself. Nowhere was the pool more than three feet deep and he wallowed like a river-horse. The sticklebacks and water-boatmen dived into their holes along the bank and stayed there, leaving him undisputed king of the pool. He felt like a king, and forgot that at any moment someone might amble along the path and discover him. Later he climbed on to the bank and stretching his shirt over his loins he let the sun dry him. The heat sent him to sleep, and when he awoke it was nearly noon.

The road leading through the valley joined a wide main road. Mr Finchley began to think about lunch. In the bright dining-room of a pleasant country hotel half a mile farther on he enjoyed a simple meal, with a tankard of beer to give it zest. Then he pulled out his pouch and pipe.

He smoked for some time before he was aware that something must be happening in the gravelled space at the side of the hotel. He could see some men pointing and laughing and then they crowded backwards, holding out their hands to form a part of a ring.

A small boy in hobnails came bounding round the corner of the bar and ran past the window shouting:

'Come on, Dicky! Come on, there's a fight!'

Mr Finchley decided to go and see the fight. He paid his bill and when the waitress brought him his change, he said:

'What's the trouble outside? There seems to be a great commotion.'

The waitress, who had not been expecting a tip from this crumpled-looking man who cheerfully brought a shabby rucksack into the dining-room, smiled wearily.

'I should say it's another of the Bosker's fights! He's the barman. He was a boxer before he joined the hotel, and whenever a poor feller goes into the bar and can't pay for his bread and beer Bosker fights 'im. We get a lot bein' on the main road. Bosker never lets 'em off or calls the police. They just 'as to fight and the boss – if the man shows spirit – makes bets on Bosker, if he can find anyone fool enough to lay 'em. Disgustin' it is – though I've got too much sense to say so to the boss!'

When he reached the car park, Mr Finchley found that the fight had already begun. He wormed his way through them to the edge of the ring.

The fight was being conducted without rules or regulations. The two men were in the ring, and there they were to stop until one of them was vanquished.

Bosker, a massive fellow with long swinging ape-like arms and a face red from the atmosphere of the tap-room, was making fierce rushes at his opponent, who was a tall, fair-haired man, very thin, and seemingly no match for the burly bartender. Both men had stripped to the waist. The sunshine slid off their sweating bodies.

Every time that Bosker rushed, his arms slashed in and out like flails and each stroke was strong enough to floor a man; but his blows never landed effectively. The tall boxer avoided the mad rushes and, when Bosker caught him against the ringside, he covered his head and body skilfully, so that the blows glanced harmlessly from his arms and shoulders.

'Come on, Bosker – finish him off! Me dinner's waiting,' called a man beside Mr Finchley.

Bosker rushed again. The tall man feinted and ducked under Bosker's arms to reach the opposite side of the ring. Mr Finchley, for the first time, had a clear view of his face. He started. It was John! There was no mistaking the little goatee beard. John, who had left him in the night – and here he was fighting because he couldn't pay his bill. Mr

Finchley, in spite of his surprise, wondered if John's drawing of Bosker had not been flattering enough.

Bosker made a rush and John stopped it with a well-aimed blow that drew blood.

The crowd howled angrily: 'Eat him, Bosker! Eat him!'

Mr Finchley was maddened at their crude partisanship.

'Good old John!' he cried, without quite knowing that he was shouting. 'Good man, John! Hit him on the nose again! Hit him!'

'Eh, mate, what yer yellin' for him for?'

The man at his side looked down upon him in wonderment.

'Why shouldn't I?' retorted Mr Finchley fiercely. 'I can shout for whom I like!'

'Sure – but he ain't got a chance.'

'Perhaps he hasn't, but he's my man and I'm shouting for him. I believe in fair play.'

'Good for 'ee, mister. So do I,' answered his neighbour, and he shouted in a voice which Mr Finchley envied: 'Come on, Johnny!' to prove his sense of fair play. Hearing him, the crowd around also gave a shout for John.

The issue was not long in doubt. Bosker cornered John and there was no escape. One of his swinging blows caught John in the chest. He went down like a ninepin, and, for all Mr Finchley's loud pleas, he stayed down.

The fight was over and Bosker, grinning triumphantly, magnanimously leaned over, picked his victim up, and carried him to a seat, anxious to show that there was no ill-feeling.

He held a glass to John's mouth. John seemed to recover at the sight; he struggled upright and drank the beer. The drink revived him.

'Thank you,' he said. Seeing Bosker standing over him, he smiled. 'You were too good for me, Bosker; but it was a good fight, eh?'

'You bet!' replied Bosker, emphatically.

The crowd drifted away, and Mr Finchley was left on the seat with John.

'It seems, John, that the barman was no lover of the arts,' he said softly, when they were alone.

John turned round.

'Good Lord! Where did you spring from?' Then he laughed shortly. 'No, Bosker did not like his portrait. He prefers fighting. For that matter, so do I.'

'But you're not so good at it as Bosker, eh?'

'It is not wise to believe all you see. It may sound paradoxical, but I'm better than Bosker and, had I wished, it would have been he who touched gravel first. I haven't drawn men for years and not learnt to assess them at sight.'

Mr Finchley did not understand.

'What do you mean? That you could have beaten Bosker?'

'Yes! But I didn't Why not? Now that the crowd have left I'll tell you. You saw what happened when Bosker floored me? They bore no ill-will, and even gave me a glass of beer. If I had beaten Bosker I should probably have had to run for it – and there would have been no glass of beer to refresh me. Understand? I waited my time and then let Bosker put me down with an easy blow. Now I am quite fresh and ready to go on again. I might have been haring up the road!'

They looked at one another and then burst into laughter . . .

They wandered along the main road together, keeping the sun before them. Sometimes they passed through villages, and once through a small town.

At last they came to where a huge oak tree stood beside a little mill stream, and hung its branches over the main road.

John spoke.

'For the rest of the day I shall lie beneath this tree and rest, and, perhaps, think a little. You must go on!'

'Go on? Why?' asked Mr Finchley. 'I've only just found you again!'

'That is the reason. I am not on holiday. You must understand that a man of many friendships can never be a genius – it leaves him no time for the indulgence of healthy egotisms!

It is better for us to part. Otherwise, we should spoil our individual pleasures by trying to please one another. Some day in London, I will hunt up your name in a directory and visit you, and we shall laugh together again, but now we must part. You are holidaying, and to be happy I must be selfish. Goodbye!'

He shook Mr Finchley by the hand and then threw himself down under the tree and shut his eyes.

Mr Finchley, too surprised to reply, looked down at the careless, colourful figure. He could not entirely appreciate John's logic, his heart was, at that moment, too full of sentiment, yet he recognized the other's sincerity.

'Goodbye, John,' he murmured and turned away. In a few minutes John opened his eyes. Mr Finchley had disappeared. He sat up with a frown on his face. The frown faded and he shook his head sadly.

'I didn't think he would. I didn't think . . .'

The rest of his words was lost as he sank lazily back to the grass.

TWENTY-ONE

How Mythology and Mist may make a Bicycle Skid

THE white road slipped round the edge of the tors, slanted gratefully to the slight valleys and then, as though tired of the continual undulation, struck straightly across the land and lost itself in the sky. A curlew mewed as it circled. In the heather behind Mr Finchley a sheep called. He leaned back against his green hummock and felt the grandness of the scene sweep over him. Hills, hills and, beyond the purple slopes, more hills and tors that sloped away into the distance to find the sea.

This was Dartmoor. The wind whistled by Mr Finchley's ears, as long ago it had whistled through the unkempt hair of druids moving in ceremony round their stone circles. The pool where a mountain stream flowed round two huge granite boulders once had mirrored the aegis and greaves of Caesar's infantry as they stooped to drink. Now it held but the blue of the evening sky and the shaking leaves of the drooping ash. Five hundred feet above the stream a kestrel hung upon the air, its pinions beating in slow arcs against the waves of light, its eyes bold with a far-sightedness that marked each movement of the browning bracken, each flutter of small wings from ling tuft to stunted thorn, and took in the distant sea beyond Plymouth Town where great liners drew pennants of smoke above their wakes.

The hawk closed its wings and slanted away with the wind flattening its breast-feathers. It disappeared behind the tor-side, and Mr Finchley saw a man working his way up the side of the hill towards him. He watched the figure climbing laboriously in and out of the rocks and ploughing a way through the bracken. Presently the man stood by his side, admiring the view and regaining his breath. Mr Finchley saw that he was of his own height, dressed in a quiet grey suit. His round, chubby face lost its redness as his breathing slackened to normal. The man's hat attracted Mr Finchley's attention. It was a shooting-cap with side-lapels that were buttoned across the top of his head, while fore and aft two wide peaks sloped down to protect the wearer from sun and rain. If Mr Finchley had been less absorbed by the cap, and possessed a knowledge of his own appearance, he might have been astonished at the similarity of the man's appearance with his own.

The man turned to Mr Finchley and smiled.

'Good view,' he said.

Mr Finchley smiled in return.

'Yes, it is. I've been lying here watching it for a while. It certainly sets one at peace with the world.'

The man took a seat by his side, and presently lifted the odd cap from his head and dropped it to the turf, in order that the cool breeze might blow across his skull. Mr Finchley saw that the other was bald. They sat watching the silent moors. Two, bald-headed, short-bodied, middle-aged men, and the eyes of one held a growing contentment as he viewed the beauty and peace of the scene, while the eyes of the other were dark with shifting shadows, as though the joy of the hilltop were not enough to drive from his mind the thought of some unpleasant memory that was almost a fear. The stranger's eyes as he turned to Mr Finchley, were surprisingly furtive and held a queer spark of light that flickered vagrantly.

'Peace with the world?' murmured the stranger. 'That would be a fine thing. Peace doesn't come to stay with any nation, any town, or man; she just passes by, and passing, throws a light for a little while. When she has gone the land is altered, and nothing seems quite the same. Things, my friend, alter considerably with the years.'

Mr Finchley was impressed, as he was always impressed by anyone who could handle words to form conversation that appeared free and erudite. He answered, more from courtesy than hope to start a debate. 'Things alter ... only some things, perhaps you mean? Look at this moor. Here it is as it was a thousand years ago. Peace and warfare have passed over it, but it remains unchanged.'

The other slewed round on his turf mound at Mr Finchley's remarks. He shook his head sadly.

'You talk in terms of thousands of years; but peace, my friend, is universal. Peace in some form or other lasts for ever and outwears the very rocks. Peace is as old as the Universe, and in the age of the Universe a thousand years is no more than the dropping of a stone from a boy's hand. These stones, these hills and the bracken – what do they signify? Nothing. Soon they will be dust or ocean-bed. Listen, and I'll tell you a story that will prove my words. A well-known story and a true one. And when I have done you will see that in another thousand years this land we call England may well not be England at all, but a sunken shoal in the Atlantic and North Seas. You have read of Atlantis?'

Mr Finchley nodded. He had heard vaguely of the one-time continent which had formed a land connexion between the New World and the Old; but he was not sure whether the story was myth or fact.

His new acquaintance enlightened him. He told Mr Finchley the story of Atlantis. The story of an imperious race, strong in wisdom and body, which had built its cities of gold. His voice was alternately rich with pride and dull with sorrow. He spoke as though Atlantis had been but yesterday. When he described the end, how either the gods, in anger at the hardened hearts and proud voices of the people they had raised, or subsidences in the earth's surface, had brought about the obliteration of a whole race and an entire continent, his voice held a regretful note, and his eyes burned with a curious fire.

His passionate manner of telling the story aroused Mr Finchley's sympathy.

'I can see you have a very real feeling for this place, Atlantis,' he said, in an effort to convey his understanding. The effect was surprising.

The man sat bolt upright, and transfixed Mr Finchley with a fierce blue eye.

'You don't dispute, I suppose,' he said with a harshness that grated on the ear, 'that there *was* such a place as Atlantis?'

Mr Finchley felt very anxious to placate the fierce little man.

'No, no! Of course not! Why should I?' he answered, twirling his cap nervously between his hands.

'Why should you, indeed,' answered the other, smiling. 'You could not! Why should anyone deny what Plato has affirmed in his *Timaeus*? You know nothing, I presume, about burrowing amphisbaenidae?'

'No, no! I'm afraid not; but it sounds interesting – what is it?' asked Mr Finchley, dropping his cap to the turf at his side.

'Another proof,' answered his companion shortly. 'But people refuse to believe in insects. Biology, mythology, and even hagiology – no, they still refuse to acknowledge truth. And when men shut their eyes to truth, what hope has peace? We were, if you remember, talking of peace.' He was silent.

A car crawled along the road far below them. It stopped and three men descended from it. In the distance they

176

looked like ants. Their arms wavered above their heads, caressing the air antennae-wise.

'I must be leaving you.'

The man rose and began to descend through the bracken on the far side of the hill, away from the road. Mr Finchley rolled over on to his tummy and watched him climb down and finally disappear over the edge of a small valley. He sat up after a while, and saw that the men who had descended from the car were making their way up the hill. There were three of them, and they had spread out in a fan-shape along the skirt of the slope. Slowly they converged towards the top of the hill. Mr Finchley watched them idly and wondered for what they were searching.

The sun dropped behind the edge of the moors and the wind grew cold. Little clouds crept round the fringe of the horizon and, growing temerarious at the death of the day's sun, wriggled a slow way across the sky. The cold wind struck Mr Finchley's bald head. He reached for his cap, to discover that it was no longer where he had dropped it. Instead, at his side lay the odd shooting-cap of his Atlantis friend. He laughed.

He picked up the green horror and turned it over. It was almost new. A colder shaft of air struck his head and, anxious not to take cold, he put the cap on. It fitted him, and was comfortable and warm to his bald pate.

He was halfway down the hill, walking in the direction of the road, before he realized that his appearance had excited the three men. Until that moment his thoughts had been occupied with his Atlantis friend and the problem of a night's lodgings. He breasted a dip in the hillside, and rising above the bracken saw that the men were closing in upon him quickly and shouting to one another. He came to a halt and waited for them to reach him.

Probably, he thought, they want to ask me something.

The first man to reach him was a tall, well-set fellow, dressed in dark blue serge. The man halted at a distance of three yards from him. Mr Finchley could see the blunt

177

square toes of his heavy black boots squinting through the bracken stems. The man's conduct amazed him.

He stood his distance from Mr Finchley and, holding up a conciliatory hand, intoned clearly:

'All right now, all right! I believe every word you say and I know it's true. I know it's true. All right . . .'

He continued this motive with variations upon the original words for some time. Mr Finchley began to feel alarmed. He was about to speak or go up to the man, when the other two arrived, panting. Without any warning, they swept forward to him and bowled him over. The foremost got him by the throat and held him in a gentle manner, half a degree removed from throttling. The others pinioned his arms. Mr Finchley was too surprised, and the grip round his throat too tight to allow him to speak.

'Easy, there, Sam, easy! He ain't goin' to fight.'

'Now then! Up with him!' said the man who had reached him first, and who appeared to be in charge of the three. They lifted him to his feet. Sam released his grip round Mr Finchley's throat and stepped back. The other two men still gripped his arms.

'And I'll tell you, now that we've got you again,' said Sam, smiling slowly, 'that I don't really believe it at all! There, that puts us square? Come on, boys, lead him back to the van. I've wasted enough time on him!'

He trotted off. The two men jerked Mr Finchley by the arms and forced him to follow between them. Now that his throat was free he spoke. It said a lot of his last few days that he was still more or less self-composed.

'Would you be good enough to tell me exactly what all this means? What are you doing with me?'

The man at his right-hand side laughed, a delightful laugh, such as a schoolboy might make when a teacher commits a mistake in a sum on the blackboard. 'Good for you, Professor!'

He laughed again and his fellows joined in.

'But I insist upon you telling me what all this is about,' demanded Mr Finchley. 'Obviously, you've mistaken me for someone else. I'm on holiday!'

'Ay, and we've been on holiday since five this morning, looking for you. You ought to be ashamed of yourself,' scolded Sam.

'Now, look here!' stormed Mr Finchley, losing his temper. 'I can forgive your making a mistake, but this thing's going a bit too far. In a few minutes I shall have lost my temper and then ... and then – there'll be hell to pay!' He snapped his last words defiantly and tried to shake off his oppressors.

The outburst had a surprising effect on the three men. They stopped walking and looked, first at him, and then at one another with questioning glances. The leader shook his head as he eyed Mr Finchley's reddened face.

'All right,' he said at length, and he nodded to the other two. 'Better do it. I thought he was coming sensible.'

The other two hustled Mr Finchley along again, but now they gave him no time or opportunity to speak for as the three walked they intoned, in serious manner:

'Of course, we believe you! We've made a mistake. You could never be mistaken at all, Professor!'

And the refrain, which went, 'Of course, you're right. Of course, we've always believed you. Of course you're right. Of course, we've always believed you!'

Mr Finchley's anger was forgotten in his amazement. He was in the company of madmen! They might appear rational. They might look human; but they couldn't be. Otherwise, he argued, why should they have thrown themselves upon him and then forced him towards the roadway, singing as they went this idiotic refrain, telling him that they believed him, when up till that moment he had not opened his mouth or even seen them in his life before?

Still chanting, they reached the road. A small van was drawn up near the grass edge and in the low ditch by the roadside was a bicycle.

Sam stopped his chanting and the others did likewise.

'Never seen that bicycle before, have you, Professor?'

'Of course not!' snapped Mr Finchley, wriggling in their grip. 'And I'm not a professor!'

'Of course you haven't seen it. I was wrong,' apologized

Sam. 'No, you're no professor. I was wrong; we were all wrong!'

The man roared and slapped his thigh. At the same time a thought entered Mr Finchley's head, and the darkness of the situation was lightened. The man these fellows wanted was his Atlantis friend. Mr Finchley almost laughed, but he would not have been so confident could he have seen what a striking resemblance he bore to the other now that he was wearing the shooting-cap.

Mr Finchley had enough sense to know that he could not immediately persuade the men that they had made a mistake. All his assertions would be taken as proof of his insanity. They would just humour him. He decided to allow things to come to a head. When they reached the institution, then there would be time enough to make them see what a ridiculous mistake they had made. He enjoyed the prospect of Sam's ugly face all confused, and he pictured his stammering apologies. Perhaps, to atone for their behaviour towards him the authorities might offer him a bed and food. He had eaten nothing since lunchtime, and his stomach was aching. Perhaps they might . . .

'Come on, Professor,' urged one of the men, as Sam went round to the front of the old car to crank the engine. 'It'll be bread and water for you, I guess.'

Bread and water! A doubt crept into Mr Finchley's mind. If these men, who had probably known the other man intimately could make such a mistake, what might not the institution authorities do? Supposing, he thought, they refused to believe his story and treated it as a vagrant manifestation of his insanity? There had, he knew, because he was a solicitor's clerk, been many cases of quite sane people wrongly entombed in lunatic asylums . . .

While these thoughts were running through Mr Finchley's mind, the clouds, which at first had only fringed the sky, had now crept over the moor, bringing with them a gloomy darkness. The wind dropped and Mr Finchley felt a spot of rain on the back of his hand. At the same time, Sam who had been having some bother to start the engine, managed to do so. He jumped into the driving seat.

'Push him into the van,' he called.

The two men took him round to the rear of the van. One of them got in first and pulled Mr Finchley after him, while the other stood with his hand on the door ready to follow. The interior of the van was dark and smelt of dust and leather. The unpleasantness of the van seemed, to Mr Finchley, to be a promise of what he might expect when they reached their destination. His doubts were strengthened to convictions, and Mr Finchley's reaction to his convictions was admirable and dangerous.

'I won't stand this any longer!' he cried, and he gave the warder by his side a mighty dig in the stomach which sent him gasping into the corner of the van. Mr Finchley sprang forward towards the warder at the door. The look of incredutility on that worthy's face lasted two seconds and was terminated by a hard punch on the nose that sent him backwards upon his heels. Mr Finchley jumped to the ground and slammed the van door, which immediately locked on one warder.

An exultant feeling welling within his breast, Mr Finchley saw the bicycle. In a trice he had fished it from the ditch. As he rode off down the road in the opposite way to which the van was pointing, the imprisoned warder gave a bellow of alarm.

Sam's head came round the edge of the van like a marionette's.

'Whasermarrer?'

'He's gone!' cried the other warder, picking himself up. He pointed to where Mr Finchley was pedalling hard down the road. There came a hammering and thundering on the van door from the imprisoned warder.

'Quick, jump in!' shouted Sam, the man of action. 'He's a cute old bird, ain't he? Trust him to ride that way so we've got to turn the van first. Uh!' The 'Uh' was a curious mixture of admiration and scorn.

Ignoring the warder in the back, who continued his fulminations, they turned the van to pursue Mr Finchley.

At any other time they might have easily overtaken him. But now the weather was against them. By the time they had turned the van Mr Finchley was half a mile down the road and almost out of sight.

From a slight drizzle the rain had changed to a steady downpour, and high up round the tors a faint mist began to form and move slowly down the valley rifts and slopes. Dartmoor was on Mr Finchley's side. An hour before, the sun had been throwing long shadows across the ling and stone-crop; and now, the moor was veiling its face in tears and vapours with the suddenness of a child's mood.

Sam pressed the accelerator hard, and the van, quivering, leaped forward.

Mr Finchley's mackintosh was in his rucksack on his back and he was getting wet. The water from the road swirled up from the front wheel with a pleasant susurrus and played a graceful jet on to his legs. In three minutes his trousers were wet through and he could feel the shooting-cap growing heavier.

'Got to stick it if I don't want to spend the rest of my life in a lunatic asylum,' he muttered through his tight lips. He bent his head to the bars and pedalled furiously.

The road dipped and he travelled downward over the gleaming surface at a dangerous pace. At the bottom of the hill the road forked. Mr Finchley tried to take the left fork but the back wheel wobbled and induced the front wheel to follow its example. For one long, breath-taking, soul-frightening, heart-stopping, nerve-rattling instant the machine slid under him, jumped round him, spun about him and bucked like a mustang. Later, Mr Finchley swore that the handlebars had, in the brief moment of miscontrol, turned completely round and laughed in his face. He miraculously managed to retain his seat in the saddle, and when the wheels assumed their normal equilibrium and Mr Finchley felt more at home with the law of gravity, he found himself bowling down the right-hand fork straight for a large patch of mist which obscured everything before him.

He entered the mist. When only one yard of road is visible twenty miles an hour is a mad pace. He applied the brakes too vigorously and skidded. This time the bicycle won easily. The back wheel made a gallant attempt to caress the front wheel and, when the attempt was over, Mr Finchley was sitting in the ditch with a large boulder near his head and the machine settling comfortably around him so that the spokes of the front wheel formed a grill through which he surveyed a startled world.

The shock demoralized him and he sat in the ditch, resigned to his fate. Even a lunatic asylum would be safer than such a bicycle.

The malicious gods had not done with Mr Finchley!

Sam had seen Mr Finchley take the right-hand fork and he followed. Four minutes after Mr Finchley had hit the blanket of mist, the van charged into it like a juggernaut. The sudden murk forced all Sam's attention on the road, and Mr Finchley, still in his ditch, was surprised to see the grey shape of the van hurtle by him and vanish with a rattling into the distance.

The appearance of the car started him to action again. The rest had restored his courage and beating heart to normal. They had missed him that time, but they would soon be back.

'Come on, Bertha.'

He wriggled from under the bicycle and lifted it over the low hedge. He left it lying flat on the grass, where it could not be seen from the road. Taking his coat from his rucksack he buttoned himself closely about, and pulling down the side-flaps of his shooting-cap he started forward into the mist and moor, sure of one thing – he did not intend to be taken to any lunatic asylum that evening! He had not then, of course, realized that his only alternative was a night on the moors.

Mr Finchley had known London fogs. He knew the area a normal fog might cover. He knew that sometimes fogs upset the bus services. In London, however, even if the bus services stopped, there was always the Tube railway. He plunged into the mist, confident that before very long he would find his way out of it, and once out – a night's lodgings and the food he craved.

TWENTY-TWO

Of Flora Macdonald and Green Apples

MR FINCHLEY had been walking for two hours. During that time he had seen nothing but the grass and stones immediately beneath him and heard nothing but the sound of his own breathing and the steady drip, drip from every unseen blade of grass, from every rock-crevice and branch. Around him hung the mist. It played with him and made his feet catch in the gnarled roots of furze bushes so that he tripped and lay full length on the wet earth, glad of a rest he had not sought. It annoyed him, when he began to walk warily with an eye for roots, by painting continual curtains of mist drops on his eyelashes so that he walked and saw as one gazes through a hoar-rimmed window on a winter's morning. And when the mist had finished with his vision it produced tricks in his hearing. Little gurgles of laughter would burst from the gloom by his side, making him swing round and stiffen with fright. Once he could have sworn that he heard a man laugh and then a woman scream. His nerves were strung to such a pitch that when at last he fell wildly across a sheep curled away in a hollow, he leapt to his feet with a scared yell and relieved his feelings by fetching the animal a satisfying kick across the rump that sent it scurrying into the farther darkness, regretting its slow get-a-way.

He struck a match – the mist put it out for him. He struck another match and, guarding it from a breeze which had not existed until that moment, saw that it was gone ten o'clock.

At the end of another hour he had to admit he was lost, and looked like being lost for the rest of his life unless the mist lifted.

As he was now safely out of reach of his pursuers – if the warders had been foolish enough to assay pursuit on such a night – he determined to shout occasionally, in the hope that someone might hear him.

The effect of his first shout was electric and nearly prostrated him with fright. It was immediately answered by a chorus of echoes that bellowed back at him from the surrounding mist in countless variations and distortions.

'Hi!' shouted Mr Finchley.

'Hi! Eeyah! Hi! Yeeha! Hi! Hi! Hi! Hi!' laughed the mist.

He tried again, but always the mocking echo of his shout came back to him, and he decided to abandon the effort. Even if anyone heard him, and replied, he would probably mistake it for an echo.

He walked, for what seemed like a century, in pitch darkness, feeling his way cautiously forward. He was tired, he was hungry and – although he would not have admitted it – he was growing desperate and frightened. At half past eleven – he struck a match immediately afterwards to see the time – he walked into a low stone wall and drove the breath from his body. The blow gave him an excuse to vent his desperation and annoyance. He kicked the wall, regardless of the hurt to his foot, and swore. Calmed by this action he leaned against the stones, knowing that he could not go much farther.

Leaning there in the darkness and solitude, the wall, still warm from the day's sun in spite of the mist, came to him like an allegory of stability and shelter. He decided not to leave the wall. Walls meant civilization. Some man must have built it. He would stay there, and in the morning, when the sun came, perhaps the mist would be gone and he could find a house and food. The food problem was worrying him. He searched in his pockets and found some chocolate. It was warm and soggy and small pieces of fluff adhered to it. He ate it, fluff and all, and wished for more.

Slowly he felt his way along the wall. He had gone about a hundred yards when the mist and gloom before him took on a firmer, darker appearance. His outstretched hands saved him from walking into the side of a tin shed. Mr Finchley made his way to the front of the shed . . . he was saved! It was empty and dry, and quickly he decided to spend the night there.

Covering his wet coat with his rucksack he made a pillow and then drew for warmth over him a couple of sacks that smelt of manure. He went to sleep quickly. His whole body and mind cried for rest, so that the hard floor and filthy sacks might have been a feather mattress and blankets.

He awakened once in the darkness and thought that he could hear cattle lowing at a dog's bark. The idea of a house nearby almost tempted him out into the darkness, but the warmth of his sacks and the security of the shed proved a stronger attraction and he dropped his head and slept with gentle snoring.

Mr Finchley wakened with the sun shining through the open doorway of the hut upon his face. He sat up and stared about him. During the night the sacks had disengaged themselves from his body and were now crumpled about his feet. He felt cold and stiff. He stood up, and the effort almost crippled him. Never again, he thought; never again would he sleep on the ground. He looked down at the hard, earthen floor, tramped to brick-like solidity by the hooves of cows and the hobnails of labourers. Only darkness and despair could account for his sleeping in such a place.

He gathered up his coat and rucksack, and moved out into the sunshine. He was grateful for the warmth that spread around him as he left the hut.

He discovered that he was in a field at the head of a small valley which sloped downwards until it met, at right-angles, a larger valley. At the junction of the valleys was a small cluster of houses. Quite close to Mr Finchley was a gateway leading from the field in which he stood to a farmyard, where the white walls and grey roofs of a clump of barns, stables, and byres gleamed. Towering over the other buildings was a large white house, which was apparently the farmhouse.

'Well, I'll be . . .!' Mr Finchley exclaimed. If he had followed the wall another fifty yards he would have bumped into the end of the farmhouse. Last night those few yards had held for him all the terror of the dark Atlantic to a flyer, but now in the vivid sunshine they occasioned in him a pathetic querulousness. The analysis of his own inaction might have been pursued deeper, had he not been interrupted by a barking dog which tore round the corner of the farm and galloped towards him.

'Hullo! Hullo, old fellow!' Mr Finchley cried bravely, yet fearful that the dog might resent the familiarity. He distrusted dogs that barked and bounced.

'Hullo, old fellow!' He stretched out his hand to the circling dog, not very far, yet far enough to indicate to the dog that if he could reach him then he would pat him. The dog barked scornfully and continued to circle about Mr Finchley.

As Mr Finchley reached the gateway three small boys came running towards him from the farm.

They wore hobnailed boots, stiff ungainly creations that failed to control the impulse of their dancing, eager feet, and black jerseys and brown corduroy shorts.

'Hullo!' they said in chorus; and as the dog still kept up its barking, the tallest, who seemed to be the eldest, stepped forward and cuffed it on the flank. The barking stopped. The dog joined the three who had ranged themselves before Mr Finchley and barred his way to the farm.

'Hullo!'

They repeated their greeting.

'Hullo!' replied Mr Finchley, the sight of their round, healthy faces cheering him after his horrible night in the dark mist. 'Nice weather!' he added, as they continued to regard him curiously.

They looked at one another. The senior member, perhaps ten years old, with large owlish eyes and dark, crisp hair, said:

'It won't last long. I could hear the train coming up the valley from Plymouth this morning.'

'There weren't any rabbits feeding in the big field this morning, either,' added the middle one – a brown tangle of hair and dirty knees, although it was still not eight o'clock.

'And the barometer in the hall's going back!' finished the youngest. 'I heard them say so!'

'Well, well, you're all very cheerful, I must say,' laughed Mr Finchley.

They ignored his optimism.

'Where are you going?' asked the eldest.

'To find some breakfast,' answered Mr Finchley.

'What for?' asked the middle boy.

'Because I'm hungry.'

'So am I, and I've had breakfast!' The youngest shifted his pose and scratched the dog's head.

'Do you think your mother would give me some breakfast?' asked Mr Finchley. He nodded in the direction of the house.

'She couldn't,' replied the eldest.

'Why not?'

'She not here,' said the middle one.

'We're orphins,' finished the youngest.

'I'm sorry,' said Mr Finchley, genuinely touched by the pathetic group.

At this they all laughed and the dog barked unrebuked. Mr Finchley was perplexed by their outburst.

'You need not be sorry, really,' explained the eldest.

'Why . . . aren't you . . . but why not?'

'Because it's all a mistake,' went on the middle one.

'A mistake?'

'In the book, chapter ten,' finished the youngest, 'the three orphins was really three princes who got stoled in their cradles.'

'We thought you might be the king come to discover us.'

'Did I disappoint you?' Mr Finchley was relieved to discover that they were playing a game with him.

'You're not a king. You've got a tummy like the vicar's.'

Mr Finchley bowed before the inevitable.

'And you haven't had any breakfast. The king had bank . . . bank . . . feasts.'

'Since I can't be a king, perhaps I can get some breakfast. Let's try and see what we can do about it, eh?'

Mr Finchley stepped forward, and they drew themselves about him and followed in silence.

He made his way to the house and knocked on the door. A

short man, with bowed legs in riding breeches, his hands deep in his front pockets and a rakish red handkerchief round his neck, came out of the doorway.

'Good morning,' said Mr Finchley. 'I've just come across the moors; do you think the good lady could find some breakfast for me?'

The man stopped and looked him up and down.

'Ay, I 'spects so. Missus!' he called into the house. 'There's a gentleman here wants some breakfast. See what 'e can do for un. She'll fix you up,' he said cheerfully, and stepped by Mr Finchley.

'Hey, you robbers!' he called as he saw the three boys. 'What are you staring at? Come here!' He swept forward and gathered one under each arm, while the other jumped and clung to his neck. He turned and winked at Mr Finchley and then made his way across the yard, with a wriggling load of life and devilry clinging about him. The laughter of the boys remained in Mr Finchley's ears while he was eating the breakfast the good wife prepared for him.

What it was to be happily married and to have children. The proud way in which the farmer had looked back at him ... the solemn, deliberate looks of the boys. At that moment Mr Finchley regretted his bachelor fate. It was a selfish thing to let life die barren within one's breast at the going down of the sun ...

Mr Finchley ate his bacon and eggs reflectively, and eyed his green shooting-cap over the top of the *Western Morning News* which the woman brought him to read.

'The master hisself will be back in a minute to read it, but maybe you'd like it to look at while youm eatin'?'

'Thank you.'

He opened the paper, and turned to the cricket scores; then he folded back the middle page to read the political and chief news. The first thing he saw was a picture, full in the centre of the page, of the man of Atlantis. There he was, short and tubby, and dressed in the identical grey suit, and upon his head he wore the shooting-cap, which at that moment lay on the sofa at Mr Finchley's side. Under the picture was a headline:

189

With a peculiar sensation gripping at his stomach, Mr
Finchley read. The account was very short. Early in the preceding day an inmate of an asylum on the Plymouth fringe
of the moor had escaped on a bicycle and taken to the moors.
Acting on reports from various villages and other sources,
warders had followed the man and had caught him on a tor
quite close to Princetown. Mr Finchley, reading the description, recognized the incident in which he had played a
prominent part. The paper described his escape and then –
to Mr Finchley's horror – he learned that early in the night
the lunatic had broken into a cottage, stolen food and had
half killed a burly cottager who had disturbed him. The lunatic was still at large and dangerous. The paper gave a
detailed description. It might have been Mr Finchley they
were describing. The paper spoke of the man's idiosyncrasies;
his Atlantean theories, and how he invariably attempted to
strangle those who disagreed with his views. Mr Finchley's
throat contracted as he read.

He dropped the paper with an unpleasant feeling of guilt.
He stared across the room and saw the green shooting-cap
on the sofa. The whole countryside would be on the look-out
for the lunatic; and there was one thing which would
identify him! He stared in horror. There it was, crumpled and
damp, the cap which would set half the county about his
ears if he appeared in it. If he took five steps down the village
street he would be surrounded by an eager mob, men with
guns, men with pitchforks, men with rakes, men with
manure prongs; all eager to still him before he could explain. He breathed a prayer that so far he had met no one
but the farmer and his boys.

He rose to his feet and reached for the cap, and was standing with it in his hand when the woman came in.

'Do 'e mind if I have the paper for the master, sir?' she
asked pleasantly.

Mr Finchley smiled absently, he was thinking hard.

'Thank you, sir,' she said as she took the paper.

'Oh, before you go, I might as well settle up with you,' Mr Finchley said quickly. He did not want to be in the house while they were reading the paper.

'Just as you like, sir,' she said, and mentioned the amount due from him.

Mr Finchley felt in his pocket for his money. The action caused him to loosen his grip on the cap. It fell to the ground, and the woman, good-naturedly, picked it up for him.

'Reminds me of the hat me father used to wear,' she said. She counted his money.

'Yes ... yes ... they are a little old-fashioned nowadays,' admitted Mr Finchley, cursing the providence which had sent the conversation in such a direction.

He left the farmyard hurriedly. He did not know in which part of the moor he was, or in which direction he wished to go. He blindly followed a little trail which started away from the gate up the hillside, and passing through two fields of sainfoin, finally met the moor. Halfway up the hillside he sat down to think. He had a lot of thinking to do.

Mr Finchley sat for nearly a quarter of an hour. One thing was obvious, he must get rid of the cap. So far he had escaped detection, but if he continued to wear it, he was merely asking for trouble, and trouble, since he was on holiday, was the last thing he wished to meet. That much decided, Mr Finchley felt a little happier. Almost happy enough to perceive the droller side of the affair. He knew now why the warders had volubly insisted upon agreeing with him ... and where, he wondered, was the real lunatic? The immediate danger having passed by, Mr Finchley sat on his hillock, enjoying the morning and the pleasant afterglow of a good breakfast. Recently he had missed his meals so often that when he did eat it was with a voracious, healthy appetite which he had never known in London. His indigestion had not worried him for a long time.

From where he rested, the hillside moved slowly down to the broken line of hedge that marked the beginning of the fields, and below the fields the land dipped sheerly away to the valley. It fell so sharply that Mr Finchley could no longer see the farmhouse. He could just make out the faint blue tail of smoke drifting up from the hollow, and see the tips of the elms in the yard, and hear the distant stir of cattle and fowls. On his left the moor came tumbling down to the valley in a riot of royal ling and gorse. High above the far line of the moor hung white shell-puffs of clouds.

He took out his pipe and lighted it. A pipe that drew well was Mr Finchley's greatest aid to the appreciation of beauty. He took two or three draws and then tossed the green cap into the bracken at the side of the path. He regretted having to jettison it, but necessity compelled him to do so. He was tired of being a lunatic. He wanted to be himself again.

Mr Finchley was roused from his musings by a shout. Not a friendly shout; but a loud, ragged shout that came from the throat of more than one man. He looked up, startled.

In the gateway of the field below him, and already swarming upwards to the moor along the path he had taken, was a bunch of about ten men. They all carried sticks or weapons of some fashion. Two of the men had guns. The cold barrels signalled to him in the sunlight.

'Eeeeeeeeeyah!'

The cry came again and Mr Finchley thought of wolves. He did not stop to reason; he knew what had happened. The farmer had read his morning paper, and it had not taken him long to get help.

Springing to his feet, Mr Finchley started to run up the hill. His flight confirmed the suspicions of the men, and with another howl they set themselves to the chase eagerly. They were tough, long-limbed, wiry labourers and moorsmen, who could run tirelessly over the uneven ground.

Mr Finchley dipped over the brow of the tor and for the moment had the whole of the moor on that side to himself. He hesitated. The path led downhill for about a hundred yards into a small fir wood, emerged lower down and finally crossed a stream. Mr Finchley was hunted, and fear sharpened his wits. He knew that he was no match for these men when it came to running. As he left the crest of the hill he had an idea. They would assume that he would make straight along the path for the wood, so he decided not to do so. No sooner was he out of sight than he turned sharply at right-angles to the path. Stooping low in the bracken, and skirting the clumps of furze, he made his way along the side of the ridge. He had travelled a good two hundred yards before the first man came dashing into sight. Mr Finchley dropped flat on his chest in the grass, well hidden by a piece of outcropping stone. The man was almost instantly joined by three others. They stood for an instant, baffled.

Mr Finchley saw them point to the wood and simultaneously they dashed down the path in that direction. Mr Finchley smiled: though he was not aware of it himself. The rest of the pursuers soon appeared and, noting the direction the first men had taken, they hurried after them. When they smell blood, men act as stupidly as Panurge's sheep.

Lying in the grass, Mr Finchley watched the men reach the wood. The dark line of trees swallowed them up one by one. From the tips of the firs a couple of wood-pigeons rose and clipped a quick way down the valley. A vixen, frightened at the noise of shouting and trampling feet, slipped out from the far end of the wood and came lolloping up the hillside, to pass within a stone's-throw of Mr Finchley.

Mr Finchley started to wriggle backwards up the hill. Carefully he wormed his way through the deep undergrowth. Unbending furze bushes pricked his skin: black vetch pods burst around him with malicious explosions, but he took no notice. Once a little brown lizard, basking on a flat stone, flipped its red tongue at him and then disappeared like magic. The lizard reminded him of vipers. He sweated. A huge spider with a white cross on its back threatened him where it swayed in a web which it had slung between two whin bushes. Mr Finchley made a detour and discovered an ants' nest. Not daring to raise himself, he crawled over the mound, and was rewarded by little stinging sensations in his hands and ankles. A leveret lying out in the sun nearly occasioned his downfall as he put his hand into a clump of tall grasses on to its warm fur. His heart thumped in time to the animal's jumps as it sprang away. To add to his discomforts and fears a ladybird got wedged under his shirt and tickled him until he was forced to release it by pulling his shirt free, at the front, from his trousers. His rucksack kept slipping from his back and impeding his progress. Yet, in spite of everything, he managed to move up to the tor top, with a craftiness worthy of an Indian.

He reached the top of the ridge as the men, exhausting its possibilities, left the wood on the far side and headed for the stream.

Mr Finchley slipped over the ridge and breathed again now that the whole of the tor was between him and his pursuers. He worked his way along the hill until the farm was far below him on his left, and then, throwing caution to the winds, he stood upright. Following a sheep-track, he rapidly made his way into the heart of the moor.

Now that he was free of his pursuers, Mr Finchley was not anxious to encounter any more trouble, and he decided to find a quiet spot where he could lie hidden during the day. There was a fairly good moon and, if he were spared from mist, he could put a good twenty miles between himself and the farm during the night. The moment he reached a town or bus route he knew he would be saved.

Mr Finchley's action, although he did not fully know it, was a wise one. The farmer had informed the police of his discovery, and a forty-mile cordon was quickly drawn round the farmhouse.

It did not take Mr Finchley long to find a hiding-place. The moor was full of pits and hollows that were overgrown with bracken and bushes. He found a hollow, sheltered at the back by a leaning slab of rock, moss-covered and grey, and on its other sides by tall bracken growths and stunted sloe trees. Into this hollow Mr Finchley crept and, cool in the shadow of the stone, he settled himself to pass the day. He had plenty of tobacco and matches; his one anxiety was for food. Drink he could get by crawling to a nearby stream which, from his retreat, he heard trickling merrily. The whortle-berries were not yet ripe and the sloes looked hard and sour, so he would go hungry.

It was eight o'clock when he left the farm. By twelve o'clock he was feeling hungry and cramped and wondering how he would survive until the evening. Only once had he been disturbed and that was by the passing of a shepherd. The man had ridden by on his long-haired horse, not ten yards from Mr Finchley's hollow. Mr Finchley held his breath, but the other did not suspect his presence. He would have been less fearful had he known that the shepherd had just come up from the farm, where he had been told that the real lunatic had recently been caught at Mary Tavy, nearly ten miles away. The news had come through to the village Post-Office, and the whole village was endeavouring to solve the mystery of the green shooting-cap, which had been found where Mr Finchley was seen sitting; endeavouring to solve, indeed, the whole mystery of Mr Finchley.

Meanwhile, Mr Finchley, unable to eat, tried to forget his hunger by sleeping. He dozed fitfully for a long time before he finally dropped off to sleep; and then he slept peacefully for nearly two hours. The certainty that no one had observed his clever elusion of the men made his sleep deeper and calmer. No one would dream of looking for him in this part of the moor.

Mr Finchley was mistaken. Three persons had seen him come back over the top of the tor and had watched him slip into the moor.

Mr Finchley wakened, with the vague feeling that he was being observed. He looked at his watch. It was three o'clock. As he raised his head he saw a face staring at him from the opposite side of the hollow. He imagined momentarily that he must still be partly asleep and seeing things. He rubbed his eyes and looked again. The face was still there. It moved slightly. A round, solemn, dark-eyed face, that made Mr Finchley think of pixies; only the pixies whose pictures he had seen in books never wore poke-bonnets. This face was crowned by an old-fashioned poke-bonnet, caught up on one side by a tenacious thistle and tied under the chin with ribbons.

'Who are you?' said Mr Finchley, suspiciously and fearfully. He was still not sure about the face.

'Sssssssssh!'

The face developed arms and a warning hand was lifted.

The movement proved too much for both the soft crumbling edge of the pit and the poke-bonnet. They collapsed, and a small boy was shot ungracefully on to the grass at Mr Finchley's feet. He recognized the youngest of the farmer's three boys.

'Sssssssh!' the boy repeated. 'The king's men are about!'

'The king's men?' queried Mr Finchley, wondering what was going to happen now that he had been discovered.

'Yes; they're looking for you with swords!'

Mr Finchley began to understand, and he entered into the spirit of the game.

'Are they? Then they'll never take me alive! Who are you?'

'I'm Flora Macdonald,' replied the boy, 'but I didn't want to be!'

He wriggled himself to a sitting position and produced a paper bag from behind his back.

'I've brought you your provisions. We were going to kill a fowl for you, but Roy's penknife wasn't sharp enough, so they gave me a back to get through the pantry window.'

Mr Finchley unwrapped the paper and found a huge pasty. Food!

The boy looked at him, all eyes. Mr Finchley's mouth twitched humorously. He took a stick and stood up, carefully.

'Although I'm only an outcast prince,' he said, in as grand a voice as he could command, 'one day I shall be King of England and that day shall see you an earl at my side!'

He tapped the youngster lightly on the head with the stick, and then turned to the pasty.

The boy was impressed. His thin body wriggled ecstatically. He did not even question the possibility of a king being able to pronounce a woman an earl.

'My men are ready to die for you, sire,' he piped, and added: 'That was the biggest pasty I could find.'

He watched Mr Finchley eating, and there was a deep admiration in his eyes as he measured each mouthful.

'I suppose,' said the boy, when Mr Finchley was halfway through the pasty, 'Flora didn't really want to be a girl, did she?'

'No, no!' replied Mr Finchley, out of the corner of his mouth. 'Her greatest wish was to be a man so she could fight with the prince's forces.'

'Do you mind if I take this off, then?' He tugged at the crumpled poke-bonnet.

Mr Finchley shook his head.

'They said I had to wear it all the time. It's too hot!'

'How,' said Mr Finchley, when he had finished the pasty, 'did you find me?'

'We saw you from the top of the elm. You can see all over the tor from it.'

The boy told him how they had climbed the elm which stood in the corner of the farmyard, and had watched Mr Finchley and the pursuing party. They had seen him double back over the hillside and had conceived the idea of playing Bonnie Prince Charlie with a real fugitive. For the once, the favourite part of the prince had not been available for either of the three, but this had not prevented the old poke-bonnet from descending on the youngest boy again. The others, he told Mr Finchley, were hunting for food for the prince.

They talked for a while and then without any excuse the boy put on his bonnet, and with a backward wave of his hand, climbed out of the pit and wriggled away into the bracken. Mr Finchley watched him go, and in his heart was the same mixed feeling of envy and disappointment which had assailed him that morning. He had no qualms of being discovered. The boys would treat him as a secret and he might lie hid without fear until nightfall. The rest of the afternoon passed slowly.

The boys respected his secret – due partly to the fact that their parents had refused, at lunchtime, to tell them what all the commotion had been about – but Mr Finchley knew that they were still hanging about. At five o'clock he heard a scuffling in the tangle at the right-hand side of the pit, and suddenly four green apples, a chunk of stale cake and a weighted match-box containing a note were tossed into the hiding-place. Mr Finchley collected the things and opening the match-box discovered the note. It was written in a round-hand, and read:

'Lie hid till nightfall. We will yet save you from the glutine. The aples is better bruised first.

THE SCARLET PIMPERNEL.'

Mr Finchley chuckled. Evidently they had tired of Bonnie Prince Charlie. He looked at the hard, bright-green apples and, taking the boys' advice, commenced to bruise them methodically on a stone before eating them.

Left to himself again, Mr Finchley's thoughts recurred to his awkward position. As long as he stayed on the moor and knew not if the lunatic were still at large, he was unsafe. It was too late now, he felt, to hope to make a satisfactory explanation before some injury was done to him. He was an outcast, with every man's hand against him!

Night came at last. There was a moon, five days past the full, and striking sparks of quicksilver from the outcrops of stone. Taking his direction by the moon (he had to think for a few moments – did it rise in the east or west?), he set out across the moor in the direction of Plymouth. He had no idea how far he was from the town and his map helped him not at all. Since being chased by the warders he had lost all sense of direction.

The night was cool and made walking pleasant. At first Mr Finchley proceeded cautiously. He met no one, and emboldened by the spreading solitude and peace of the moors, he strode vigorously across the ling and soft turf. The action of his muscles, the easeful sweep of his legs, and the feeling of hard ground beneath him came like a balm after his cramped day in the pit. There was little wind, and the only life he saw came from the sheep that browsed in the moonlight and the rabbits that flashed dim signals before him in the night. A great velvet moth *burred* into his face, and sent a spasm of quick fear volleying down his spine, and he almost screamed.

He walked for three hours while above him the moon moved steadily and the Bear shone feebly, low on the horizon. Once from the pale sky a shooting-star drew a curve of instant fire, and Mr Finchley stopped, caught up in its beauty. The wake of flame died like the fading of a note in a still room.

Slowly the nature of the country began to change, and he knew that he was leaving the moor. The land was broken into mad geometric sectors by crumbling walls of flat stone. Low oaks and copses of beech and sycamore gave way to tall chestnut and elms. He came into a grass-grown lane and passed a silent cottage. A dog barked and he hurried on. The lane led into a field, and at the far side, Mr Finchley, now tired with his long walk, saw a haystack, and beyond the haystack a row of concrete posts that guarded a railway track.

He reached the rick and stopped to take his bearings. The rail track, he knew, was a main one, because there were two sets of lines. He pulled some hay from the rick and lay down to have a quick nap before continuing his walk. He woke once to hear a train rattling by, and as he opened his eyes he saw the brightly lit windows swirl before him like a cinema screen, saw nodding heads and faces that gaped through the glass into the blankness of the night and the red eye of the guard's light bobbing into the distance. He slept again.

TWENTY-THREE

The Influence of a Scarlet Bathing Costume

MR FINCHLEY jumped a train. He had seen it done on the films – and it looked dangerous. He had read in magazines of men who did it – it was said to be simple for a real hobo – but now he had done it himself. He found that it was one of those acts which happen with such rapidity that one is unconscious of the effort and conscious only of the subsequent heart-beating and pride. It had all happened very quickly and while he was still thick with sleep. He had wakened to find a goods train pulled up alongside the field in which he had slept. The signals were against it. Fifty yards up the track the engine puffed jets of steam and shoals of cascading sparks into the air. Far down the line the green eye of a signal twinkled.

'If this were America I should jump that train,' Mr Finchley murmured to himself.

'This ain't America, so don't try it!' the engine seemed to snort.

'You're not going to take that lying down, are you?' something whispered to Mr Finchley.

'He's got to!' rumbled the engine. 'This ain't America!'

Maybe it was the defiant attitude of the train, maybe Mr Finchley was still dreaming a little, or perhaps it was the very low truck opposite him on the line.

'What is a holiday without change and excitement?' Mr Finchley asked, as he collected his mac and rucksack.

'You sheer off!' warned the train and whistled fiercely. The green eye nodded the train on. Pistons jerked. The train moved off and with it went Mr Finchley. To step on the axle grease-box and clutch the top of the truck was easy. To wriggle inboard was a little harder, but he did it, and found that he was in the company of five thousand, methodically arranged, roof tiles. Their serried rectangles gleamed at him like friendly slabs of anaemic chocolate. Thinking of chocolate made him hungry and he settled down in a corner of the truck on a tarpaulin to sleep. Mr Finchley had discovered that sleep was the best anodyne for hunger, and he found sleeping easy to achieve.

For all the concern which he showed Mr Finchley might have been an old hand at train riding. The motion of the truck rocked him to a deep slumber, and the clang of meeting buffers as the goods train pulled in and out of stations and stopped at points went unheard by him.

He was roused early in the morning by a sharp shower of rain. It was light, and the train was passing at a fair speed through a country of viaducts and deep woods. Once, as they rumbled across a viaduct, its five fingers reaching down firmly into the valley sides, he caught a glimpse of a narrow, mud-lined creek, and up the valley came a stiff breeze, carrying with it the tang of the sea. Sheltering from the rain by pulling the tarpaulin round his shoulders, he tried to catch the names of the stations, being careful not to show himself. Presently they sped through a large station and he read – St Austell. The name was familiar. While he had slept the goods train had carried him far from Dartmoor and Devon, through Plymouth and Bodmin down into Cornwall. He wondered how he should escape without attracting attention.

It was well past breakfast-time when the train slowed up with a signal against it. The puffing engine calmed itself, and presently there was a crescendo of clanging buffers. Mr Finchley was jolted on to his back as his truck came to a standstill. He was on his feet in an instant. At one side of the truck was a huge mound of clay and slag, and above the line of the mound he could see the upper works of a pit-head. The other side of the track was dark with trees.

He peered over the edge of the truck; no sign from the guard's van. The engine-driver had his head out of his cabin, looking up the line. Mr Finchley gripped the truck-side and swung himself over. His feet felt for the grease-box, found it, slipped on the waste grease and he fell backwards from the truck to the safety of a bank of nettles in the ditch at the side of the track.

Two minutes, two of the longest minutes in Mr Finchley's life, passed, and then the signal flicked, the train grunted and the trucks commenced to trundle from him. The guard's van swayed by and he was left alone.

He jumped from the nettles and danced. He sought dock leaves to wrap about his hands. There were no docks, only a coarse plant with leaves like those of a large rhubarb. He plucked these and, holding them around his wrists, climbed through the rails into the woods.

He emerged from the wood to find himself on a main road. A little way down the road was an inn. Mr Finchley ordered breakfast, though it was nearer lunchtime, and while it was being prepared he washed himself and tidied his appearance.

With a morbid satisfaction he noted that his nettle stings were coming out on his wrists and hands in large, ugly white patches. He learned from the landlord that he was ten miles from St Ives, and that a bus passed the inn every half-hour.

The mental picture of a bus, and comfortable, well-sprung seats, contrasted strongly with the dust of a main road and the heat of a fierce sun which had taken a notion to appear. He gauged his eating to enable him to catch the next bus. At one o'clock he stepped from the bus to the flagstones of St Ives.

The clean, crowded town, the happy holidaymakers, and the spirit of warmth and fraternity in the air stirred Mr Finchley. The men he saw were all brown and healthy, in clean white shirts and comfortable sports jackets, and the women floated by in light summer frocks. Seeing his own reflection in the plate glass of a shop after the man had passed, Mr Finchley was seized with shame. He was happy, healthy and brown, but he had to admit that, although he might personally be clean, his clothes had suffered terribly.

It was a different Mr Finchley who, two hours later, wandered through the narrow streets to the beach. He had been busy. He had found a lodging for the night, but before doing so he had made various purchases.

He went into the lodgings, our Mr Finchley, his tonsure brown and shining, his trousers creased into easy folds, and his khaki shirt bravely hiding its wealth of dirt. He still carried his rucksack and his mac. He also held in his arms a large paper parcel. His landlady, a tall, angular woman, with suspicion in the place of a soul, eyed him doubtfully. Her qualms vanished as she watched, from behind the parlour curtains, the spruce Mr Finchley who stepped jauntily down the front steps and made for the bathing beach, with a newly-purchased scarlet bathing costume dangling from his arms.

That scarlet costume had been a final gesture. He was wearing new grey flannels (ready-made, but they fitted everywhere except where it did not really matter), a brown-checked sports jacket, open-necked cricket shirt of a faint blue tinge, and a pair of comfortable shoes (his old ones were worn thin with so much walking); but not a hat. He had grown to like the feeling of the wind and sun upon his head . . .

He swung down the rocky steps into the bathing cove and

felt rather sorry for, and superior to, the crowd of laughing people, who were so obviously content to rusticate in one spot for a couple of weeks and call it a holiday.

Mr Finchley bathed. The edge of the surf was noisy with happy bathers, and he swam slowly and laboriously out to sea to escape the hubbub. His feeling of superiority was still with him and he was loath to splash and gambol in the shallows with the other bathers. He fell into a contemplative state of mind and swam on, not realizing how far out he was going. After the mad, rushing action of the last few days he was glad to escape into this quiet corner, where he could lie still on his back with the waves rocking him gently. To think and feel the lazy hours floating by as the idle gulls floated by him overhead . . . Mr Finchley wanted nothing more than that.

From the middle of the bay the tall brown cliffs, the red-and-white ice-cream stalls and the bathing huts might have been the creations of a child. A toyland of coloured plasticine and bricks. The jumbled houses and scattered beaches . . . mused Mr Finchley; they had nothing to do with him. He was alone and supreme with all the sea to call his own. So he thought until there came a gentle splashing behind him, and a small apologetic voice said aloud with the obvious intention that Mr Finchley should hear:

'I really don't think that I shall be able to reach the beach without help!'

Mr Finchley rolled over and discovered behind him another swimmer.

'I beg your pardon?' he said politely, treading water.

'I said that I don't think I can manage to reach the shore without help,' repeated the other. The speaker was a woman.

'Do you mean that you are drowning?'

The woman trod water weakly. She smiled as Mr Finchley asked his question, and the little trace of concern on her dark features faded.

'Hardly; but I think I very soon shall unless I get back to the beach. You see, I swam out too far – and now – I know it's very silly of me – I can't swim all the way back. Would it be spoiling your bathe if you helped me?'

Mr Finchley laughed gallantly, and swallowed water.

'Not at all! I shall be delighted! Let me see . . .' He swam slowly round the woman, his brows contracted in thought.

'I think,' he said after he had completed his circuit, 'that the best thing for you to do is to lie flat on your back with your arms resting on my shoulders and I'll float you back.'

'Oh, thank you so much!' she smiled, a wonderful smile that made Mr Finchley understand why St George killed the dragon.

'Well, let's try it, shall we?'

She lay floating on her back and Mr Finchley, pushing her before him, started in an eager breast-stroke for the beach. For the first fifty yards her weight was no strain to him. The woman was very light and Mr Finchley was quite fresh.

They were still a good distance from the shore, when Mr Finchley began to find that the woman was not so light as he imagined. At every stroke he felt the pressure of her body, where her hands rested upon his shoulder, growing heavier. He said nothing. They struggled for another ten yards and Mr Finchley realized that he was slowly sinking deeper into the water. His arms were aching with the strain and he had great difficulty in keeping his head above water.

'Is it,' the woman said suddenly, 'very far now?' She could not see the beach from her position.

'Not far,' Mr Finchley gasped. The beach was a good twenty yards distant from them.

'Perhaps I could manage by myself,' she said. 'I feel much rested now.'

Her sentence was terminated by an ominous *plop!* as Mr Finchley's head went under water definitely and deeply.

'Ooooch!'

He came to the surface and blew. His face was red and his eyes were wide with momentary panic.

The woman came to his side.

'Are you all right?' she asked anxiously. She, herself, now appeared to be recovered.

'Yes, I'm all right. What about you?' Mr Finchley splashed weakly and did not attempt to say any more. A lean, strong arm came under his own and supported him.

'Let's see if we can do it together.' Saying no more, she set out for the beach, swimming with one arm and supporting Mr Finchley with the other. Mr Finchley, appreciating the fundamental truth of the old saying that discretion is the better part of valour, did likewise.

To anyone watching from the beach there did not appear to be anything unusual happening. If two people liked to swim a fantastic breast-stroke there was no law against it. Fortunately they were not far from the beach. Presently Mr Finchley felt bottom. He stood up and blew a mighty breath of relief.

'I'm a fine fellow to offer to save you, and then finishing by letting you save me!' he said shamefacedly.

'Oh! It was nothing of the kind!' she asserted vigorously as they left the water. 'I think it was very brave and noble of you to help me when you must have known that you, too, were tired. I shall never forget it!'

Mr Finchley looked at her quickly. He did not stare at her because she was in a green bathing costume and it would have been rude, but he looked at her long enough to see that she meant what she said. Something about her seemed familiar to him.

'Anyone would be only too happy to be of some small service to you!' replied Mr Finchley handsomely, and then, abashed at his own gallantry, dived into his bathing tent with a mumbled ' 'Scuse me!'

He finished his dressing and stepping outside his tent found her waiting.

'Oh!'

'Oh!'

The exclamations came simultaneously from them.

'But you're Mr Finchley!'

'But you're Mrs Crantell!'

They began; and then realizing how funny they must appear to one another they laughed together.

'Well I never!' said Mr Finchley, when they had finished

laughing. 'Fancy my not recognizing you. I never expected to see you here.'

'And I didn't expect Mr Finchley to rescue me from drowning.'

'Not quite that. It was the other way round.'

'We won't argue about that. It is so nice to meet you again.'

Mr Finchley was pleased. Mrs Crantell was a valued client of Bardwell & Sprake. On her husband's death Mr Finchley had taken charge of her papers.

'Are you on holiday?' she asked.

Mr Finchley nodded. They moved along the beach. The dry sand scrunched beneath his new shoes and, though he would not say why, he was glad that he had treated himself to a new outfit.

Mrs Crantell the client was one person, but Mrs Crantell on holiday, Mr Finchley discovered, was quite a different person. She was a small, dark-haired little woman with vivacious eyes and lips and a pretty manner of looking up into a person's eyes as she spoke, so that it seemed as though she spoke alone for them. Mr Finchley found her manner most attractive.

She was, she said, stopping in St Ives for another week. She was all alone. Was he, Mr Finchley, by himself, too? Mr Finchley said that he was.

In a quarter of an hour Mr Finchley felt that he had known her for a long time, and she was beginning to feel that, had she known Mr Finchley before, her life since the death of her husband might not have been so dull and lonely.

They had tea at a little café. Mr Finchley watched her pour for him. He almost blushed as she said: 'One or two, Mr Finchley?'

She was staying at an hotel, quite close to him. She asked him what he had been doing and how long he had been in St Ives, and gradually Mr Finchley found himself telling her the long story of his adventures since he had left London. Her merriment or sympathy, the understanding with which she met each recountal and the interest she took throughout his tale made talking a pleasure to him. He boldly coloured a few incidents to his own advantage, and her eyes opened wide with wonder, but a little smile played about the corners of her mouth the while.

At six o'clock they were still talking, though the tea in the pot was stone cold.

At seven the slight wind died away as the tide went out. The heat of the town and the warmth of the evening air drew them to the beach for another swim. This time they swam together and kept close inshore.

They spent the whole of the evening together and when the moon brightened in the night sky they were still together, making their way back along the cliff to St Ives.

Mr Finchley left her at the door of her hotel and went home happy and humming to himself. He undressed and sat on the edge of his bed for a long time before he thought of sleep. He was thinking of Mrs Crantell and the outing which they had planned for the next day to Land's End by charabanc.

Mr Finchley slept. Down on the deserted beach the tide crept back again to claim for a few hours the sands that during the day teemed with the invasion from the town. Over the sea hung the quartering moon. Across the mirrored surface of the water moved the noises of the night and the flitting shadows of cormorants winging their black way low over the sea.

TWENTY-FOUR

How Mr Finchley finds one Thing and loses Another

MR FINCHLEY was disappointed with the ride to Land's End. He had expected the whole of Mrs Crantell's company and resented sharing her with another man. Henry Fadewaite was his name, a tall, ageing, grey-haired man with a slight stoop, who was staying at her hotel. He, too, appeared not to relish the presence of Mr Finchley on the other side of Mrs Crantell as they all sat in the long back seat on the coach.

Mrs Crantell, with an impartiality that was amusing to

everyone, except Mr Finchley and Mr Fadewaite, showed that so far as she was concerned, she had no preference at all. She might advise Mr Finchley of balms for his nettle-rash when he showed her his white-plotched wrists, but it was no more than a humane interest, and Mr Fadewaite found it hard to tell whether her concern for a slight cold which he had been unfortunate enough to contract, arose from a genuine interest in his condition, or from a fear that she might possibly be affected by his ailment. So they talked amiably to her as the coach rumbled through the narrow dusty lanes, and glared at one another whenever she was not looking at them.

Perhaps Mrs Crantell saw Mr Finchley's hostility. It may only have been a whim on her part, or she may have definitely resolved to rouse Mr Finchley's jealousy; he was not to know, but as they neared Land's End he sensed that she was paying far more attention to Mr Fadewaite. Mr Finchley was disconsolate. For long intervals he found himself sitting silently, holding her spectacle case while she chattered to Mr Fadewaite. Sometimes seeing the hardly concealed misery in his eyes she turned round and lightened his worlds with a smile and some remark, and then, as Mr Finchley took fresh hope, turned to Mr Fadewaite.

Mr Finchley's gloom increased. It seemed to him that the warm, confiding woman of the previous evening had never existed. There was only this hard, merry, laughing person who talked to Mr Fadewaite as though he were the only other person in the coach, as though there were not twenty other people around them, and following close behind another coach similarly loaded.

Mr Finchley decided that it was a hard world. He decided that he did not care if she would not speak to him. Why should she? he asked himself belligerently. Why should she? Although he could not prevent himself from being down-hearted because she did not show him the same consideration as she did the other, he knew that he had no reason – except for private little romancings in his own heart – for expecting her to do so.

He repulsed with a polite snarl the effort of the man on his left to talk to him. This other, a retired schoolteacher, smiled and left him alone.

At Land's End the party split into groups that wandered away over the turf and cliffs to look at the views, and to buy postcards or crested vases. Mr Finchley, in a group composed of the retired teacher, Mrs Crantell, Mr Fadewaite, and two maiden ladies, with withered dewlaps like lizards, headed for the extremity of the cliffs.

Mrs Crantell and Mr Fadewaite walked in front. Mr Finchley walked behind, with his head hung down a little.

They stood on the cliff-edge and watched the green waves beating against the jumble of rocks below.

'Oh! How pretty those gulls look floating below us!' cried Mrs Crantell, as the gulls wheeled over the sea on steady wings.

'They look,' said Mr Finchley, with a desperate effort to force himself into the picture, 'almost like washing which has escaped from a line to float about in the air . . .'

Mr Fadewaite laughed nastily.

'To me they seem more like the souls of forgotten seamen. To compare them with washing is almost a reflection upon their beauty and grace. What do you think, Mrs Crantell?' he asked.

'Oh, I agree with you!' echoed Mrs Crantell, giving Mr Finchley a swift sideways glance which in his annoyance he did not see.

Mr Finchley swore under his breath. The idiot! What, he demanded of himself fiercely, did that old fool know about sailors if he imagined that their souls were as white as the flashing wings below?

They moved away, and Mr Fadewaite caught Mrs Crantell's arm to help her over a rock. Mr Finchley saw the action, and decided suddenly to remain upon the headland and let them go on.

The party was fifty yards from the headland before Mrs Crantell discovered that Mr Finchley was not with it. She looked round. He was nowhere to be seen. Behind her the ground sloped upwards a few yards, and the rest of the headland was hidden by some upstanding rocks.

'Wherever,' she said, and for the first time with interest, 'is Mr Finchley?'

'Oh, he'll be along in a few minutes, no doubt,' answered Mr Fadewaite.

'Don't you think we'd better wait for him?'

'I don't think I would if I were you!'

The retired schoolteacher thrust himself forward, and there was a humorous wrinkle to his mouth. 'He knows that we're having lunch at the hotel and if he loses us now he'll be there when we get back.'

Mr Finchley, meanwhile, had wandered away in the opposite direction.

He came to a place where a steep rift made a way sheer into the cliff-side. He climbed down a few yards and found a comfortable patch of moss.

At his side a hidden stream sang its way under the turf, and bulbous campions shook their white balloons in the breeze. He lay still and enjoyed the warm sun. Around him the great rock sides of the cliff stretched their blue and grey arms to the sky.

Mr Finchley filled his pipe. It was half past twelve. The party had agreed to lunch at the hotel at one. He decided to smoke for half an hour. He wondered how Mrs Crantell would receive him. The coach was leaving at half past two to return through Penzance. He made a pillow with his mackintosh and lay back to enjoy himself. For a time he smoked and was happy. The minutes passed and he grew drowsy.

He was genuinely surprised when he awakened to find that it was quarter past two. He grabbed his pipe and started to climb up the valley. His long sleep had deprived him of his lunch, and unless he hurried, he would miss the charabanc. He wondered whether the others had missed him.

They had. His absence at lunch had worried all but Mr Fadewaite. Mrs Crantell had been exceedingly distressed, though she was careful not to show it. After lunch they had spent half an hour looking for Mr Finchley, without result.

Mr Finchley came panting up to the gravelled square

before the hotel, in time to see one of the two coaches that made up their party swing out on to the roadway. He glimpsed Mr Fadewaite and Mrs Crantell in the back seat and shouted. The coach was gathering speed, and they did not hear him.

'They might at least have stopped to see I was safe,' he murmured angrily to himself. Apparently if he had fallen over a cliff it would have given them little concern.

Muttering to himself, and feeling very bitter about the loss of his lunch and Mrs Crantell, he mounted the coach behind and pushed his way to an empty seat. The people were unknown to him and he made no attempt to join in the conversation which rattled up and down the seats. He sat gloomily occupied with his thoughts as they started. For the first few miles he kept one eye on the road, hoping to see the other coach, but it had started too far ahead and they did not come up with it. Mr Finchley settled down to a lonely ride. All around him people were laughing and joking. One man wore a coloured paper hat, and a small boy, with a large adam's apple, that parted his cricket shirt at the neck, leaned precariously over the side of the coach to float a long blue paper streamer on the draught.

Mr Finchley looked at his watch. It showed half past three. They reached Penzance and stopped for tea, but there was no sign of the other coach. Mr Finchley ate a solitary tea and then resumed his journey. He was quite definitely bored with the last stage of the ride and took no interest at all in the journey. When he returned to St Ives, he decided, unless Mrs Crantell had considerably changed her attitude towards him, he would not stop in the town. It did not occur to him to ask himself why so much depended upon Mrs Crantell's attitude. In fact, it never did occur to Mr Finchley to ask himself questions which might prove embarrassing. The jolting of the coach prevented him from sleeping, but he lay comfortably across his seat, enjoying the blur of flying hedges and the soothing drone of the engine. They were returning by a different route and, it seemed to him, a much longer one.

The road widened suddenly. Houses appeared, and Mr

Finchley sat up to see that they were entering the town. They swept through the streets and finally brought up outside a tall building with a huge garage on one side of it.

The joyriders picked up their baskets and coats and filed out of the bus. Mr Finchley politely let them pass by and joined the tail. As he stepped down the driver slammed the door hard behind him, then climbed back into the driving seat and drove the coach into the garage.

The street in which Mr Finchley now found himself was completely unfamiliar. He walked to the end of the road and asked the first passer-by to direct him to the street in which his lodgings were situated.

'No street of that name in Falmouth, sir. Perhaps yer got the wrong name?'

Mr Finchley jumped.

'Falmouth! Am I in Falmouth?' he asked.

The man looked at him curiously.

'Dotty,' he said at last, and hurried away.

Mr Finchley soon discovered that it was true. He was in Falmouth.

'What a fool!' he muttered to himself. This was what happened when you started thinking about women. Upset you altogether! A fine thing to have to admit, that he had got into the wrong coach.

He went into a restaurant and ordered a coffee. He sat down to think over his position. It was going to be ignominious for him to face Mrs Crantell and confess that he had been foolish enough to get into the wrong coach. The thought struck him – did he have to tell Mrs Crantell at all? Did he have to tell anyone? Who cared, anyway? Not Mrs Crantell. It seemed to him that there was no need to return to St Ives. He had nothing to return for.

Mr Finchley did not know that the coach in which he had seen Mrs Crantell departing had been the second of the two and she, after searching for him fruitlessly for some time, had come back just in time to see the first moving off and, glimpsing what she imagined to be the back of Mr Finchley's bald head, had followed in the second without any qualms as to his safety. Mr Finchley did not know this. He knew only that he could buy a new rucksack and map, and that he no longer wished to return to St Ives.

It took him some time to come to this decision. He thought of the past days which had been so mad and wonderful; he thought of London looming nearer with each day's end. And, thinking, he determined that what was worth doing was worth doing thoroughly. He adopted a fatalistic attitude and told himself that he was not intended to stagnate in St Ives for his last week; besides, he mused, he had grown to like the wandering and leisure, the quick fears and laughter of the countryside. St Ives and comfortable beds faded before the stronger vision of long roads, brown beer and rich hours from which to mould adventures.

TWENTY-FIVE

How Mr Finchley plays for a Bed

MR FINCHLEY had spent the night at a small hotel. He sent a letter to his landlady enclosing payment for his lodgings, and instructed her to forward his old clothes and walking kit to his London address.

Sunday ... and the last week of his holidays had commenced, and as he walked slowly down the hill towards the riverside Mr Finchley was a little saddened at the thought. He must, it seemed, turn his mind to London. He had to return, but just how he was not able to say. He could always get on a train. He remembered his last train ride and rubbed the place where his nettle-rash still lingered.

Half past nine found him sitting in the clear sunshine on a small pier and studying his map. London. He must go east. To go east, however, was difficult as three steps in that direction would take him over the side of the pier into the green tide that washed about the iron pillars. He stood on the end of the pier and looked across the wide estuary that was white and blue with dancing waves that swept in from the Channel before a fresh wind and strong tide.

213

Mr Finchley folded his map and consulted a ferry time-table.

The rest of that Sunday passed like a pleasant sunny dream ... The ferry-boat to St Mawes; the beautiful monot-ony of the boat's engines, colourful groups of passengers in summer clothes, a boy sucking plums and throwing the yellow stones at the wheeling gulls, and Falmouth, dropping away into the wake and churn of the ferry's stern, growing more beautiful with every yard that merged houses, ware-houses and buildings into a kind grey.

He lingered a long time in St Mawes, watching the boat-men rowing about the estuary and the people bathing. It was late in the afternoon when he left by a road that led over the hill and away from the river and sea.

That night Mr Finchley slept under canvas on a waterproof ground sheet and wrapped in two thick Army blankets.

He was passing down a narrow, deeply rutted roadway overhung with trees, tall beeches that shut out the evening sun, when a man overtook him.

'Nice weather for tramping,' the man said.

'Very nice,' murmured Mr Finchley.

'Going far?'

'London,' replied Mr Finchley absent-mindedly, for as he walked he had fallen into a dreamy state of mind.

'You've a long walk in front of you!'

Mr Finchley woke up.

'I mean, of course, that I'm ultimately going to London,' he explained with a smile. The man whom he was address-ing was tall, sandy-haired, wearing corduroy shorts, a shirt of khaki and a red scout's scarf round his neck. From the top of his lip a sandy-coloured moustache tickled his nose and kept a perpetual smile upon his face.

'I'm going back to London, too – but not for another fort-night, thank God!'

'You're a scout, aren't you?' asked Mr Finchley, staring at the man's brown knees.

'Scoutmaster,' corrected his companion. 'A vastly different thing. A scout goes to camp and eats and never asks where

214

the grub comes from; a scoutmaster goes to camp and eats sometimes, but mostly he's worrying about little Johnnie who's got to be careful about damp because he suffers from neuralgia, and little Dicky who thinks turnip much better fodder than porridge and consequently is in constant conflict with his stomach. Boys eat an awful lot! Have you ever faced twenty starving scouts armed with bowie knives and each scout determined to secure the last tin of bully-beef which you have hidden for emergency in your kitbag?'

'I can't say I have. Have you?'

'Yes, and I'm getting used to it. At one time I used to have far worse dreams!'

'Still, I expect you find that even that is preferable to London life.'

'I'm sure it is!'

The scoutmaster's name was Michael Grady. He was, so Mr Finchley learned, a clerk in the Shell-Mex offices somewhere in London. Each year he gave up the two weeks of his annual holiday to bring twenty youngsters to Cornwall to camp.

They walked for some time talking.

Mr Finchley, under skilful pressure from Michael, told him of what he had been doing.

'You mean you've had two weeks just floating around waiting for things to turn up and then doing 'em?'

'Something like that,' agreed Mr Finchley. 'Generally I found I couldn't help doing them.'

'What a holiday!' The other was enthusiastic. 'Where do you intend to sleep tonight?'

'That,' said Mr Finchley, 'I am not sure about, but I expect there are good hayricks in this part of the world!'

He said this with a touch of pride, the arrogance of a trouper who cares nothing for the banal comforts of the world, though actually he was on the look-out for a bed-and-breakfast sign!

'Oh, no! You're not going to do that!' Michael said firmly.

'I'm not – how do you know?'

'Because you're going to sleep in my tent – that is, if you're willing to make a bargain.'

Mr Finchley rubbed the top of his pate.

'Bargain?'

'Yes. Can you play cricket?'

Now Mr Finchley could play cricket. It was one of the few games at which he had ever showed any aptitude.

'I can – though I haven't played for some time.'

'That's good enough! I'll give you a bed and food for tonight if you'll play cricket for us tomorrow. You see,' Michael explained, 'every year we have a match with the village here and generally we lose. This year we want to win. In fact, we should certainly have won but unfortunately our star bowler very cleverly managed to cut his hand yesterday and now we're left in the soup. The only thing to do is to rely upon our batting, but you can imagine what chance youngsters of twelve and fourteen have against the villagers, especially as the squire – an old university man – generally plays for them. With you to stiffen the batting we might stand a chance.'

So Mr Finchley made a bargain to play cricket in return for a bed. Michael led him to the camp that was set in a small field at the side of a creek which at low tide was only a mud-lined stream, surrounded by a waste of cotton-grass and sea-feverfew.

The boys disregarded introductions. He had come, and in five minutes they accepted him with the healthy animal disregard of conventions which boys share with puppies. He was a friend of Mr Grady's; he was going to play cricket (there was a slight rumour that he was some relation to Hobbs); and very soon two of the old-stagers warned him against the squire's under-hand lobs.

He had his supper with them, bread and jam and a huge enamel mug full of steaming hot cocoa, at an open table supported on log legs.

After supper there was a camp-fire, round which they sat wrapped in groundsheets. The singing was lusty and eager and occasionally tuneful. Mr Finchley went to bed with his head reeling and until sleep claimed him he was in imagination still at the fire singing *Clementine* and *Green Grow the Rushes O!*

He was roused in the morning by Michael rolling him from his blankets.

'Good morning!'

'Good morning,' replied Mr Finchley. 'Why the bathing costume?'

'Bathing parade. Here's a slip for you if you want to come.'

Michael left the tent with Mr Finchley following.

In three minutes the camp was awake, the cooks for the day were already in the camp-kitchen at the top of the field, lighting the fire and getting breakfast under way. The rest of the camp raced from the field to the creek, where the tide was now full.

The creek-side echoed to the splashing and cries of the bathers. The sun gleamed across the tree tops and smiled as the water was split into silver shards. Mr Finchley climbed on to the bank after his swim and watched the little bodies turning, diving, wriggling, splashing, jumping and shining. The sight of their fresh faces and eager brown bodies, of their bare limbs and the cool water running through their hair as they swam, set him thinking of the three farmer's boys and Mrs Crantell, and for a moment he experienced again the odd, lonely sensation of the morning in the farm-yard . . .

After lunch they proceeded in a sober procession to the village. The serious business of the day had begun.

The cricket field was in a corner of the squire's grounds. It was a delightful field, as ordinary fields go, but its only pre-tension to being a cricket field existed in the form of a strip of worn turf in the centre of an acre of good, stout arable land. The outfield, as Mr Finchley found later, contained, beside a fine proportion of nettles, a particularly virile species of thistle that laughed at the thick stuff of trouser-legs.

The village batted first. Mr Finchley, in grey-flannel trousers, and a white shirt (lent to him by Michael), was placed at fine leg, where he stopped for the whole of the innings. At first he was insensible to the long walk-over when the bowlers finished their overs, but after twelve overs he grew just a little weary of walking over the same strip of ground. He knew each plantain that clung close to the turf and greeted each nettle, as he plunged into the outfield, with a sad smile. If only a ball would come his way. But no ball came.

The squire and a rotund villager started the innings. Michael and a tall scout bowled. After six overs the squire was still batting, but the rotund villager had given place to another. After two hours' play the score was forty-eight, the squire was still in with a total of thirty, and there were three more men to go in.

The whole interest of the game was centred round the squire. The villagers greeted each of his hits with bursts of cheers and each of his mis-hits with groans; they groaned at the rate of three groans every twenty minutes. Michael changed the bowling, but nothing seemed capable of dismissing the squire. The other wickets fell with a satisfying frequency, but not the squire's. He was sterner stuff. Long hops, lobs, leg-breaks, off-breaks ... they all came alike to him. Michael began to despair. The squire knew his ground and was careful not to lift any balls within reach of the fielder. At four o'clock the last man came in and the bowling was concentrated upon him. The scouts had abandoned the idea of dislodging the squire.

Mr Finchley watched from his outpost in the long grass.

The squire was taking the bowling from Michael. Michael bowled loose to the leg, trying to tempt the squire to hit and run so that the bowling would come to the last villager. The squire did hit. Despite his fourteen stone, he swung round on his ankles like a top and smacked the ball hard back to fine leg. There was a cheer from the crowd and Mr Finchley woke from his reverie as a miniature cannon-ball struck him in the chest and knocked him backwards into the grass. For a second or two he lay dazed, his hands clasped tightly across his belly. He was not allowed to stop in this position long. He was gradually aware of the squire standing over him, and a

crowd of scouts, villagers, girls, small children, and Michael
– all grinning down at him and cheering.

'Jolly good catch, sir! Jolly good!' The squire boomed and
stretched out a hand. Mr Finchley realized that his clasped
hands were folded over the ball and he understood. He had
caught out the squire.

'Oh, that's nothing,' he said, and struggled to his feet,
wondering when sensation would return to his stomach. He
walked back to the pavilion, followed by the reverent gaze of
small boys who dreamt of such catches.

The village had made fifty-six, and it was the scouts' turn
to bat. What followed was an awful calamity. Mr Finchley
was conscious of sitting in the darkened pavilion, staring out
at the bright green fields. The smell of bats and pads rose
thick in his nostrils. Michael and one of the scouts were
opening the innings. There was half an hour before the tea-
interval. Mr Finchley was second wicket down, and did not
anticipate going in until tea was done.

Michael took centre. A dark-skinned villager – greeted
from the edges of the field as Haymaker – took the ball, spat
on it, walked five yards from the stumps, walked back and –
so it seemed to Mr Finchley – threw the ball with a crab-like
action straight at Michael's head. He expected to see
Michael go down like a ninepin. Instead, Michael got his bat
to the flying ball and lifted it over his shoulder into the
churchyard. Six!

The scouts went wild and Indian calls rattled across the
field. Haymaker was unconcerned. He took the ball, spat
again, and repeated his action. Michael swung his bat. There
was a crisp – *whack!* Mr Finchley saw that the three stumps
had spread themselves at fantastic angles to the ground.
Haymaker spat on his hands and grinned.

Two minutes later Haymaker bowled another man, with
the score still six. It was Mr Finchley's turn to go in. Haymaker was still spitting and rubbing his hands as Mr
Finchley took his stand at the wicket. The fielders crowded
closer and eyed Mr Finchley over their grass stems, chewing
and watching.

Mr Finchley was not nervous, although it was fifteen

years since he had handled a bat. No, he was not nervous, only he was apprehensive. He took centre, dug himself a neat hole and smiled at the umpire, who took no notice of him.

Haymaker walked to the wicket and bowled. The ball spun down towards Mr Finchley in a long curve, swinging to the off-side of the wicket. His bat came forward swiftly and – plonk! The ball rolled back to Haymaker, who spat and walked backwards. Haymaker bowled again, and Mr Finchley's bat came forward to meet the ball. This time the ball wasn't there, and looking round he encountered the sad eye of the wicket-keeper and saw that one of his bails was missing and a stump hanging backwards. He walked away slowly.

'Sorry, Michael,' he murmured as he took his pads off.

'That's all right, old man. I know that fellow – he's a beast to play. He generally skittles us out. It doesn't look too rosy, does it?'

The situation was not rosy. Ten minutes before tea, the last two men were in and the score was nine. Haymaker was having a field day.

'Nine runs and the twins in.' Michael shook his head at the pair at the wickets. They were twins and as irresponsible as magpies. But for once the twins appeared to be cognizant of the serious situation. Their freckled faces were furrowed and their sweaty little hands quivered about the bat-handles. One may only be thirteen, still show an intelligent interest in mice-breeding, catapults, like sticky sweets, and prefer *Dan Dare* to the *Tale of Two Cities*, but even so the harshness of life is apt to obtrude roughly into the bliss-fulness of childhood. Flit and Flut were worried; they guessed what was coming to them from the eighteen other savages if they walked back from the wickets with the score still at nine.

Haymaker bowled to Flut. He decided that shutting his eyes and waving the bat vigorously was the best procedure. It was. He opened his eyes to see the ball sailing across the field for a four boundary. The experiment cheered him up. His hands quivered less. At the next ball, emboldened, he kept his eyes open and waved the bat. There came a rasping

'Aaaah!' from the spectators. The ball had narrowly missed the top of the stumps. Flut's hands trembled.

Haymaker spat and bowled. Flut reverted to normal, and shutting his eyes waved the bat again. A roar from the crowd. He had hit another boundary: though for all he knew, the bat in his hand might have been a feather. Haymaker was ruffled, and the last ball of his over flew high above Flut's head. The scouts breathed.

The postman was bowling from the other end. The sight of Flit's golden hair and blue eyes filled his rough heart with pity. The innocent! He tossed Flit a gentle lob. Flit – if you are unfortunate enough to possess golden hair and blue eyes you soon perceive such things – saw the maudlin pity and understood why he had been bowled a girl's lob. His heart filled with rage. He stepped forward and smacked at the ball. It flew like a piece of shrapnel from the bat, whizzed over the postman's shoulder, eluded a fielder's grasping hands and trickled over the boundary.

'Good ol' Flit! That's the boy!'

Flit waved a lordly hand to the mob; his honour was satisfied.

The postman banished pity from his heart and hurled the ball. But Flit had secured a moral superiority. The ball was almost a full-toss and it came straight for Flit. Self-preservation demanded that he should guard himself. He raised the bat before his face. The ball skimmed the bat and shot away to fine leg. There was no hope of stopping it. All the force of the postman's arm was behind it. Another boundary. The next ball was a better one. The postman controlled his feelings, and Flit's middle stump broke from the wooden trinity.

Flit and Flut walked away from the wickets, conscious that they had done more than their due share. Twenty-five runs and they had made sixteen of them. They used their fame as a means of procuring the tastiest and best cakes at tea.

Both teams sat down to a tea provided by the squire. The long board creaked with food. There were huge piles of new bread, raspberry, strawberry, apricot and plum jams, thick cream, paste of four kinds, fish sandwiches, fresh cool lettuce and plates of cake – fruit cake, madeira cake, saffron cake, honey cake, ginger cake, chocolate cake, cherry cake, cakes unnamed and so good that no name could even adequately describe them. And at one end of the table stood a great tea-urn, guarded by the squire's housekeeper, from which tea flowed in an endless stream into cups.

They all ate noisily, hungrily and unduly. In five minutes the table ceased to creak, and the wooden benches on which the teams sat took up the song. In less than ten minutes Mr Finchley felt that he was full of the most horribly delicious medley of food that a man who suffers with his digestion could imagine. The squire stood up and welcomed the scouts to the village and Michael stood up and replied. But all the while the eating continued. By now it was not the eager, desperate affair which it had at first been. The twins alone still ate with a voracity that astonished everyone but themselves. They were still eating when Mr Finchley left the room to put on his pads.

The village had put them in again – the squire was out for an innings' defeat. Mr Finchley and Michael were to open the batting.

'Remember,' said Michael as they went out, 'we've just a chance. We've got to make runs, otherwise this will be the first time we've been beaten by an innings. You keep your end up and stonewall – I'm going to get the runs.' He meant it. These villagers were going to see something. And they did.

Mr Finchley might have been a block of stone. For three overs he stopped at one end and played a straight bat to everything while Michael hit – boundaries. It was useless to keep the ball low because the rough outfield stopped it almost as soon as it left the turf.

The Haymaker hurled his cannon-balls, the squire bowled breaks, lobs and googlies, the postman squinted at Mr Finchley and tried yorkers and full-tosses; but he was not tempted. If he started to hit he knew he should miss and be out.

Michael did the hitting. He did it carefully and whenever a ball was safe. The score mounted steadily from ten to twenty. At thirty the squire took the Haymaker off and tried his other bowlers. Michael had his eye in and was not affected. Mr Finchley plugged along. The excitement along the edge of the field grew rapidly. The scouts formed a band outside the pavilion and under the direction of the twins cheered every stroke.

It seemed as though the two were set for ever. From thirty the score jumped in three overs to fifty – and Mr Finchley's contribution to the total was two. Then Michael tried to send a ball from the postman over the church tower. The direction was good but the hit was badly timed. It dropped softly into the hands of a fielder on the boundary.

One wicket for fifty runs. After that, so far as the scouts were concerned their innings was finished. The remaining wickets fell for six runs. The twins, over-gorged and self-confident, fell easy prey to the Haymaker, and Mr Finchley finally returned to the pavilion with the grand score of three – not out!

The villagers started to bat with twenty-two runs to make. Although there was not to be a total innings' defeat the match was in their hands. So the squire thought, so most of them thought; but cricket is a game of chance and luck and as fickle as an English summer.

Mr Finchley retired to his outfield and the game went on. The village made ten before a wicket fell. Then four men came and went like may-flies. A lanky scout with long hair that dropped into his eyes as he bowled, found his length and a soft spot on the wicket. The sun started to climb down over the trees. Another three men went for two runs. The squire came in to join his lodge-keeper. A ball came down to the keeper and he snicked it round to leg in Mr Finchley's direction, where it was lost for a moment in the deep grass, and they ran three. The last ball of the over passed and the squire faced the bowling.

'Finchley!' Michael called to him, and tossed the ball. 'You have a shot!'

'Me!'

'Yes, you – you bowl, don't you? See what you can do.'

Mr Finchley showed them what he could do. The squire crouched over his bat and stood ready. Mr Finchley measured his run and gripping the ball bowled. When you have not bowled a ball for years the first one is strangely intractable and wayward. Mr Finchley's first ball was no exception. It flew high and wide on the leg, but not too wide for the squire. He jumped out and caught it square on his bat, driving it well over square leg's head into the churchyard – six!

'And that,' murmured Michael to himself, 'has lost the match for us. They want one to win.'

Mr Finchley took the ball again and cursed under his breath. If they lost now it was his fault. He had let Michael down. A bitter feeling of despondency and remorse gathered about him. He walked back from the wicket. The sun was still hot and he was sweating. He looked up and the sun, catching his eye, dazzled him for a second. He turned and in his eyes was a gleam. The sun had given him an idea.

He trotted to the wicket and bowled. The onlookers gaped. The ball went sailing high into the air. Up and up it went until it seemed as though it were suspended between the wickets. The squire followed it with his eyes, and at the height of its trajectory the sun struck him full in the face and the black spot which was the ball was lost in a slashing mist of silver and red. The squire tried to focus his eyes as it slowly gathered speed in its fall. The sun was too much for him. The ball fell full on the wickets and knocked the bails flying.

'Whow!' the scouts yelled. 'Bowled by a donkey-drop! Hurrah!'

A smile came to Mr Finchley's face as he watched the squire walk back to the pavilion.

Michael bounced over to him and the fielders crowded round.

'Good ball! We've got a chance to tie at least. This is their last man!'

It was the postman. He was prepared for Mr Finchley's

donkey-drops. Mr Finchley – playing for safety – bowled three more and each time the postman shaded his eyes with a hand and carefully patted the ball. One run meant victory to the villagers.

The last ball of the over. Mr Finchley trotted to the stumps. The postman, anticipating him, raised a hand to his eyes. But Mr Finchley was filled with a machiavellian cunning. His arm swept upwards, but not for a donkey-drop. This time the ball travelled straight and true for the wickets and, while the batsman was still staring into the blue waiting for the ball, it had spread-eagled his stumps. The scouts went wild. They rushed across the ground and, finding Mr Finchley was too heavy to chair, they mobbed him, rolling him on the ground, and punched and slapped him in a good-natured, heavy-handed fashion. When Michael rescued him he was in a breathless condition, but happy. He was finding cricket and Cornwall exhilarating.

TWENTY-SIX

Of the Potency of Cider and the Vagrancy of Music

A CAR climbed the long hill in bottom gear, reached the top, and swept by the shoes. The driver did not notice them. Five minutes later a boy with a bag of rabbit gins over his shoulder cycled past them down the hill. He saw them but he was going too fast to pull up. Another five minutes passed, and the left shoe nodded wearily to its neighbour, and then was still. Somewhere a church-tower bell struck two. The notes came vibrating up the wind.

The dusty grasses nodded sleepily with the heat. Men in the turnip field thought of beer but, in spite of the heat, still wore their waistcoats. Holidaymakers shrank from the torture of hot sand under their bare feet and tried to recall the bitterness of November squalls. Everywhere, in field and pasture, on beach and headland, beside stream and sea, man and beast shrank from the pitiless glaze of the arid August sun; the tropic sun that frightens England for a week and then is gone, taking summer with it.

Another car came slowly up the hill. It breasted the crown, and the engine note died away as it came to a standstill alongside the shoes. The three men who were in the car descended.

Three men, and three strange men. Had they carried dirks and flat targes one might have been forgiven for supposing them to have stepped straight from a Waverley novel. They were dressed in long plaid shawls, short coatees and tartan kilts. Their knees might have been brown or dirty. The man who had been driving the car, and whom his companions addressed as the 'Duke', was tall and handsome and seemed more at home in his dress than the others. Of the other two, one carried a bugle under his arm and pressed it closely to his skinny body which contrasted strangely with the Falstaffian rotundity of his fellow. This last was a huge man whose kilt stretched despairing round him and was lifted high above his knees to reveal a pair of pathetically plump legs.

The Duke threw off his shawl and, spreading it on the grass at the roadside, sat down.

'Bring the beer, Bengy!' he said in a haughty voice.

The thin man with the bugle leaned over the side of the car and brought to view three bottles of beer. They all sat down, and for a while there was a silence as they drank.

'Ahhhhhh!' the fat man breathed comfortably, and put down his bottle.

'Must you express your satisfaction in that vulgar way, Reddy?' asked the Duke, wiping his lips with a handkerchief.

'Cut it out, Duke,' said Reddy; 'we've heard it before.'

The Duke raised a haughty eyebrow.

'You're indulging your low habits again. Remember, I'm in command of this band. We may be only street-players, scraping out coppers from the gutters. We're low enough as it is, but, Reddy, we give of our best—'

'—which is more than we get!' Reddy interposed.

'—and we earn an honest living!'

'Says the Duke! Listen, Duke; I like you because you're a lovely hypocrite; and I like beer and I like me vulgar habits whatever they are, and if I got to choose, I choose beer and habits. And you can't do without me because there ain't another drummer like me in the world. So let's be sensible and not talk of honest livings – for you and me and Bengy there, with his lean legs, knows that we're as honest as a bunch of jackdaws. If we ain't – why did we have to leave poor old John back in Truro?'

'There is no need to continue,' put in the Duke. 'The incident to which you refer was unfortunate. I have no objection to you at all, Reddy, but I dislike belching.'

'All right, all right, you win.' Reddy waved a hand and, dropping backwards on his rug, he grinned at the sky and belched loudly. The Duke wisely took no notice of him.

Having drunk their beer the three settled down for a sleep. The Duke slept motionless on the shawl. Bengy twitched and muttered, and Reddy breathed loudly and rolled his huge body from one side to the other. One of his rolls took him over the edge of his shawl on to the grass. The ground, which sloped a little, caused him to turn a complete revolution, and he hit his face against something hard. The blow wakened him. He raised himself and found himself staring at a pair of shoes that protruded from the ditch. From the shoes sprang a pair of legs and following the legs Reddy discovered the body of a man; hidden almost completely by the long dusty grasses, lying half in and half out of the ditch.

'Hey – look here!' Reddy sat up and shouted to the other two. They were awake instantly.

'What's the matter?' asked the Duke.

'I've found a body,' said Reddy in a scared voice.

'Why wake us?' inquired the Duke. 'You found it, you keep it. We don't collect dead bodies!'

Laughing, the Duke and Bengy turned to their rugs again.

'Hey – you're wrong!' cried Reddy before they could lie down.

'Wrong?'

'Yes! It's a living body.'

They were still eyeing Reddy mistrustfully, when there was a rustle from the ditch. The shoes withdrew slowly, the legs bent, and, like a mummy rising from the ground, the sleeping man was suddenly awake and sitting upright in the ditch. The man stared straight at the three, saying no word. Lazily he started to shake his head from side to side.

Reddy looked at the Duke and the Duke looked at Bengy, and from them all came the same word in a soft whisper: 'Drunk.' The man must have heard them.

'That,' said Mr Finchley, rising unsteadily from the ditch, 'is a gross libel. I am not drunk.' Finding himself weak upon his legs he sat down again.

'He looks like a tramp to me,' said Reddy, eyeing the worn shoes, crumpled trousers, and Mr Finchley's general air of disreputableness.

'Sir,' said Mr Finchley, rising again with difficulty, 'whatever I may be, I am not a tramp. I am at present on holiday.'

'Don't you think you'd better sit down again,' said Bengy anxiously, as Mr Finchley swayed and looked like toppling forward upon him.

'Thank you, sir, I will.'

Mr Finchley sat down again.

'Sir,' said Mr Finchley, again addressing Reddy, 'I am not drunk. I repeat it. I am not drunk. A man who is drunk has no control of his faculties, while I am in perfect control of myself.'

'Mr—?' began the Duke, whose eyes had become bright and eager as he watched Mr Finchley.

'Finchley, sir, Finchley is the name, and a very fine old name indeed.'

'Listen, Mr Finchley,' said the Duke, who saw in Mr Finchley a way out of a troublesome situation. 'You say you're doing nothing at present . . . just on holiday, eh?'

'Precisely . . . on holiday.'

'I wonder if you'd like to join our band. You would get your share of the takings, and I can promise that you would find it more profitable than being on holiday . . .'

'Band ... you mean that you have a band?' asked Mr Finchley.

'Yes, we three, bagpipes, bugle and drum.'

'But, my dear, good sir, I should be only too happy to join you if I could play. I am afraid though, that beyond *Paddy Get Out of the Donkey's Way* on the piano, I am no musician.'

'But, Mr Finchley,' continued the Duke, 'you would join us as a collector. We play in the streets, of course, and you would go round with a box, collecting.'

'And why is there this vacancy for a collector?'

'Unfortunately we were forced to leave our last one behind at Truro. He was taken ill, poor fellow.' The Duke winked at Bengy.

'Ah, very sad, very sad! I hope he is progressing. Well, in the circumstances, I have not the slightest objection to assisting you. One tires of holidays, you know, one tires.' Mr Finchley yawned. 'When do I start collecting?'

'As soon as we reach Plymouth. Now, Mr Finchley, I'll introduce you to the other members of the band, and then we'll start for Plymouth. This – the Duke waved to the drummer – is Charles Frederick Redfern Mahon—'

'Call me Reddy,' said that worthy, with a grin.

'And this is Benjamin Xavier Striker, and I am known to my friends as the Duke. My real name I prefer not to disclose—'

'Because his mother never knew it!' put in Reddy, and winked at Mr Finchley, who took no notice of this interpolation.

'Ah, Mr Duke, I think I shall enjoy working for you,' he answered, and without waiting for an invitation, he stepped lazily into the back seat of the car. Settling himself comfortably into a corner, Mr Finchley promptly went to sleep.

'And that's settled the difficulty of a collector,' said the Duke, nodding at Mr Finchley. 'I thought it was going to be difficult to get a man in a hurry.'

Mr Finchley began to wake slowly. About him there was the

quick sound of voices, and the clanking of chains. Occasionally he heard a sound as of the slap of waves against the sides
of a boat. He shook his head and tried to force his stirring
mind into action. What was happening? The names of
villages floated up to him: Portscatho, Veryan, Portloe ...
pinafored children, a general store, crushed by a two-foot
window of bottle glass and a toothpaste advertisement, a tall
clock tower that had lost its church, and somewhere at the
end of the village a public-house. He had walked himself
into a strong thirst. The dark room closed about him like
cool green depths round a diver. The man behind the bar
laughed, and his laughter was like a runnel of water, cool
and refreshing ... and Mr Finchley was thirsty. He drank a
pint of cider before the plate of bread and cheese appeared,
and then there was more cider. The man was still laughing,
like falling water, and Mr Finchley sat for a time, his body
tied to the bench with fatigue and sun-weariness. The laughter had moved to him and told him to go. There was the sun
and the hot street again, its gutters untidy with cigarette
cartons and bus tickets. His feet left him and lived a life of
their own. He walked behind them as they made their way
up the hill. People glanced at him and smiled. He knew they
were smiling at his feet that walked before him. The hill
stretched on, and the sun bored little holes through the back
of his collar. The sun, he thought, will ruin my collar. And
at the hilltop his feet leaped forward and disappeared over
the horizon. He stood in the black roadway, helpless, and
everything jeered at him. The sun jeered, the weary flowers,
and the tired hedges, they all jeered – and far away on his
left the huge white clay mounds above the Luxulian valley,
they turned their dazzling pyramids from him and jeered,
pityingly. A green beetle tipped itself backwards on the
melting tarmac and looked up at him. Behind him the
laughing man chuckled, and Mr Finchley stood helplessly
without his feet. With a sigh he sank into the cool grass and
the shade of the ditch. If I sleep, he thought, perhaps my
feet will return.

But his feet did not return.

Time passed, and there were three giants talking to him. Three Scotch giants and he was not afraid . . .

He opened his eyes cautiously. He was in the back seat of a car. At his side was a fat man in piper's dress and two men, similarly dressed, occupied the front seat of the car.

'Where are we?' asked Mr Finchley.

'Torpoint Ferry – just going over to Plymouth,' answered the fat man. 'Slept it off?'

Mr Finchley saw that the man spoke the truth. They were on a ferry. Before and behind the car were wedged other cars and wedged between the cars were motor-cycles. Above him on both sides rose the decks of the ferry, and above the decks seagulls flew in the bright sky. The smell of the sea mixed with the acrid exhaust gases, came back into his face. Mr Finchley knew then that he was no longer dreaming. The effects of the cider he had so injudiciously imbibed were gone. He was Mr Finchley again, with the horrible thought gnawing at him that, while he had been under the influence of the cider and heat, he might have acted strangely or contracted obligations which Edgar Finchley, Esquire, might find it difficult to honour. The ferry neared the opposite bank, the Devon border.

Mr Finchley's impressions of the past few hours were hazy and he was anxious to clarify them.

'What exactly am I doing with you?' he asked Reddy suddenly.

'Doing? What do you mean?'

'Why am I here?'

'Because you chose to come. Because you accepted the Duke's offer of a job as collector for us – and because you like the sight of my handsome dial!'

'Collecting! Do you mean collecting money for you while you play . . . that?' Mr Finchley touched with his foot the big drum, which was jammed into the car at Reddy's feet.

'Sure! You aren't going to back out now – are you?'

'Back out!' The Duke turned round at the words. 'Whose backing out? Mr Finchley – what, after we've brought you nearly sixty miles to Plymouth? You can't do it! Besides, we

231

didn't take advantage of your condition. You said – didn't he, Reddy? – that you were in perfect control of all your faculties. Say, you can't back out now!'

'Back out!' Mr Finchley was instantly indignant. 'Who said I was backing out? What's all the bother about? If I said I'd be your collector, then I will be—'

'Good for you, Mr Finchley,' cried Reddy, and he tried to shake him by the hand, only the movement of the car, as it left the ferry, jerked him backwards and defeated his project.

No more was said. The Duke apparently knew his way about Plymouth, and drove through the streets as though he were anxious to reach some particular place. There were many curious glances at the car as it passed. Three men in outlandish Highland costumes, and a fourth man – bald-headed, sunburned, with a worried look on his round face and long creases across his brown jacket and dirty flannels – this was something at which to stare. Mr Finchley did not enjoy the promiscuous publicity, though the other three did not appear to notice it.

Presently they were in a busy thoroughfare, midst a mêlée of clanging trams and tall omnibuses. Then the car shot round to the left and pulled into a garage that ran back from the roadway, like the quiet arm of a creek.

'Here we are!' cried the Duke.

'Here we are,' echoed Bengy, 'and now to earn our suppers and a bed, eh?'

'More than that, I hope, if the good folk of Plymouth appreciate music,' said the Duke.

Reddy winked at Mr Finchley, and pulled the big drum from the car. The garagehand appeared to know them, for he said nothing and watched them in silence. Mr Finchley saw by the garage clock that it was five o'clock. He wondered what Michael was doing, and Mrs Crantell, and John . . .

'Here y'are!' The Duke broke in upon his musings and handed him a collecting box. He outlined Mr Finchley's duties. He was to keep level with the band as they marched and was to shake the box in the faces of the passers-by. He must watch the windows and keep an eye open for young girls, because the kilts always fetched them. And, above all, he must keep moving, otherwise the police would jump on them for begging.

'Got that – keep moving with us!'

'I understand,' said Mr Finchley, and in his stomach he had a vacuum. If he had been given half an excuse he would have thrown down the box and run away, but there was now no escape. He had given his word and the thing must go through, but he vowed to himself that it should not be for long. Within the next day or two he had to break away.

A sports car roared a merry staccato at the entrance to the garage. In the steel girders of the garage a sparrow chattered, and from somewhere the sporting gods looked down at the four and chuckled. Mr Finchley was to have his opportunity for escape sooner than he anticipated.

'Ready?' questioned the Duke and he surveyed his band.

He was to lead with the bagpipes, behind came Bengy with his bugle, and in the rear was Reddy, his stomach now swollen to three times its normal size by his beloved drum. On the left flank shivered Mr Finchley, collecting box in hand. He looked very miserable.

'Don't forget to smile, Mr Finchley,' chuckled Reddy. 'A smile always gets 'em. If you look as though you're starvin', they'll let you starve, but grin as if yer tummy's bung full of grub, and they'll undo their purses. I know. Bang!' He whacked the drum as the signal for the march to commence.

A thin skirling of pipes wailed from the Duke's direction, the bugle broke into song and with a bang, bang, bang from Reddy the band marched into daylight, to the strains of a tune which Mr Finchley eventually identified as *Annie Laurie*.

TWENTY-SEVEN

How Mr Finchley throws Good Money to the Winds

THAT afternoon marked a period in Mr Finchley's education. For an hour he followed the band, shaking his box, and in that hour he learned more of the true nature of his fellows than the whole of his life so far had taught him. When one has passed one's life on the pavement it is a revelation to be suddenly forced into the gutter, and made to look at people, instead of looking with them. Mr Finchley soon realized why it was difficult for the Duke to procure collectors. The members of the band were doing something for their coppers, but the collector was just a necessary parasite.

At first Mr Finchley had shaken his box hesitantly, and his face had glowed a rosy red. Then the first shame went, and he forced himself to accept his position.

He shook the few coppers in his box – which had been placed there by the Duke to form a rattling decoy – and thrust it under the noses of the passers-by who generally, in a sudden excess of myopia, feigned unconsciousness of its presence. The three players in their flowing plaids and bare knees, the pipes skirling, drum beating, and Bengy fluting like a hurricane so that one wondered at the wind which came from such a thin body, made a fine show, but a poor band.

Even in the midst of his embarrassment Mr Finchley could not altogether repress his amusement. The Duke was the leader and called the tune. He started with *Bonnie Prince Charlie*, and after the first four bars changed his mind and slurred the pipes into the *Londonderry Air*. From this the tune would wander into some popular dance number, and so, with incredible gymnastics, the Duke kept them going. Had he played alone he might have called it a medley and achieved a faint success, but the unfortunate Bengy was slow to perceive the change of tune and consistently remained four bars behind the Duke. The result was a lovely noise, pleasantly chaotic and punctuated by the rhythmic booming of Reddy, who beat away on his drum impervious to any change of tune and conscious only of the pretty girls who passed.

The children loved them, and little girls speculated upon the possibility of the existence or otherwise of shorts under the kilts. The boys were disappointed at the absence of dirks from their stockings, but found consolation in the Duke's regal strut and the Scotch reel which he did at the corner of every street that yielded more than one and sixpence.

They entered a small park for a rest, and the Duke took Mr Finchley's collecting box, which was satisfyingly heavy.

'Twenty-two shillings and sixpence – not bad for an hour and a half!'

'Some of the London dance bands,' said Bengy, scratching the ground with his toe, 'get paid a pound a minute . . .'

They ignored him.

'Another hour and we can knock off for today. Come on, let's get back to it.'

The Duke rose, the money concealed about him, and handed the empty box to Mr Finchley.

They left the park and started again.

Mr Finchley saw a stout lady, with plentiful pouches of fat wreathing her face, fumbling in her bag. He darted across the pavement and stood by her side.

'There you are, my man! I love the Scotch.' She dropped a shilling in his box.

'Thank you, lady,' said Mr Finchley. He was about to dart back into the road when a curious thing happened. The band was playing on the right-hand side of the street. From the left pavement four policemen sprang into existence, crossed the road, and with a calm sureness laid hands on the three bandsmen. Two took Reddy in hand, and the others looked after the Duke and Bengy. Instantly a crowd formed round the band. Mr Finchley pushed his way forward impetuously.

'Hey!' he shouted, and attempted to push his way to

Reddy. But the crowd was too thick and no one took any notice of him.

'Hey, Reddy!' he shouted again and this time Reddy heard him. The drummer half turned and saw Mr Finchley. Instantly there came over his face a warning look, a look pregnant with meaning. Mr Finchley faltered ... what ...? He heard voices around him in the crowd.

'Probably wanted for something.'

'... You can't tell with those sort of chaps ... Do anything for money!'

The police had hustled the three away, and the crowd was breaking. Mr Finchley was conscious of the box in his hand. If anyone saw that, he would be connected with the band and then ... Suddenly he was anxious to get away. He did not want to be mixed up in any police-court proceedings. With a quick look round he slipped across the road, holding the box tightly to his coat, and reached a waste-paper bin by a lamp-post. He dropped the box into the bin and heard it strike with a faint rattle the debris at the bottom. The next minute Mr Finchley had slipped out of the thoroughfare into a side-street. He was determined to get well away from the neighbourhood before any more trouble started. As he worked his way back towards the centre of the town he wondered why the police had arrested the three.

The explanation came to Mr Finchley two hours later as he was sitting in a public-house in Union Street. He had booked a room for the night in a hotel in the same street. Fortunately for him, even while he had been collecting, he had persisted in wearing his rucksack, and all his belongings were still secured to him.

Mr Finchley ordered a beer and, leaning back into the seclusion of a little wooden box compartment, of which there were several in the room, he counted his money. He had over forty pounds. With a slow feeling of pride he realized that for nearly three weeks he had lived on less than ten pounds ... and he wondered what Mrs Patten would say if he told her.

He had not been sitting over his beer long when he was

aware that a man was looking at him. The man stood at the
bar, and occasionally Mr Finchley saw that he turned and
watched him curiously, almost as though he expected Mr
Finchley to acknowledge his presence.

Mr Finchley finished his beer and, looking up, caught the
man's eye. He was a tall, well-built fellow, dressed in a navy-
blue jersey with a high collar, grey trousers, and short sea-
boots. On his head, and tilted to show unruly yellow hair,
was a dilapidated old felt hat, wavy and stained, and obviously on good terms with its owner. The man nodded,
stepped forward, and took Mr Finchley's glass.

'What are you having?' he asked.

'Beer,' replied Mr Finchley, who was too surprised to say
other.

'Beer it is, then,' said the man, and called to the barman.
'Two bitters, please!'

He brought the glasses and sat down by Mr Finchley.

'Here it is,' he said. 'Let's drink.'

They drank, Mr Finchley sipping and his companion
almost draining his glass.

'This is very kind of you,' began Mr Finchley as he put his
glass down.

'Not kind – call it natural, eh?' laughed the other. 'I expect
you're rather wondering who I am and what I mean by
squattin' down by you without so much as a by-your-
leave.'

'Yes, I am. I don't think I know you.'

'Pitt's my name. Captain Pitt.' He rubbed the hard
moustache above his lip. 'Now you know me. But the reason
for sitting down by you? Ah! That's different. There's only
two things that ever made a man take a seat by a perfect
stranger and buy him a drink. The prospect of pleasure or
profit, or sometimes both. Let's call it pleasure – shall we?'

'Call it,' answered Mr Finchley, raising his glass, 'what you
like. In the last few weeks I've become so used to odd things
and strange happenings that I begin to feel that soon I shall
find I can't live without 'em. Tell me, Captain Pitt, did you
ever feel that you couldn't live without adventure; that if
luck or fortune jerked you from a comfortable existence by a

237

weird accident into a life of thrills and fears you would want to go on living the new life for ever . . .' Mr Finchley stopped, overcome by self-consciousness.

'You mean,' said Captain Pitt, who was not at all nonplussed by Mr Finchley's plunge into philosophy, 'do I prefer blizzards to bus tickets, and white-topped breakers to porcelain-tiled bathrooms? I did, I do, and I shall – and my one hope is to drop quietly overboard at the end of my time into water that shoals quickly and deeply, so that I can rest for ever on the white sand and surrounded by waving seaweeds – which, for me, is pretty good talking, seeing that I'm more for doing than saying, Mr – what did you say the name was?'

'Finchley.'

'Mr Finchley, I can see that I wasn't wrong about you. You're a man after my own heart. I didn't waste that beer.'

'I think,' said Mr Finchley heavily, 'that most men feel like that in their hearts. They want something different; they want to take a risk, but life won't let 'em. Life didn't ask me, I was just thrown into it – and I haven't regretted it!'

Captain Pitt leaned closer to him. 'That's the man – take a risk, eh? You like danger, you like excitement, you want to live fast? You're my man! What are you doing for the next few days?'

'Doing!' said Mr Finchley bitterly. 'I'm going back to normal. That is, I'm on my way back to London. I've got to be there by Saturday . . .'

'Saturday, eh? That's fine—'

'Fine?'

'I mean, that let's you in on this. Listen, Mr Finchley, I've got a boat – a small twenty-footer with an auxiliary engine, and I want to do a trip round the coast as far as Seaton. Are you on?'

'You mean a sea trip?'

'I do! Go out on the tide first thing tomorrow morning and land you at Seaton on Thursday evening, and you can make London easy. And I'll promise you plenty of adventure.'

'But why,' questioned Mr Finchley, 'do you ask me?'

'We don't have to go over that again, do we? Why do I ask

you? Aren't you the man after my own heart, aren't you the one fellow that I would choose to take on a pleasure trip like this?' Captain Pitt stressed the word 'pleasure' in a curious fashion.

'And, besides, I should think you would be glad to shake the dust of Plymouth from your feet. Ever seen this?' As he spoke he thrust deeply into his coat pocket, and banged the familiar wooden collecting box on to the table.

Mr Finchley jerked backwards, and a look of horror spread over his face.

Captain Pitt burst into a cheerful roar.

'Forget it, Mr Finchley, forget it! Same as I shall! That was very clever of you to slide away like that, but I saw. Yes, I saw, and I knew you were my man.'

'You saw . . .'

'Yes, and I admire you. You're clever. Here' – he took the wooden box between his big hands and wrenched off its cover – let's have another drink to seal the bond.' He slid the copper and silver coins on to the table and from there into his pocket.

Mr Finchley was perturbed. He could not understand this Captain Pitt, and found it hard to assess his real intention or character.

Captain Pitt returned with the drinks.

'To our voyage,' he said, and they drank. His face was shining with gaiety and companionship, and there was a rollicking assurance in his swaggering stance that convinced and reassured Mr Finchley. He decided that the man was gay-hearted, eager for adventure and the life of the sea, and badly in need of company. The fact that he had asked him to make a trip titillated Mr Finchley's pride. He began to suspect in himself qualities of which until now he had never dreamed.

He walked back to his hotel accompanied by Captain Pitt, and, while the other talked of the sea, the harbour and harbour dues, chandlers' prices and mackerel, Mr Finchley's head was drowsy with the thought of Hawkins and Grenville, and Drake who had made the name of Plymouth famous . . . He entered the hotel with shining eyes and firm step, and the thought of London lurking four days away was swept completely from his head.

Captain Pitt, with a bulky kitbag over his shoulder, called for him at the hotel next morning, and they were being rowed across Sutton Pool to the mooring where Captain Pitt had his boat before seven o'clock.

TWENTY-EIGHT

How Friendship, not Charity, is the Currency of Liberty

THE *Florence* crept round the Cattewater, and past the high granite walls of the Citadel which turns its guns upon the town and heeds not the sea. Once fairly in the Sound, Captain Pitt set the main-sheet, and quietly the long, white boat moved out to sea. The land slowly sank back and the sea swept in to welcome its own again.

On the right the green slopes and woody side of Mount Edgcumbe Park gleamed in the clear air, and close on their left, darkening the water and alive with the wheeling and cries of gulls and diving cormorants, the high cliffs of Stadden climbed to the sky and dipped their crests in the golden glory of the morning sun. Before the boat was the long line of the breakwater with its ugly grey fort and toy-like wreck-cage, and behind them stretched the high ridge of the Hoe, lazy and gay, its statues and lighthouse standing out like colourful monoliths.

They passed a cargo boat flying the yellow quarantine flag. She floated black and silent as a dead sea-beast. Little waves ran hissing along her rusty sides, and a line that dangled from the stern into the dark sea under her beam, swayed and moved with the pull of wind and waves. On top of the deck-house a shirt flapped, white and pathetic, like the sloughed skin of a dead sailor. Four days later the flag would be run down and the boat would wander off into the seas again.

Early as it was, the Sound was moving with slow craft;

fishing boats coming in late to the Barbican, rowing boats with boys straining at heavy oars, and between the glass-backed pier and Drake's Island, a tall-masted, white-sailed yacht tacked to and fro in the aimless fashion of pleasure boats.

The *Florence* neared Stadden Point and lost the security of the breakwater. A long swell set in that rocked the boat gently. Plymouth grew more distant, and the white houses, church spires, and blue morning smoke, wrapped themselves together into a hazy smudge. A hooter sounded a long way up the Hamoaze in the dockyard. Then they were in the open sea, and there was only the rise and fall of the swell and the quick glimpses of the land that was fast fading from them.

'How are you feeling?' Captain Pitt popped his head from the small cabin and grinned at Mr Finchley.

'Fine,' sang Mr Finchley, and his hand was tight upon the rudder-bar, where he had been stationed.

'Good! Though, if you're going to be sick, this swell will soon find out—'

Mr Finchley ignored the remark. Half an hour later he did feel queasy in his stomach, but he fought the feeling, and to his relief it gradually passed away. For the rest of the voyage he was not troubled by the slightest symptom of sea-sickness. He came to the conclusion that he must be a good sailor. Mr Finchley could see that even Captain Pitt was impressed.

The *Florence* was a twenty-footer. Not a beautiful boat; in fact, she was a long, ship's boat with a big cabin built into her, forming almost a superstructure. This cabin was the living and sleeping quarters and also housed the engine, which was never used while there was a wind. She carried a big, clumsy mainsail, a foresail, and sometimes – when Captain Pitt was in a hurry – a small jib. If she was not beautiful, she was seaworthy, and Mr Finchley soon saw that Captain Pitt loved her like a child, and it was not long before Mr Finchley began to appreciate the other's feeling for the *Florence*.

There was a steady south-westerly breeze blowing, and

Captain Pitt held a dead south course out into mid-channel. For the next two days Mr Finchley lived a new life.

Confined to twenty feet of shipboard two men must either become enemies or friends. Mr Finchley and Captain Pitt became friends. They cooked their food over a little primus stove and drank in turns from the same huge enamel mug. The cutlery was as defective as the crockery. Mr Finchley ate with the fork, while Captain Pitt used a clasp-knife, because he was more of a hand with it.

That afternoon, with the sea all around them, and only stormy petrels and gulls to watch, they bathed over the side, while the *Florence* lay hove-to, and Mr Finchley knew the indescribable fear and joy of bathing in a long swell, of being rocked high and low by waves that had their birth in the wildest Atlantic, and would meet their death on some popular beach, knew the joy of cool water sweet upon his skin and strong waves that held him up and broke an occasional white horse over his face, and the fear of unknown fathoms of water, dark, mysterious, cold and silent, lying directly beneath him. He trembled with a quick dread. Then Captain Pitt climbed the cabin-top, and dived into the green waves, shouting and bellowing as he broke water. Mr Finchley's fear was gone as the water hissed under the other's firm strokes and thrashing feet.

They ate enormously of corned beef and biscuits, and Mr Finchley forgot indigestion and sea-sickness. Captain Pitt showed him how to steer the *Florence* well up to the wind and yet keep the sails trimmed. He taught him to watch for the shaking canvas that told of wind spilled, and to keep his eye upon the surrounding water for the swift black patches, cat's paws, that told of squalls; taught him to ease the mainsheet as the squall struck and to watch for the swinging boom.

As darkness fell they put out a sea-anchor and slept by turn, each taking a watch. When Mr Finchley came up from his bunk to watch, the moon was on her back in the sky, and all about her blazed a glory of stars. He sat in the stern and watched the phosphorescent wake go rippling backwards. The sea rose and fell like lead, cold and heavy under the night, and a chill wind played on muted notes through the sails. From the dripping counter came gurgling noises and little trills of water laughter, and all about the boat the night and the sea, the stars and the moon, made a grey and white picture of fantasy. For long he sat, warm in a borrowed top-coat, and his red pipe-dottle was all the life in the moving periphery of sea and sky. At five o'clock the night lost interest in the sea and began to leave her. The moon gave up her strength to the growing day and retired with the waning stars. The light spread westwards round the horizon, and the pitching sails that had been black shades upon the sky were now dirty white sheets, and the fore-deck that through the night had gleamed like ebony, was a waste of wet planks. For a while the *Florence* sailed through the monotony of the twilight, until the sun rose like a maiden from the rosy horizon, and the new day swept the grey clouds together into one corner of the sky, and blew them away like broken cobwebs.

Captain Pitt relieved Mr Finchley, who went below and slept for two hours. When he awoke there was the smell of frying bacon in the air, and the sound of spitting fat.

'Ready for some grub?' Captain Pitt looked up from the pan.

'Am I!'

'Good – well, I've let the sheet down – so off with your togs, and I'll race you three times round the *Florence* – we swim in opposite directions. The winner takes two eggs. Go!'

And, without waiting for Mr Finchley to agree, he began to strip where he stood. Mr Finchley leaped from the bunk. A few seconds later two pink, shouting figures squeezed themselves from the cabin and dropped with a splash to port and starboard.

Later, as Captain Pitt was eating his second egg, Mr Finchley said, with simple directness:

'Have you a private income?'

Captain Pitt looked up quickly. He shook his head.

'How do you manage to live this sort of life then – don't you work at all?'

Captain Pitt's eyes avoided Mr Finchley. In the short while they had been together he had developed a liking for the little, bald-headed man, but he had also found out that Mr Finchley was not the man he had first imagined him to be. He shook his head again quickly.

'No – I haven't a private income! I wish I had. I manage to make a do of things by picking up odd jobs when I can. It doesn't cost me much to live. A tin of biscuits and bully-beef, and wind enough to fill the old girl's canvas is all I want.' The tone of his voice was somehow not convincing.

Mr Finchley was puzzled, but said nothing.

'It's a hard thing,' said the other, rising to clear away the meal, 'but if I had to take a shore job I should go mad. I belong out here, and whatever anyone says or thinks, I can't help. I'm going to stick out here until I die—' There was a belligerent note in his voice now. 'I don't like towns, and I hate the smug-faced chaps I see in towns! I want to be where I can be alone to act as I wish ... I suppose it's a jealous and unsocial life, but I can't help that – that's me! And that's how I mean to stop!' He left the cabin.

It was some time before they forgot the conversation. Gradually, however, the strangeness which had crept between them wore away and vanished altogether in their excitement at a school of dolphin that suddenly appeared on their port bow. For twenty minutes, by Mr Finchley's watch, the sea was alive with dolphins; huge, shining gentle creatures which broke water without a ripple all around the *Florence*. Then suddenly, they were gone, and the two were alone again.

At two o'clock Captain Pitt got out a sextant and took a reading. Mr Finchley watched him with interest as he jotted down their position on a chart. He turned to Mr Finchley.

'In another half an hour we should pick up with a Frenchy about here. Keep your eye skinned for a big boat – red sails like a trawler.'

'Why – have you arranged to meet it?' Mr Finchley asked innocently. The reply to his question startled him.

'See here, Mr Finchley, I like you.' Captain Pitt faced him. 'You're a decent little chap and a sport, but that evening I met you in the pub I got you mixed up completely. It was my fault, so I'm not blaming you . . .'

'I don't understand you.'

'Don't try,' cut in Captain Pitt. 'I'll tell you. When I saw you give the police the slip, I thought you were well in with that gang – they were wanted for two or three robberies, you know – and I reckoned that you might be glad to give me a hand for a while.'

'I'm afraid I still don't see what you mean,' said Mr Finchley. 'I was under the impression that you invited me to sail with you to keep you company – just a pleasure trip.'

'I know,' nodded the other, 'but I didn't. Mind, I'm not blaming you! It was my fault. This isn't any pleasure cruise. I said this morning that I wouldn't take a shore job and that I meant to live this life as long as I could – and you asked me about a private income.' He laughed cynically. 'I've got no private income, but I make a living – you'll call it dishonest – by smuggling!'

'Smuggling!'

'Yes, smuggling. It's still done, you know, and sometimes it's very profitable – profitable enough for me to give it up for three months and live as I wish; but I always have to come back when funds get low. That's what I'm doing now. The trawler we're going to meet will transfer a small cargo of spirits and silk and, perhaps, tobacco, which I shall land late tonight somewhere in the neighbourhood of Lyme Regis.'

Mr Finchley realized how very dull he had been. This genial Captain Pitt who loved the sea and his boat more than most men loved their wives and children was a smuggler. And he smuggled merely that he might live the life he desired. He did not know what to think. Smuggling quite definitely was wrong, and in his usual awkward fashion he, Mr Finchley, had become mixed up in it.

'Why don't you become indignant or revile me? I shan't mind. In fact I should be relieved, because I feel that I've pulled you into this, though you said you wanted danger and excitement.'

'Danger and excitement . . .' repeated Mr Finchley slowly. 'I know. And it seems to me that it is hard to get those things today without breaking the law somewhere or in some way.'

'Breaking laws isn't the danger and excitement that I want. It's this—' He laid his hand on the tiller and nodded at the racing seas.

'I know,' replied Mr Finchley, feeling unutterably wise. 'So you make a compromise. Well,' he said with a smile, 'it seems that I can't do much more than you do. I must make a compromise with my situation. It seems that my innocence led me into this so I might as well see it out, but I hope that it doesn't end disastrously.' From the way in which he spoke, it might have appeared that Mr Finchley's decision had given him very little concern. This was not so. He was not, it was true, as concerned about breaking the law as he would have been two weeks before; but he had realized that whatever he wanted to do, there was only one thing he could do. During his holiday he had faced the same situation so many times that now he just smiled – and hoped that his luck would stay by him.

'You mean you'll see it through?' cried Captain Pitt.

'Why not – don't you think I'd make a good smuggler?'

'Good smuggler – you'll make an ideal one. But I must say you've surprised me. I fully expected you to shout and demand to be landed right away. You look, you see, in spite of your unshaven face and greasy bags, too damned respectable to break the law ... If I'd had any sense I should have known that in the pub.'

So Mr Finchley accepted his position and became a smuggler. If he had expected to find danger in doing so, he must have been disappointed, for it proved to be a very ordinary affair. They soon picked up the Frenchman. A large bale was swung overboard into her small boat, and finally dumped well forward in the *Florence*'s cabin. The whole operation took fifteen minutes, during which the two boats stood by tossing and dipping to one another. No one spoke. A man in blue blouse and beret pulled the boat alongside the *Florence*. Captain Pitt threw him a rope which was made fast round the bale, and he and Mr Finchley took the strain. The bale came inboard and was carefully stowed away. The small boat went rocking back across the lane of water. Someone waved from the wheel of the trawler. Captain Pitt returned the wave and then ran out the mainsail. In five minutes the trawler was hull down on the skyline, and the *Florence* was running north for the English coast with contraband aboard.

There was a stiff breeze swinging between the south and west and the *Florence* made good time. Now that the chief business of the run was over, the zest seemed to slip from the adventure, so far as Mr Finchley was concerned, but Captain Pitt's spirits were, if anything, higher. If the cargo were landed safely he would have enough money to loaf about the coast again for another two months. Mr Finchley, despite the growing pessimism of his own thoughts, could not refrain from smiling at the other's enthusiasm. He wished, with the desperation of those who can only wish and not act, that he could do something for this big, boyish man whose only responsibility in life seemed to be the satisfaction of his desire to sail and go on sailing until he died.

As the sun went down the clouds gathered, and by nightfall, the *Florence* was running through growing seas and driving rain. Mr Finchley crouched in the doorway of the cabin, watching Captain Pitt who, hidden in oilskins, sat at the tiller with one eye on the sails and the other on the darkness ahead. Occasionally from the darkness a light flashed out and helped Captain Pitt to verify his position, but he said nothing to Mr Finchley. Still the *Florence* drove on northwards to the land.

Hours passed, and Mr Finchley slept while the other maintained his watch. At three o'clock Mr Finchley awakened. He moved to the doorway. The dark figure was still at the rudder.

'How are things going?' he asked.

Captain Pitt grunted friendlily. After a while Mr Finchley realized that the *Florence* was no longer making northward but was passing up and down on a short tack. Captain Pitt was in fact running up and down a stretch of coastline waiting for a signal. It came.

Away on their port quarter a green light burned low in the night.

'Ah, there she is!'

The tiller went back, and the *Florence* swung round and headed in the direction of the light. The light showed again and nearer.

'Are we near land, then?' asked Mr Finchley.

' 'Bout two hundreds off it,' came the reply.

Mr Finchley was surprised, but before he had time to say anything there came a soft hail from the darkness, and Captain Pitt rose to his feet and flashed a torch. Mr Finchley heard the sound of rowlocks, and a small boat emerged into the nearer gloom and drew alongside the *Florence*.

Without a word Captain Pitt lashed the tiller up and nodded to Mr Finchley. Together they went into the cabin and fetched the bale. Holding it between them they brought it out and lowered it by the rope overboard. No word was spoken at all. There were two men in the boat, indistinct figures. One held the boat against the *Florence* while the other manipulated the bale. At last it was settled and then Captain Pitt spoke to the man at the bale.

'Are you running that straight up to London?'

'Going away as soon as we land— Why?' came the reply.

'Then you might give my friend a lift up with you,' answered Captain Pitt, and he indicated Mr Finchley.

'Is he all right?'

'I'll answer for him.'

'That's good enough for me,' said the man and turned to where Mr Finchley leaned over the side. 'Come on, mate, can't stop about all night.'

Mr Finchley looked round at Captain Pitt and would have spoken only the other interrupted.

'Don't try to say anything. You want to get to London, don't you? There's your chance.'

The tone of his voice was almost forbidding. Mr Finchley disappeared into the cabin to get his rucksack. He came out after a few minutes and silently climbed overboard to the small boat. Captain Pitt dropped his rucksack after him, and with a wave the two craft fell away – the *Florence* dipping back into the sea and darkness, taking with her Captain Pitt, and the row-boat scudding under the oars of the two men towards the beach taking Mr Finchley. He sat in the stern, and rubbing against his knees was the bale of contraband goods.

The keel grated on shingle. One of the men leaped overboard and ran the boat high on to the shore. The night prevented Mr Finchley from seeing more than the dim outlines of a little cove before his help was needed on the bale. Getting their shoulders under it they bore it up the beach, through a maze of scrubby sand dunes to a road. Mr Finchley saw that a small lorry was waiting.

'Up!' And up the bale went to find a lodging on the floorboards of the lorry, where it was soon hidden under sacking and long rolls of linoleum.

'Ready, mate?' asked the man to whom Captain Pitt had spoken.

Mr Finchley nodded and climbed to the seat beside him. The other man was apparently staying behind to look after the boat, and Mr Finchley guessed that he was possibly a local fisherman.

The engine purred quietly, and without any lights the lorry started a slow way along the road. The driver winked at Mr Finchley.

'Can't risk lights until we get away a bit,' he said. Mr Finchley's knowing smile convinced him of his passenger's illicit authenticity.

Once clear of the cove the lights were switched on, and the lorry began its long journey back to London. Mr Finchley arranged his coat as a pillow and made himself comfortable. At last, he mused, he was on the final lap towards London, and soon all these mad days would have slipped into the obscurity and unreality of the past. Soon ... and he smiled sadly ...

And two miles out at sea Captain Pitt was smiling as he tore open an envelope which had been pinned to the cabin table. It was addressed to him in Mr Finchley's handwriting and read:

This is part of my savings for a holiday. The holiday is

249

nearly over and I shan't want it. Perhaps it'll keep you off smuggling for a couple of months – or always?

Inside were twenty pound notes.

Captain Pitt shook his head slowly. Then he picked up the notes and went back to the tiller. He glanced up at the small pennant flying at the mast-head.

'He's a good chap, isn't he, *Florence*?' he said softly. 'A damned good chap, but he doesn't know the sea, eh? We don't want charity, you and I – we want freedom . . .' And he dropped the notes over the stern where they tossed for a while on the churning wake and then, saturated, sank slowly through the ebony sea to find the peace of the quiet ocean-bed.

TWENTY-NINE

How the End may be the Beginning

It was half past three when Mr Finchley started on his lorry journey to London; half past three on Friday morning, August the eighteenth. At that time he was in need of a wash; there was a two days' growth of beard on his chin, a rent in the seat of his grey trousers caused by a projecting nail in the *Florence*'s boards, bacon fat and cocoa stains down his jacket front, and the upper of his right shoe was working away from its sole. Beneath his dirty, scrubby face, however, there was a healthy tan, and the long lines under his eyes were from dirt alone; he was leaner, though still stout, and the tonsure round his brown head was turning golden with the bleaching action of the sun.

It was half past three on Saturday morning, August the nineteenth, when Mr Finchley slipped up the steps of his house and let himself in with his latchkey for five hours of sleep before he prepared to face the office again. Mrs Patten was in bed, and he did not disturb her. But it was a different Mr Finchley who surveyed himself in the glass as he commenced to undress. He still had his healthy tan, but he was clean and shaven. He still had a browned scalp and bleached hair, but they were hidden by a light trilby hat which he had forgotten to remove. And his clothes – although they were borrowed – were clean and well pressed and fitted him as though they had been made for him. He eyed the reflection in the glass with satisfaction. Smart and spruce; he told himself that he looked as though he had had a good holiday. He felt well and could eat anything, and he knew that the moment he threw himself down on the bed he would sleep – because he was tired. He remembered the last sleep he had taken ... in the lorry. How the jolting over the road had slowly swept him into forgetfulness. He must have slept for a long time while the lorry tore on towards London.

He had awakened in a deep stillness. The lorry was stationary. Slumped against the opposite side of the driving cabin the driver was taking a nap. Around them the morning had blossomed while they slept. The lorry was drawn up on a piece of waste grass by the roadside. Mr Finchley got down from the cabin and looked round. They were in the middle of a long white road which stretched across an undulating plain. By his side was a tall coppice of fir trees.

He entered the trees and sat down on the soft brown needles and watched the sun painting the plain. He was happy and contented and the feeling of the turf and good ground around him filled him with peace. He could sense the stir of the earth and the movements of the living creatures all about him. The insects that worked through the pine needles and moss, the birds that cut flashing arcs from the bright air and filled the morning with music, the slow shuffle of cattle in the distance ... he was drawn towards the beauty of the land and living. This, he mused, was his ... he belonged in this land and he was glad of it.

He no longer thought regretfully of London as he once had done. He saw the two existences no more as contrasts, but as complements one of the other. When he reached the city and the smoke, the discordant jangle of noise and the hurry of action, he would always have this memory of peace and beauty to soothe his harassed soul ... Before he had had nothing ... nothing beyond his uneasy emotions and indistinct desires. Three weeks had changed that. And so, thinking and musing, Mr Finchley – though he had but just awakened – went to sleep again; and the gods laughing in the coppice sent him his last adventure, an adventure which was to sweep him right up to his doorway in a borrowed suit and with good food and wine inside him; but it is not an adventure which can be recounted here. That is a part of his story which Mr Finchley keeps always to himself. It began with an aviator and petrol, and Mrs Crantell's spectacle case which he had kept since their parting at Land's End was no longer in his rucksack when Mrs Patten discovered it on top of the wardrobe that same Saturday morning.

Mrs Patten always nursed a healthy suspicion of Mr Finchley's holiday at Margate; and when the people at the office greeted him effusively with – 'Have a good holiday, Mr Finchley?' – they read no mystery into his quiet affirmative.

If you have enjoyed this PAN Book, you may like to choose your next book from the titles listed on the following pages.

Victor Canning

Dick Francis

'Dick Francis's novels are probably the best sports detective stories ever written'
— NEW YORK TIMES

'The best thriller writer going'
— SUNDAY TIMES

Arthur Upfield

BONY, or to use his proper name, Inspector Napoleon Bonaparte is the unforgettable, half-aborigine detective created by Arthur Upfield.

Bony's work is demanding and tough – to combat crime in the sprawling Australian outback.

'If you like detective stories that are something more than puzzles, that have some solid characters and backgrounds, that avoid familiar patterns of crime and detection, then Mr Upfield is your man.' – J. B. PRIESTLEY

Arthur Upfield's books include:

THE MYSTERY OF SWORDFISH
  REEF   25p
THE BACHELORS OF BROKEN
  HILL   25p
DEATH OF A LAKE   25p
MURDER MUST WAIT   25p